C000049373

Thread of Hope

Choices and Consequences: Book 2

By Rachel J Bonner

What if your secrets are so dangerous they could destroy the one you love?

This is a work of fiction. Names, characters, organisations, places, events and incidents are all used fictitiously. Any resemblance to actual persons, places or events is purely coincidental.

Text copyright © 2019 by Rachel J Bonner

All rights reserved

No part of this publication may be reproduced, or stored in a retrieval system, distributed, or transmitted in any form or by any means including electronic, mechanical, photocopying, recording or otherwise, without prior express written permission of the publisher except in the case of brief quotations for review purposes.

Published by Isbin Books, Lancashire

Cover artwork and design by
Oliver Pengilley © 2019 by Rachel J Bonner

Editing by Sarah Smeaton

ISBN: 978-1-912890-02-6 (ebook – epub)

ISBN: 978-1-912890-05-7 (ebook – mobi)

ISBN: 978-1-912890-06-4 (paperback)

All Scripture quotations, unless otherwise indicated, are taken from the Holy Bible, New International Version®, NIV®. Copyright ©1973, 1978, 1984, 2011 by Biblica, Inc.™ Used by permission of Zondervan. All rights reserved worldwide. The "NIV" and "New International Version" are trademarks registered in the United States Patent and Trademark Office by Biblica, Inc.™

Lyrics quoted from Blessed Be Your Name by Beth Redman and Matt Redman and 10,000 Reasons (Bless The Lord) by Jonas Myrin and Matt Redman, both © Capitol Christian Music Group

Dedication

To my Mum,
who taught all us kids that life is made up of choices.
And choices have consequences.

In loving memory of my Dad

1934-2013

And of my friend, Ronnie

1935-2019

Rest in peace and rise to glory.

Description

What if your secrets are so dangerous they could destroy the one you love?

Is honesty always the best policy?

Leonie may have run away but Prospero *will* find her. He loves her and he wants a future with her by his side whatever the consequences. Only when he does find her, he ought to tell her who he really is, outside the monastery. That'll make her run again. Dare he risk it? But if he doesn't tell her, someone else may...

Marriage to Prospero is what Leonie wants most and the one thing she knows she can't have. If he found out what she was really like, what she'd been, what she'd done, he'd despise her and she couldn't bear that. Better to leave now than live a lie – but it's harder than she expected. If only...

Gabriel is starting to discover the secrets inherent in Leonie, secrets that not even she knows, secrets that will tear the world apart. And the secrets he is keeping are tearing him apart. How can sacrificing those he loves possibly achieve peace when everything he discovers risks the death of millions?

Table of Contents

Prologue 1

Chapter 1 7

Chapter 2 20

Chapter 3 33

Chapter 4 43

Chapter 5 55

Chapter 6 62

Chapter 7 70

Chapter 8 77

Chapter 9 92

Chapter 10 99

Chapter 11 113

Chapter 12 124

Chapter 13 133

Chapter 14 144

Chapter 15 153

Chapter 16 166

Chapter 17 175

Chapter 18 183

Chapter 19 187

Chapter 20 198

Chapter 21 211

Chapter 22 216

Chapter 23 226

Chapter 24 238

Chapter 25 252

Chapter 26 267

Chapter 27 271

Chapter 28 282

Chapter 29 294

Prologue

She found him pacing between the stacks in the library; for all his other faults he was a conscientious student.

"What are you looking for?" she asked, sensing his frustration.

He brushed her off. "It doesn't matter, just something I heard about."

"Tell me. Maybe I could help."

He thought about that; maybe she could. Although they were both student doctors, she was several years older and nearing the end of her studies. "Someone mentioned power stones and master stones. I want to know more."

Now she understood. Such things would be irresistible to him. "You won't find anything here. They aren't stones. You're looking in the wrong place."

He rounded on her. "You know about them? What class are they covered in? Where can I find out more?"

"They aren't taught in class. You'd only find out about them at the very end of your training, depending on the specialism you choose. Or if you became a monk."

That made them both smile; anyone less likely to become a monk was hard to imagine.

"Or a High Lord," she added.

That took the smile off his face. The risk that might happen was something that both kept him awake and tormented his dreams. Their world was feudal; individual establishments pledged their loyalty to Low Houses, who in turn pledged to High Houses. And the High Houses pledged to Great Houses, each of which was ruled by a High Lord. He was eligible to be heir to one of those High Lords, and just the thought of the responsibility gave him nightmares.

"So how do you know?" he asked.

She shook her head. "Not here. Somewhere private. Come on."

He followed her eagerly, lengthening his stride to catch up and wrap an arm round her waist. Although they weren't a couple they had been lovers on and off for some time; he had no problem persuading her to talk.

"I overheard my mother and him talking about them years ago, when he became Abbot. His ring is one, you know," she confessed, referring to the High Lord of the Great House they both currently lived in. Here, the Great House was based around a monastery and the High Lord was also the Abbot. "Then I made it my business to find out all I could," she continued. "Most of the information is hidden away but I tracked it down."

That didn't surprise him. There was no one quite like her for getting into places she wasn't allowed and finding out things she shouldn't know.

"They aren't jewels like that," she told him, gesturing at the emerald in his signet ring. "They're constructs, a sort of miniature cross between an EEG machine and Shields."

As doctors, this couple were both familiar with machines that sensed, measured and tracked brainwaves. As a part of the quarter of the population that were Gifted with extra abilities, such as telepathy or telekinesis, they also were familiar with what the mind could do and with the Shields that could contain or prevent the use of such Gifts. He nodded, understanding, and urged her to carry on, his thirst for knowledge consuming him.

"They're about linking two or more Gifted people together," she said. "You activate them by touching them with your mind, a bit like telepathy, and they transfer the energy you'd normally use for your Gifts to one dominant person, from all those who are connected."

"So that one person has more energy and it enhances their abilities?" he asked, eagerly.

She nodded. "Yeah, but they're limited. Power stones restrict how much energy is transferred to protect their users. And they only work over a short range. Master stones work over a much greater range, and they collect the energy and store it, like a battery. But they take all the energy they can from their user, too. People don't survive using a master stone."

"What do they look like? Have you seen them? Where can you get hold of them?" he demanded.

She laughed. "I've seen them and so have you. They are always disguised to look like jewels set in silver or gold. Some say the setting helps them transmit and receive energy."

"So? Where are they?"

"Each of the Gifted monks or nuns has a power stone in the cross they wear. And I told you, his Abbot's ring is one. I think it's a master stone. And my mother has a power stone too, in that brooch she nearly always wears."

"How can you tell? How can you be sure it's not just an ordinary jewel?" His curiosity was overwhelming.

She shrugged. "If you touch an ordinary jewel with your mind, it's just that, a stone, inert and non-responsive. If you touch a power stone you can feel it hum, a bit like the Shields do." His disbelieving look stung her. "I can prove it," she insisted. "Meet me on top of the Abbey Tower at midnight. I'll show you." With that, she was up and off, leaving him to ponder over all that he'd been told.

***

He met her at midnight, as she had known he would, still insatiably curious. They made love first, at the top of the tower, another private place where they wouldn't be found. She was insistent and he was hardly averse. Afterwards, she showed him what she had brought. First, one of the crosses worn by the monks and nuns. He didn't ask how she'd got hold of it. *Best not to know,* he thought.

"That central stone is the power stone," she told him. "Just touch it with your mind."

"How can I?" he asked. "It's night time and this is the Abbey. The place is shielded."

The whole campus – monastery, college, House and hospital – was shielded at night for protection but those Shields didn't stop an adept using his or her Gifts within the area. The Abbey itself, the focus of the campus, was shielded at all times so that no adept could use their Gifts within it.

"Not here, it's not," she said. "The Shields don't reach this high. Try it and see."

Still not sure, he did as she had told him and found the stone hummed gently at him. Now that he looked with his mind he could see it was a construct, and it was obvious how to use it should he wish to. He withdrew his mind and looked again with his eyes. However hard he tried he could see no visible distinguishing marks; the stone looked like a small sapphire.

Reading his discoveries in his face she was satisfied and brought out her other find, a long thin box. She opened it in front of him to reveal two identical necklaces. Both were finely wrought in silver, intricately woven in the crossed keys pattern symbolic of House St Peter. Each had a large central sapphire, with smaller blue stones set elsewhere in the design.

"One is a copy," she said. "Silver and sapphires, just what it looks like. The other... He said the central stone was a master stone. I heard him tell my mother."

"Have you touched it?" he asked, his voice almost a whisper in awe.

She shook her head. "I haven't dared," she confessed.

He dared, though. Like a moth drawn to a flame, he was unable to ignore it. Gently, slowly, delicately he touched it with his mind. Like the power stone it hummed quietly and in that moment he understood it was a lock to which he didn't have the key.

"Wow," he said reverently as he withdrew his mind. "Where do they come from?"

"I don't know," she said. "Traders brought his ring and this necklace when he became Abbot. That's all I know. Apparently, they said this was for his daughter."

That made him look up, tearing his eyes away from the jewels. "He doesn't have a daughter. How could he?"

"Well, no," she agreed. "Unless there's some terrible secret we don't know." She closed the case over the necklaces. "We should leave separately," she told him. "You go first. I'll follow in a bit and put these back where they came from."

He nodded and left.

***

Alone on top of the tower, she reopened the box and

looked again at the necklaces. His daughter, she thought. He had been her guardian; she was as close to being his daughter as anyone. Perhaps this master stone was hers by rights. Without thinking further she reached out to touch it. An explosion of colour hit her mind and then everything went black.

One of the senior monks, also a doctor, found her by chance a few minutes later. Unable to sleep, he'd been seeking a quiet place to pray but now he set about putting things to rights. He found her the medical care she needed and returned the jewellery to where he knew it was kept. He told her mother and the High Lord the bare minimum they needed to know. They chose neither to ask more nor to punish her, but she was sent away to stay with her father's family. The Abbey Shields were extended to ensure the top of the tower was now covered.

The young man from the tower assumed all was well with her, knowing no better, and their worlds drifted apart. He became involved with a young lady that his High Lord thought might make him a suitable wife. Soon after that his whole world fell apart.

Chapter 1

Easter Sunday Evening – April

Prospero

As soon as the Easter evening celebration service finished Prospero went looking for Leonie. He wasn't concerned when he didn't spot her in the congregation. There were to be refreshments afterwards and he'd already expected that she would disappear to help Pedro in the kitchens. When he found that not only was she not in the kitchen but that she hadn't been there since before the evening meal he became a little more concerned. He retreated to a quiet courtyard and started to scan the campus for her with his mind. He still didn't find her; his first thought was that he must have missed her in the congregation. As there was a Shield over the meeting place he went back to search physically again but with no success. He came across Andrew amongst the crowd and asked him if he'd seen Leonie.

Andrew shook his head. "She's not here. I've not seen her since the service. Why, what's up?"

"I said I'd find her afterwards to talk to her about something and now she doesn't seem to be anywhere." Prospero ran both hands through his hair. "I have to find her."

"Have you looked for her?"

"I can't sense her anywhere, which means she's either somewhere shielded or she's shielding, and she's not here." He gestured across their meeting place.

"Why would she be hiding from you? Have you done something stupid?"

"Maybe," Prospero confessed. "But if I have, that's even more reason I need to find her."

"The only other shielded place right now is the Old Chapel," Andrew said.

"She goes there to think," Prospero said, feeling a surge of relief at this likely solution. He set off fast in that direction, knowing that Andrew would follow. When the Old Chapel proved unyielding to Prospero's whirlwind like search, Andrew suggested that they try Leonie's room.

"She's not there," Prospero snapped.

"I know that," Andrew replied. "But it might give some clue as to where she is."

Impatient, Prospero agreed and this time Andrew kept pace with him. It didn't help that from halfway down the corridor they could see that Leonie's door had been left partway open. Prospero broke into a run, Andrew hard on his heels. Leonie's room was normally both tidy and a little bare. As Prospero pushed through the door, his first glance suggested that there was nothing out of place.

Then he caught sight of the necklace sitting on the desk and snatched it up, turning to Andrew. "She always wears this," he said, fear clutching at his throat. "If she isn't wearing it…"

He couldn't bear to think that she would be out there, vulnerable and alone, without the symbol that marked her as under the protection of this House.

Andrew grabbed a sheet of paper from the desk. "She left a note," he said unfolding it and they read it together.

Prospero sank into the chair, his head in his hands. "I've chased her away," he said brokenly.

Lost in his own fear, he barely heard Andrew's voice.

"Stay there," Andrew ordered. "Don't do anything. I'm

going to get Gabriel."

Sitting with his elbows on his knees and his head bowed, the necklace and note crumpled together in one hand, Prospero didn't notice the passage of time until they returned. He looked up as they entered, his eyes dark with pain, and silently handed the note to Gabriel.

'I'm choosing to leave. This problem can't be solved, so it's better that I go. There's no need to come looking for me. Sorry.'

Gabriel read the note and looked back at Prospero. "What did you do?" he asked quietly.

"I asked her to marry me."

"Already? What happened to being careful and taking it slowly? What did she say? Why has she disappeared?"

"She didn't say anything. It was during the service. I told her not to, that I'd find her later. It just happened but I meant it. I have to find her."

Gabriel stared at Prospero for a long moment.

Prospero stared back as determination flooded through him, hot and urgent. He stood up. "I am going to marry her," he insisted.

"And my permission?" Gabriel asked, sharply.

A small smile ghosted across Prospero's face. "She's chosen to leave your House."

Gabriel did not to react to his challenge. "Very well. You have my permission on one condition, and that is that she agrees of her own free will. No coercion." He paused for a moment. "Now, we need to find her. My office, I think, while we get organised."

Gabriel

Striving to remain calm, Gabriel knew he was out of his depth the moment he scanned Leonie's note and stared at the despondent Prospero, Andrew hovering concerned at his elbow. He reached out telepathically for Ellie.

"She's gone again, Ellie. He is distraught."

"What did he do?" Was it just the lack of nuance in telepathy that made Ellie sound neither surprised nor upset?

"He asked her to marry him."

"Yes!"

This time he was sure he caught her feelings of satisfaction. *"What do I do?"*

"Find her, of course. She's your ward, Gabe, your daughter. You don't want her lost and alone out there. Get searching with all the resources you can find."

"Last time I had to be reluctant. Sometimes I just don't understand you."

"Good thing, too. I'm on my way. Meet you at your office."

***

Gabriel stood in the doorway between his private office and the public outer office, watching Eleanor and Sister Chloe as they conferred over the search plans.

This is ridiculous. How hard can it be to find one eighteen-year-old girl with the full resources of a Great House at my disposal?

Chloe turned towards him. "She's not on campus anywhere," she said.

"I know," he replied. "I already checked. Have the Shields raised again and put perceptors at the boundaries to search as far out as they can sense. Put Philip on the town side, and Henry can check the wood side. Use Nick and Beth too."

"What about a search of the woods?" Chloe asked.

Eleanor responded before Gabriel could, "No. It's dark, it's late. There's no reason to think she's hurt so the woods can wait till tomorrow. We'll send search parties into town, where there's more light."

"There are shielded buildings in town," Chloe pointed out. "We should prioritise them."

"I should never have taught her to shield herself," Gabriel admitted, trying not to meet anyone's eyes.

To his surprise, Prospero corrected him, "She's known how for months, probably since before she got here."

Prospero had been sitting despondently with his head in his hands. Now he started pacing up and down to the extent the room would allow, checking on what everyone was doing. On the whole, Gabriel preferred it when Prospero was sitting still. At least then he wasn't interfering with the organisation and progress of the search. Gabriel strode over to beside Ellie and made a small gesture towards Prospero.

"He needs something to do, to occupy him," she whispered.

"I know that, but what? He'd be way too disruptive on a search team and right now he can't find the discipline to be useful as a perceptor. He'll not be able to stick to anything."

"If Mark pulls the Shields in as tight against the campus as possible, would the very top of the Abbey Tower be outside them?"

"You know it would, Ellie. I haven't changed that since Mel was up there, I just extended the Shields."

"So pull in the Shields and send him to the top of the tower to search from there. He'll be able to look wherever he chooses. He can pace round the top and he won't get in anyone else's way. Send Andrew to keep an eye on him."

That seemed to be as good an idea as any that Gabriel had, so he dispatched both Andrew and Prospero to the top of the Abbey Tower.

"It's going to be alright," Eleanor told him as they watched the office door close behind Andrew and Prospero. "We will find her. She won't be far away."

"How can you be so sure?"

Ellie just smiled at him. "I am though. My guess is we'll find her and have her back here before lunch tomorrow – I mean later today."

Andrew

On top of the Abbey tower, Prospero cycled through three activities – searching the surroundings with his mind, pacing up and down, and sitting in despair with his back against the parapet. None of them occupied him for long at a time. Right now he was in the despondent phase and Andrew sat beside him offering what comfort he could by his presence. Prospero tipped his head back against the wall, staring up at the stars. "Why did I do it?"

"Because you're impulsive, hot-headed, act without..."

"Andy!"

The anguish in Prospero's voice stopped Andrew in his tracks. "Seriously," Andrew continued, trying to keep his voice soft, "what I don't understand is why she ran away. You may have been a little impatient, but she loves you so what's scared her this much?"

Prospero shook his head. "I don't know. The other day I asked her how she felt about me and she almost ran. I thought I'd scared her then but it wasn't me she was scared of, it was something else. Like when she ran from the hospital; it wasn't us she was scared of, it was the hospital itself. But this time I don't know what it is."

"Commitment then? Perhaps she feels too young for marriage?"

"No, I don't think so. She's been living among Traders for the last few years at least. They tend to marry young so she'd be used to that."

"Maybe she's scared of actually being married, you know, the physical side. If she's heard about your past?"

"Has she? Who told her?"

"I don't know. She's not said anything to me but it seems unlikely that she hasn't heard."

"No." Prospero's voice was certain. "Whatever else, she's not scared of me, not in any sense, physically or emotionally."

"Maybe," ventured Andrew attempting to find his way through the minefield of Prospero's emotions, "just maybe, could she think she's not good enough? That something in her past means she can't be with you?"

"There's nothing, absolutely nothing that could possibly be in her past that would change how I feel about her," Prospero said fiercely, turning towards Andrew. "Nothing, you understand?"

"I know, I know that," Andrew said, resting his hand on Prospero's arm to calm him. "But does she?"

"Well, I can't tell her unless we find her. Come on!"

Clearly imbued with a fresh sense of purpose, Prospero got to his feet and leaned on the wall looking towards the town. Andrew scrambled up to stand next to him.

"Right," said Prospero. "Let's think about this. She's on foot and it's dark, so she can't go far, and she's got to hide both physically and mentally. She can't stay on the campus because we can drop the Shields and even if she's shielding from us, we'd see the energy pattern on the monitor. She can't go across the open farmland because we'd be able to see her, so her only choices are the wood or the town."

Andrew nodded in agreement and encouragement, although he was aware that Gabriel had already worked this out.

Prospero continued, "If she chooses the wood, she'll have to move slowly in the dark and by now she'll be struggling to find the energy to shield. And if she finds somewhere safe to stop she can't risk sleeping or she'll definitely drop her Shield and we'll spot her easily because she'll be the only person out there."

He glanced towards Andrew for confirmation, and again Andrew nodded and murmured agreement.

"So," Prospero carried on, "she must have chosen the town. There's people she knows there, places she could hide, and if she does drop her Shield there's probably only me who would be able to pick her out in a crowd."

Andrew pointed out the flaw. "She'll know that you'll be looking and able to spot her, so crowds won't help her. She'll either have to find somewhere with a Shield or get past your range. Does she even know how far you can see?"

"I don't know. She'd be able to work out it must be more than a couple of miles. But she's got Trader and Settler connections. They'd have Shields."

Again, Andrew disagreed. "They'll only have Dampener Shields. That'd stop her shielding but not you looking. She needs to find somewhere with Defender Shields that you can't see through, which mostly means churches and working and shopping areas."

Prospero shook his head. "Gabriel had the churches checked, and most working and shopping areas don't use Shields at night, when they're empty."

Their eyes met and Andrew voiced the thought they'd both had at the same time. "Does Leonie know that?"

Before they could take the thought further they were disturbed by the sound of footsteps as someone raced up the tower stairs.

Chloe appeared. Somewhat breathless, she spoke fast. "Philip's spotted something or someone in the riverside shopping area. It's at the limit of his range and it keeps disappearing and he can't be sure he recognises her, but there shouldn't be anyone there at this time. Can you look?"

Prospero turned back to the parapet wall and leaned out over it towards the town as if every inch closer would make a difference. "I can't see anything," he said. "No one inside. There's someone walking outside, but that's not Leonie."

"No," agreed Chloe. "There's a security guard there. Philip said it flickers, comes and goes. Could she be starting to fall asleep, but keeps waking? Or just getting too tired to maintain a steady

Shield?"

Andrew agreed absently that either scenario could lead to a flickering image. His eyes were fixed on Prospero's hands, gripping the top of the wall, knuckles white as the tightness of the grip reflected his concentration.

"Wait," Prospero said at last. "I saw something, just for a moment. It could be her." He paused. "Yes, I see it. It's her. We've found her." In almost the same moment he bent over, as if hit in the stomach, his hands still gripping the top of the wall. "Her colour," he gasped. "So dark. I have to get to her."

"You can't," Chloe told him, her voice worried. "We checked. We can't get into the area until morning, between six and seven maybe."

Andrew stepped closer to Prospero, standing over him as he crouched against the wall. Prospero looked up at him. "Andy," he pleaded. "She needs me. I can see her, I just can't reach her!"

Andrew reached out and placed his hand tenderly on Prospero's temple. "Breathe," he said, "and pray."

Leaving his hand there, he turned towards Chloe, meeting her eyes. Eyes that were wide in startled witness, and in which he could read her realisation that the rumours she must have heard and dismissed were probably true.

I thought she was too young to know, too new here to have heard.

He pushed the thought away to be dealt with another time and kept his voice low, his face calm. "Go and tell Lord Gabriel that we've found her," he said to Chloe. "We'll be down in a few minutes. We'll meet you at the gate on the town side."

Chloe nodded and raced off, although Andrew didn't even

wait to see her go before he turned back towards Prospero and squatted down beside him. "You hurt when she hurts?" he asked, not bothering to keep his concern and compassion from his voice.

Prospero nodded.

Andrew sighed. "Oh, Perry," he whispered, as he reached out with his mind and linked with Prospero.

If a person wasn't tall enough to reach something on a high shelf, a friend could help by lifting them up; two people could reach further than one. It was the same with the Gifts; by linking minds together, Andrew and Prospero could reach further than Prospero could alone. But, in the same way that a physical tower couldn't be maintained for long, or could become unstable the more people were involved, so such linking of minds like this was limited and of short duration. This link was strong enough for Prospero to reach Leonie's sleeping mind. Andrew felt his delicate touch as he soothed her and saw the colour she appeared in the image in Prospero's mind improve. Once he thought Leonie would stay asleep without Prospero's help, Andrew broke the link and both he and Prospero sank down with their backs against the wall, breathless from their exertions.

"I must try not to make a habit of this," Prospero muttered.

"You've done it before?" Andrew asked him, voice rising with alarm. "You understand how entirely inappropriate it is?"

"I do. But it's been for her benefit both times and anyway, I'm going to marry her." Prospero's voice was euphoric with relief at having found Leonie.

"Only if she agrees," Andrew insisted. "And anyway, at least promise me you won't do it again without telling her."

"How can I tell her when she's asleep and I'm not there?" Prospero stood up. "Come on. Gabriel will be waiting for us."

Andrew followed him down the stairs. "You know someone will have spotted us doing that?" he said.

Prospero brushed it off. "Who? Neither Gabriel nor Eleanor can reach that far and it's at the limit of Philip's ability so he won't have spotted it. Henry was looking on the other side of the campus and Beth doesn't have the experience to have noticed it. So that leaves Nick, and if he saw it, he won't tell."

Andrew just shook his head, not quite sure that the confident euphoric Prospero was an improvement on the uncertain miserable one. By the time they'd reached the gatehouse on the town side of the campus, Gabriel, Eleanor and Chloe were already there. Gabriel's look at Andrew and Prospero was penetrating enough to make Andrew wince, certain that Gabriel must know what they'd done, but at least Gabriel didn't say anything. Prospero rushed headlong through the main archway towards town.

Gabriel called him back. "No," he said firmly, his voice harsh. "She's safe enough. We're watching her from here, and I've people watching the shopping area exits."

Prospero came to a sudden halt, looking back at Gabriel in what Andrew could only interpret as astonishment and indignation.

"You have my permission to leave here at six this morning," Gabriel continued, his voice still hard. "No earlier. In the meantime, you are to sleep. You look like you've used far too much energy today already. If anything changes, you will be woken."

Prospero opened his mouth to object, but to Andrew's relief something – probably the look on Gabriel's face – made him stop.

Gabriel softened slightly. "Use the bed in the office. You'll be close to hand if anything happens. Andrew, go with him, and sleep too, if you can."

Prospero turned and went without any public comment, but he muttered to Andrew most of the way. "Sleep, if you can! I'm not going to be able to sleep. How am I supposed to sleep when she's out there alone and scared? I need to get to her. I need to be with her. She needs me. How can I sleep when she needs me?"

"Even you aren't daft enough to say you can't sleep, are you?" Andrew warned him. "You do know what will happen if you do? You won't be given any choice. You'll be given something to make you sleep and you won't be awake by six for sure. At least lie down and pretend to sleep." He drew a deep breath and started again before Prospero could answer. "And anyway, Leonie is peacefully asleep, thanks to you. Right now she doesn't know she's scared or alone, and she's safe and she's being watched. Nothing's going to happen to her in the next few hours."

Wisely, Prospero took Andrew's advice, lay down on the bed and closed his eyes. He obviously had no intention or expectation of sleep but, as Gabriel had noticed, he had used a great deal of energy searching for Leonie, fretting about her and then soothing her sleep. Andrew watched until he was sure Prospero was deeply asleep and then lay down on the couch to sleep himself.

Chapter 2

Monday Morning

Andrew

"Come on, wake up, we have to go get Leonie." Someone was shaking Andrew.

"Get off," he grumbled, still more than half asleep. "What is it? What's happening?"

"We have to get Leonie." Prospero's voice was urgent, almost panicked.

Andrew pushed him away and sat up. "I need coffee first. Not going anywhere without coffee."

Chloe, who he hadn't noticed until that point, pushed a hot mug into his hands with a smile. "Here, take this. Leonie's still asleep, but we expect them to switch the Shields on any minute. You can get going as soon as you're ready."

Slightly more awake after several mouthfuls of coffee, Andrew risked a glance at Prospero, who was almost vibrating with impatience and unable to keep still. He gulped down the coffee, deciding to be ready very quickly. They met Lord Gabriel, Lady Eleanor and several others at the gate on the town side of the campus. Prospero stepped outside the range of the campus Shields for a moment, obviously checking on Leonie for himself, and then, with a sigh, turned back towards where Gabriel was giving instructions.

"Andrew, Nick," Gabriel said. "You're to go with Prospero to the shopping area, but only Prospero is to go in to search for Leonie. Should all be well, you can return here, and bring with you those who've been stationed there overnight. Prospero, if you need help, you ask for it, understood?"

Prospero nodded. Andrew hoped he meant it.

"Should there be problems," Gabriel continued, "Nick is in charge, and I am relying on all of you to make sensible decisions."

He looked hard at Prospero, but didn't comment further before sending them off with a wave of his hand. Andrew trailed slightly behind the other two.

"I hope this works," he overheard Gabriel say. "I don't think Prospero would make any sensible decision right now, not if Leonie turns him down. I can't see him letting her walk away."

"No," Eleanor replied sounding satisfied. "Neither can I."

***

They were almost at the shopping area when Prospero increased his pace sharply.

"*What?*" Andrew asked telepathically as he hurried to catch up, Nick matching his pace.

"*The Shields have been switched on. I can't sense her anymore.*"

The main entrance was just being unlocked as they arrived, and they paused for a moment outside. Andrew and Nick glanced at each other, and then Andrew turned to Prospero. "Go on, then," he said. "I guess it's now or never. We'll be praying for you. Let us know if you need us."

Prospero nodded in thanks and acknowledgement, took a deep breath, then stepped through the entrance.

Leonie

Voices tried to find their way in. No words, just a hum of sound. Then a knock, a clatter as something dropped, hitting the ground hard. I bolted upright, not sure for a moment where I was, scanned the room with eyes and senses, then sagged with relief to find no one there. I was in the back room at the bakery I used to work at and what I could hear was the sound of the shopping area starting to come to life around me. Today was a holiday but it made little difference for this particular shopping area. It focused on fresh foods, baked goods and cafés, and most places would be open to entice those spending a relaxed day free from work.

The pain of having to leave Perry hit me sharply again but I had only a few minutes before someone would arrive to unlock this shop and catch me hiding, so I collected up my things and left. The Shields were still on, but there were a few people milling around already. I pulled my hood up in case anyone noticed my hair, and I found a bench to sit on in the central plaza while I thought things through again.

My plan had been to steal anything I might need and then catch a train out of here just as fast as I could. That would get me out of the range that Perry could search. I knew now that I couldn't do that. I'd stolen before, many times, but it was one thing to steal when it was the only way to get what you needed for survival, or for the survival of others. It was quite another to do so under these circumstances, and I wasn't going to. I could buy what I needed, but one way or another I'd be noticed and remembered – I was known round here, at least by some. It was the same for the train. I'd never been on one but I assumed I'd have to pay somebody something. Then they'd remember me too, a girl who didn't know what she was doing.

As I sat there, I realised the real problem was that I didn't actually want to leave. Even if I couldn't have him, Perry was where I belonged, the place I fitted, where I was safe. I needed to know where he was, how he was, that he was okay. And this Great House, these people I'd been with for months now, they were the closest I'd ever felt to having a family. I knew Perry had left his birth family and I'd not been able to understand it. Now I was beginning to comprehend that there could be reasons, circumstances under which that was the only option. But he always knew the right thing to do, he was strong and brave and I wasn't. I didn't think I had the strength or courage to walk away from what had been offered me, but nor could I take it up.

Unable to leave, and unable to stay, I sat there on the bench, arms around my knees, paralysed by indecision.

Prospero

Prospero came to a standstill almost as soon as he'd entered the shielded shopping area. Where would she be? The place was a maze of little streets and alleyways. Without thinking, he reached out to look for her with his mind, and hit the Dampener Shield. Idiot. He was going to have to do this the hard way.

Right, where would I hide if I were her?

He studied his surroundings, trying to concentrate, to think instead of rushing headlong. There were one or two people around, starting to roll up blinds, unlock shops, set out café chairs. Leonie wasn't likely to be in the busier areas, the ones that opened for the early trade. She'd have found somewhere quieter, one of the lanes where the shops opened later, surely?

Or, given that she'd somehow got into this place when it was locked, might she have also got into the back room of one of these shops? How could he possibly find her if she'd done that? It would be easy enough to miss her in this maze even if she wasn't trying to hide from him. With no other option coming to mind, he headed towards the central plaza.

One of the workers setting out chairs caught his eye with a smile. "Good morning, Brother," she said.

Ask, you idiot, ask for help.

Prospero turned towards the worker. "Good morning," he replied. "I wonder if you can help me. I'm looking for Lord Gabriel's ward. She's about this tall"—he indicated her height—"with curly red hair and I think she'd be wearing grey trousers and tunic."

The woman shook her head. "I've not seen anyone like that around this morning." She called a colleague over from inside the café.

The second woman agreed, "No one answering that description, today, no." She studied Prospero. "There used to be someone like that working at one of the bakeries. Leonie, she was called. But I've not seen her for a while either."

"Leonie, that's her," Prospero said. "Which bakery was it? Can you tell me where it is?" If Leonie knew one of the shops here well, that would be where she'd hide for sure. And a bakery. No wonder she got on so well with Pedro.

The woman shrugged. "Sure. You don't want to go all the way to the centre or you'll miss it. Take the next left up here, then there's a right turn. Don't take that, but go past the next shop, then up a little alleyway to your right. It twists a bit, but it opens out onto the lane the bakery is on. When you get to the end of the alleyway, you want to turn left again, away from central plaza, and it's the second shop on your right. Got it?"

Prospero nodded. "Left, alleyway to right, turn left, second on the right. Thank you so much."

He set off, trying hard not to run, at least not until he was out of sight. Left turn, alleyway – he ran through there – left again, and there was the bakery, just being opened up.

"Excuse me," he said to the man out front, "I'm looking for

Leonie. Have you seen her today?"

The man shook his head. "I'm sorry, Brother. She hasn't worked here for a while."

"I know that," Prospero replied, trying to keep calm. "She's Lord Gabriel's ward but she's gone missing. I thought she might have come here."

"She's good at hiding, that one. You'll not find her unless she wants you to."

Prospero sighed and his shoulders slumped. "That's what I was afraid of. Thank you anyway."

He turned towards the central plaza, his head down, feet dragging, not sure where to go next. He might as well sit there and think about what to do now. He looked up as he entered the space, still all but empty in the early morning.

And there she was, perched on one of the benches to one side, hood pulled over her head, knees drawn up to her chin, and looking as if she was lost in thought. As delight surged through him, he breathed out her name in relief. She couldn't possibly have heard at that distance but she looked towards him. He caught the sheer joy on her face and body language for a moment before it was replaced by overwhelming sadness, loss and rejection. She scooped up her backpack and turned away from him. Terrified she would run again, he was at her side in a moment, taking her by the shoulders and pulling her towards him. She didn't resist but nor did she move closer. He didn't know what to say and again blurted out the first words at the top of his mind.

"Leonie, marry me."

"How can I?" she said bitterly. "You are a monk, the Order doesn't marry. You can't leave where you belong for me. Even if you could, someone like you can't marry the likes of me. And Lord

Gabriel would never permit it. Let me go, it's better this way."

She pulled away from him and ran, heading out of the shopping area. He set off after her, his longer legs partly compensating for her extra nimbleness in avoiding obstacles. They were halfway down the street before he caught her up. He levelled with her, then reached out and pulled her towards him, using his telekinetic Gifts both to hold onto her and bring them to a stop. She fought back, as he had expected her to, flailing at him with arms and legs. He was prepared; he held her physically close so she couldn't get much momentum to punch or kick him, though he suspected he'd still find a few bruises later.

She gathered power around her but moved upwards, aiming her shoulder for his chin instead of pulling away. He jerked his head away. She wrapped her legs around his waist, her heels beating a tattoo on his back as she continued to push upwards. He concentrated his own energy on dampening hers, on holding her still to minimise injuries to them both. She stopped attacking him physically, but now she devoted her mental strength to combating his tactics. She pushed against his mind with all the power she could muster, a battering ram seeking his weak points, searching for where he was vulnerable. How was he supposed to deal with this when all he could think of was the feel of her arms and legs wrapped around him, the weight of her head on his shoulder, her breath warm on his neck? He aimed only to keep hold of her and keep them both unhurt while she fought out her fear and anger, loss and uncertainty against him. Just as he was beginning to think this was more than he could manage, her mental attack weakened. He relaxed a little and she took advantage, pushing her upper body away from his, although her legs were still clamped around his waist, and his arms around her shoulders.

"Let me go! Let me go! I hate you!"

Pulling her back towards him until their foreheads touched, he smiled, his eyes seeking hers. "Liar," he breathed, slipping one hand into her hair and touching her lips with his own.

Their kiss was deep and passionate, her mouth and body betraying her words to show her true feelings, her hands now caressing rather than attacking. She unwrapped her legs from his body as he lifted his mouth from hers and he placed her standing on the ground unrestrained by his hands, body or Gifts. He took one step back and she stared at him, eyes wide and bewildered, one hand unconsciously lifting to touch her lips.

He spoke softly. "I'm not going to make you come with me. We both know I could, but I won't. I will never force you. This is your free choice. One step towards me and we will face all these problems and find the best solutions we can, together. Or look me in the eye and tell me to my face you don't want to be with me. Then walk away and I won't chase after you. Your choice to make."

Time seemed to stand still as he kept his eyes locked on her face, watching her indecision as she battled with her hopes, fears and desires. Her body was angled for flight, her mouth open to frame his name, but no sound came. Then she took a step forward. Time and sound rushed back and he pulled her into his arms, holding her close, saying her name over and over again in relief. Energy swirled around them, generated by their emotions. Even though the street was deserted this early in the morning this wasn't a suitable place for that. He needed to do something with all this energy, quickly. He wrapped his arms more tightly around Leonie, touched her mind with his and teleported them both to the park along the river bank. He misjudged the landing slightly, stumbled, and they ended up rolling together on the grass. Under the circumstances it seemed entirely natural for their lips to meet.

Sometime later – it might have been minutes, it could have been days as far as Prospero was concerned – he pulled away with a great effort of will. "I'm going to renounce my vows, but I will not break them. I think I've probably bent them quite a long way already."

Leonie sat up and looked around. "How did we even get here? What did you do?"

He shrugged. "We had so much energy between us. I couldn't think what else to do with it. I teleported us. It's not far, look the shopping area is only over there." He pointed to where it was just visible through the trees.

She glanced back and forth between him and the trees with disbelief. "You can teleport?" she said, amazed. "Show me."

"Later," he said. "It takes a lot of energy and we have other things to talk about now."

She looked away from him, down at the ground, not meeting his eyes, but he reached over and pulled her into his arms again.

"Before that," he said, fishing in his pocket, "Here is your necklace back." He fastened it around her neck. "It's yours," he said. "Yours, no matter what. You didn't have to leave it behind."

She just shook her head at him, fingering the necklace and its jewels. He settled her more comfortably with his arms around her. She rested against him, utterly overwhelmed by the magnitude of the decision she had just made. He wanted to hold her and reassure her, tell her everything would be alright. But he knew that to make it alright, they had to face up to why she had run, and the longer they left that, the harder it would become.

"Now," he said. "Two of your objections I can deal with straight away. Firstly, I'm going to leave the Order anyway, whether I can persuade you to marry me or not. There are things outside that it's time I dealt with. And secondly, Lord Gabriel has already agreed to our marriage as long as it's what you want. So, what other problems can you find that we need to work out together?"

She still wouldn't look at him. "I'm younger than you," she mumbled into his chest.

He took her chin in his hand and turned her head so she had to look up at him. "I don't think you're trying very hard," he told her with a smile. "Andrew has made it quite clear that he thinks you are both more mature and have more sense than me. He's usually right. All the difference in our ages means is that I've got a few more memories and experiences than you have. And we both have blanks in our memories so that's probably not much to go on. We've both got the present and no one knows how much future they have so all the more reason to make the most of now."

He released her chin as she shivered at his words and cradled her head against his chest.

"There's something else you're really frightened of, isn't there?" he asked softly. "Can you tell me what it is?"

She pulled away slightly and this time she turned to look at him. "I... When... They..." she stuttered, then shook her head as if trying to clear it. "I want to," she said, clearly. "I can't. It's stuck in my head. Too frightened. No words."

"Okay," he said. "Are you up for trying something a little scary in your head?"

"Scary for me or scary for you?"

A quick smile flitted across his face. "Both. But we'll be right there together all the time."

She nodded. "What do we do?"

"First, just link to my mind like we've done before, and let me touch yours." He felt her touch and settle against his mind almost before he'd finished speaking and very gently he reciprocated. Her mind was wide open to him, no Shield, no barriers at all.

"Thank you," he whispered in appreciation. "Now, I'm in your head too, so take that link and show me what the thing is. I'll be right here all the time, so however scary it is, you'll be quite safe."

Leonie

Perry was giving me the opportunity to tell him everything, and I would not refuse him. I couldn't. The thought of telling him terrified me but whatever the outcome, he was entitled to know before we went further. I hoped against hope that he would still be there when he found out all about me.

I wove my mind round his link, and then guided him through the things I had been and done, my memories, such as they were, showing him the good and the bad, blanks and all. I laid out for him all the things I couldn't put into words, in the hope that he would understand them. I didn't hide anything that I could remember. There was no point; either he would see all this and leave me, or he wouldn't. I couldn't live any longer with keeping it secret from him. When we'd finished I was shaking both from the sheer effort and relief of sharing it all with someone and from my fear that he'd no longer feel the same way about me. He just looked at me and spoke, his voice soft.

"Did you really think that any of that would make a difference to how I love you?"

I didn't know how to answer that, because of course that was just what I had thought. "I thought it might change whether you wanted to be with me, whether you were even allowed to, with all the things I've been and done."

His voice was still soft, but intense. "The fault lies with the people who've treated you like this. I'm not ashamed of what you have been or done, I'm proud of you for all that you have achieved, despite so much being against you. It's your past that makes you the person you are today. What you have been and what you have had to do to survive don't matter, it's the person you are that I love."

"You really don't mind?" I found it difficult to believe, but I hoped so much that it was true.

"I mind that you have had to suffer, that you've been cold and hungry and mistreated and scared and alone and unloved. I mind so much that I don't know how to contain how I feel, and what I want to do to those responsible conflicts with all my beliefs. But it was all done to you, not by you. How can I mind what you are, when I love you?"

He kissed me again and I knew he meant what he'd said. Then he wrapped his arms around me and held me close to him again, my head against his chest.

Very gently he asked me, "There's more worrying you too, isn't there? Can you tell me what that is?"

I shook my head against him, but he persisted. "You've shown me, haven't you? It's in there somewhere, in what I've seen, I just have to work out what it is." He stroked my head as I nodded. "I will, you know. Work it out, I mean. And whatever it is, it doesn't matter. There is nothing that can change how I feel about you."

I looked up at him; I had yet another worry, and this one I could share with him. "And Lord Gabriel? Won't he mind about all this?"

He smiled. "Lord Gabriel will feel just as I do about your past and he has already given his permission. So you see, you have no reason to say no." He took a deep breath. "Leonie, my love, please will you do me the honour of becoming my wife?"

"Truly, you want this?" I needed to be certain.

"Yes, I do, if you will."

"Then, yes, yes, I will."

I twisted round, reaching up to place one hand on either side of his face. Then I did what I had so wanted to do, for so long, and this time, I was the one who kissed him.

Chapter 3

Prospero

Prospero could have sat there for a long time with Leonie safe in his arms but her skin was pale and she seemed a little shaky. He realised it must have been hours since she'd eaten and she'd been using all that energy, as had he. And he'd not told anyone he'd found her.

"Andy," he called. *"I've got her. She's okay. We'll be back soon."*

"I figured. I'll pass the message on."

"Come on," Prospero said to Leonie, getting to his feet and pulling her up. "You must be starving. I know I am and there's a café just along the path."

She came with him, compliant but quiet, gripping his hand until they reached the café. Concerned about her wellbeing, Prospero sat her at a table by the window and went to the counter to order some food.

Emmi was serving today, just as she had for many years. Prospero had been a frequent customer in his student days, often with one of his many girlfriends, and he still treated himself to a visit every few months. In his opinion, Emmi provided one of the best breakfasts around, although these days he tended to stop for coffee and cake, usually on his way back from a clinic in the town. Leonie needed something immediately, so, as well as ordering breakfast, he asked for two glasses of milk and some fruit.

"It's a long while since I've seen you in here with a young lady," Emmi said, teasing him a little as she served him. Prospero smiled sheepishly, and she went on, "Well, you take care of this one. She's well known and loved around here but she needs someone to look out for her."

Prospero was a little surprised at her comments; he hadn't thought of Leonie as having contacts in town outside the Settler group, but he grinned back at Emmi, leaned towards her and said quietly, but with feeling, "Emmi, this one I will love forever and protect with my life."

Then he picked up the milk and fruit and went back to Leonie, leaving Emmi staring after him. He sat opposite Leonie and insisted she ate some of the fruit and drink the milk. He started to relax as the food had its effect, the light returning to her eyes, and her colour improving considerably.

"Emmi knows you," he said. "Have you been here before?"

She nodded. "Usually round the back, though," she told him.

He worked it out. "Emmi gives you food for whoever it is you take it to, doesn't she?"

Again, Leonie nodded.

"Are you going to tell me who that is?" he asked.

"Sometime," she said.

He didn't push it, not today. She'd told him more than enough secrets for one day and he trusted that she'd tell him this too, eventually.

Emmi brought their food over and he realised that she'd tailored each breakfast to their personal preferences. He was impressed that she'd remembered his likes and dislikes; it also meant that she knew Leonie well. She gave them both rather curious looks but left them to eat in peace. As they ate, Prospero thought that perhaps it was both time and fair that he shared some of his secrets.

"You should know about my past, too," he said.

"What makes you think I don't? Your"—and Leonie's eyes were now full of mischief as she searched for the right word —"Brothers have been eager to share all they know."

He put his head in his hands in mock despair. "I have been betrayed. Who was it?"

"It was more than one person, and not just Brothers. But you're more interested in who than in what?"

"I know what, I was there. Mostly."

"Mostly?"

"Some of it I can't remember. I told you there were blanks in my memories. But go on, what do you know?"

She looked at him as if wondering where to begin, but started with a question. "You said your family were farmers. Things others have said make it sound like there's a lot of land?"

He was relieved she'd put this interpretation onto what she'd heard. "It is a big farm," he confirmed. "They're very successful at what they do."

If she didn't know already, more details and his full family background could wait until later. Right now, he was afraid it would make her run again.

She carried on, "You and Andrew were friends from the beginning. You had bad nightmares but to start with they were eased by your girlfriend, Lesley. Only, you split up big time, major argument sometime before your first Easter here. It must have been serious because she left and didn't come back, but no one knows what it was about, or at least they're not telling." She looked up at him, brows raised in mute question.

"Well, that's one small mercy. I'll tell you later. Go on."

"After you broke up, you started partying, drinking, sleeping around. Always got your work done well and on time, always where you were supposed to be, but hardly ever entirely sober."

To his relief her voice was factual, not judgemental. "That's rather an exaggeration," he said. "I usually only drank at night, at least to start with. It was only towards the end I started to drink during the day."

"And is the bit about sleeping with a different girl every night also an exaggeration?"

"Yes, although there were a lot and it was rarely the same girl twice."

"So I heard. Except for Melanie who encouraged you in all this. And your nightmares got worse though Andrew could nearly always calm them. He was as bad as you, by the way, and you were practically inseparable."

"That's all true enough. But don't put the blame on Melanie. I went along willingly. Eagerly even."

She looked at him with what could only be described as compassion. "It was the nightmares, wasn't it?" she asked. "You drank and slept around to try and beat the nightmares only it got out of control. That's why you warned me about not doing that, isn't it?"

He looked down at his plate, unwilling to meet her eyes. Even now the memories of the nightmares he'd had – nightmares suffered by all those who developed Gifts – were something he didn't want to think about.

"Perry?" she said softly, using his childhood nickname, and he looked up.

"Yes," he confessed. "Yes, to both questions. I could just about cope with Andrew's help, though I know now I was taking advantage of him, abusing our friendship, but then he was called to join the Order and without him I fell apart pretty quickly."

"From what I heard you went away with some girl and when you came back rather than just falling apart you pretty much blew everything apart?"

He smiled slightly at her description. "I saw myself as others saw me and I didn't like it," he explained shortly. He knew he owed her more explanation than that. "The obvious consequence of that was the worst nightmare I've ever had. I ended up in hospital, not just because of the nightmare but because I'd injured myself. I did a lot of damage too, far more than you've ever done."

Leonie just looked at him curiously, waiting for him to go on.

"That was rock bottom for me. I couldn't go on. But despite everything I'd done and everything I'd said, Andrew was there for me. He sat there and was quiet when I needed quiet and listened when I needed to talk and helped me as I tried to turn my life around. Somewhere in all that I had my Damascene moment and realised that the only thing I could do was to give my life to Jesus and follow him."

"What's a Damascene moment?" she asked him.

Again he smiled slightly. "I forget that you don't know what I know," he said. "In the Bible, after Jesus died and rose again, there was someone called Saul who tracked down believers and persecuted them. One day, on the way to a place called Damascus, he met Jesus, saw him when those travelling with him didn't. After that, Saul turned his life around and became a believer, changed his name to Paul and went on to tell many others about Jesus. He wrote quite a lot of what is now the Bible. So, a Damascene moment is a moment of insight that leads to a transformation in your life."

"Is it sudden like that for everyone?"

"No, just some. For others it's a gradual thing."

Leonie nodded her acceptance of that and went back to her recitation of his past. "Then you decided to join the Order and that caused a major rift with your family which still isn't properly resolved."

He looked at her in astonishment. "How could you possibly know that? Only Andrew and Lord Gabriel know about that and neither would tell anyone, not even you."

She grinned back at him triumphantly. "I didn't know, I guessed and you just confirmed it."

He shook his head in resignation. "Go on then, what gave me away?"

"Everyone else who has or even once had family talks about them. You don't, you barely even answer direct questions about them. And everyone else with family visits them or is visited by them occasionally; even Brother Mark went nearly halfway round the world to see his family, so don't claim they live too far away."

"There are plenty who don't visit family."

"Only because they don't have family, not because they choose not to for years and years. Anyway, I'm right, so what happened?"

Food had been what she'd needed, he thought. In the course of a meal she'd gone from scared and shaky, in need of his care and protection to the feisty, curious woman he'd fallen in love with.

"It's complicated," he said.

"Everyone always says that," Leonie complained. "And it usually turns out to be pretty simple in the end."

Prospero smiled at that. "You're probably right."

Hesitantly and carefully, he started to explain his family relationships. His mother was the youngest of four children, the three eldest of whom had agreed to arranged marriages to strengthen the family position, though the eldest sister had died before Prospero had been born. His mother had married for love; an adequate marriage by her family standards, but not a great one. That had been the beginnings of a rift with her family although Prospero thought that they had been on reasonable terms during his early childhood. Something had happened when he'd been about nine, but he didn't know what, just that they'd stopped visiting and seeing his cousins and their parents. The real trouble had started when he'd been about eleven or twelve and had then escalated through his teen years. His uncle, by then head of the family, had chosen Prospero and his cousin Brin to train as his potential heirs. His uncle's own son, Danny, had been in poor health all his life and had died when Prospero and Brin were in their mid-teens. Although Danny had a sister, she was just a small child, and Prospero's uncle had wanted to ensure the continuity of the family and the security of its assets, lands and businesses. Prospero's mother had been furious; she wanted nothing to do with her family and wanted Prospero to take over their farm from his father.

Prospero had not wanted to disoblige either faction – or indeed been in a position to – and so his teen years had been about balancing the conflict. On top of that, he'd wanted to be a doctor, which didn't fit with either his uncle's or his mother's plans for him. When he'd come to study at the college, neither party had known he had chosen to study medicine, each thinking he was taking the courses appropriate for their own plans.

His breakdown had brought everything into the open. His choice of the Order had been seen by his mother as a rejection of her and her life choices. His uncle had been a little more relaxed about it, convinced that it was just a phase and prepared to welcome Prospero back once it was over. His dismissal of Prospero's beliefs and convictions hadn't exactly helped the relationship between them.

"Maybe a little bit complicated," Leonie conceded. "But...you chose not to belong to them?"

Her voice was incredulous, and he was aware what an issue this was for her. He picked his words with care. "I chose to belong here. This is a family, too. But I still belong to the people there, just not their way of life."

"Couldn't they forgive you?"

"Oh, yes, my mother forgave me, although it took time, and Matt, my next brother, is a much better farmer than I'd ever have been. It's not that, it's me, I've never been able to face up to going back, seeing the hurt I caused to people I love. I can't forget what I did to them, even though I know I was doing the right thing for me. We write, though, most weeks."

"What do you write about?"

"I don't know, things that have been happening. They tell me about what's happening on the farm, in the family, what people I grew up with are doing, that sort of thing."

"Have you written about me?"

"No, not yet."

Prospero truly believed that he hadn't written about

Leonie. Not much, anyway. Maybe he'd mentioned her once or twice. Leonie's face fell. Far more aware now of her insecurities, Prospero reached over and stroked her cheek, making her look up at him.

"I wasn't ashamed of you," he explained. "I wanted to keep how I feel about you all to myself, not share it, or you, with anyone. Even here, the only people who know are Lord Gabriel and Andrew and Lady Eleanor."

Leonie looked up at him. "After we're married—" she started.

But Prospero interrupted her, "Say that again, I like the sound of it."

She smiled back at him. "After we're married, can I write to them?"

"Of course you can. They'll be your family too."

"My family?" she whispered. "I'll have a family?"

Prospero saw the light in her eyes and made a sudden decision. "Yes, and sometime soon, perhaps later this summer, I'll take you to meet them."

"Truly? But what about…?"

"Yes, truly. It's time I faced up to that, and I want you to meet them and them to meet you. Right now, though, I think we should go and see Lord Gabriel. Are you ready?"

"You haven't told me everything yet!" Now she sounded indignant.

His voice was full of laughter. "You think there might be more things your sources haven't told you?"

Leonie shrugged. "They can tell me what happened. Only

you can tell me why it happened."

"And that's what interests you most? You never fail to impress me. Suppose I agree to answer your questions while we walk?"

Leonie readily agreed and they headed back towards the Abbey.

Chapter 4

Prospero

As they walked, Prospero took Leonie's hand in his. "I'm not letting you run away from me again, ever," he said.

"I wasn't running away."

He turned towards her, taking her chin in his hand and tilting her face up so that she had to look him straight in the eye. "No? It looked remarkably like running away to me."

"No. I wasn't running away. Not exactly. I found I couldn't. I just thought it would be better for you if I wasn't around."

"Never better without you," he replied gently.

"I couldn't leave last night, so I just hid."

"You did that very well. You had me worried. I was frantic when I couldn't find you."

"How did you find me? I shielded until long after I was inside the shopping area, and I know that has Shields too."

Again he was very gentle. "Did you not realise that if you were able to shield, its Shield must have been switched off?"

Leonie looked crestfallen as he went on. "It only has Shields on when the shops are open, not at night. Once you dropped your Shield – when you fell asleep? – we spotted you, but I couldn't get to you until the shopping area opened. And do I even want to know how you got into a secure and guarded shopping area in the middle of the night?"

"Probably not," Leonie acknowledged with a grin, her crestfallen look disappearing. "I didn't know about the Shields not being on."

"I'm glad you didn't!"

"Anyway, I thought I was supposed to be asking the questions?"

"Go on then, fire away!"

"What made you want to be a doctor so much?"

He was surprised. "That's your first question? Most women would be asking about the other women I'd slept with."

Leonie shrugged. "Mostly they aren't important. But it was you wanting to be a doctor that started the problem with your family, so it must be really important to you."

He was amazed at her perception. "You know how to cut to the heart of things, don't you?" He carried on, "When I was about nine, my little sister was born. She only lived a few hours and my mother was devastated. She tried to put a brave face on it for us kids, but I decided then that I wanted to use my life to stop others suffering like that. I didn't realise that they had other plans for me."

"Do your parents know it was because of your sister?"

He shook his head. "They were so upset by losing Jenny, how could I tell them that?"

"Jenny, that's a pretty name. I like that."

He smiled at her, amused that she seemed to have been distracted by his sister's name. The distraction didn't last long.

"Did you tell anyone you wanted to be a doctor?" she asked.

He answered honestly. "Yes. I had a friend, Clare, and we grew up together from when we were small children. I told Clare, and she encouraged me, especially when we were older and I was applying to college."

"What about Clare? Did she go to college?"

Prospero sighed. "No, Clare's parents felt more education wasn't necessary for girls, that she should get married, raise a family, run a household. Clare said she didn't have the courage or strength to go against them for herself, but by supporting and encouraging me to do what I chose, she was doing something to move the world on. She saw my family's demands on me as old fashioned, out of date."

"What happened to Clare?"

"She got married and is running a household and raising a family, just like her parents wanted. She has three small boys, and a fourth child on the way."

"Is she happy?"

"Happy? I don't know. Content perhaps, rather than happy."

Leonie nodded and appeared to be thinking about her next question.

Prospero took a deep breath. "Leonie, you should know that Clare was the first woman I ever slept with."

She looked at him as if he were being stupid. "Well, obviously," she said.

He stopped, pulling on her hand and swinging her back into his arms. "No, not obviously. We kept it secret and since then the only people I have ever told are Andrew and Gabriel and now you. So, why obviously?"

Leonie grinned up at him, eyes full of light and mischief. "She was the person you were closest to, the only one close enough you could tell her about your ambitions, and she's female. I should think that makes it pretty obvious but also it's the way you say her name in your head."

He was astounded. "You're reading my mind?"

She shook her head. "No, but I can hear you say her name."

He protested. "But I was shielding, I always shield, it's automatic. You do too."

She nodded and shrugged at the same time, a movement he found extremely...arousing, given he still had his arms around her. "I didn't hear anything else, just her name. And the other names that matter, of course. You were thinking about them too."

He was wary now. "Which other names?"

Leonie gave him a dark look. "It's not like they are any secret. Lesley, Melanie and Marie. I mean, I've been told of loads of others but those are the only ones that are important."

Prospero released her and started walking again, though he kept hold of her hand. "If I didn't know better, I'd think Gabriel or Andrew had been telling you all my secrets."

She shook her head earnestly. "They haven't, honest. Others have, but they don't know which ones are important. That was you." Still holding his hand she half ran, half danced so that she was ahead of him and could look back at his face, her own etched with worry and concern. "Was I wrong?"

He stopped and pulled her back into his arms again. "No, you weren't wrong, don't look so worried." He bent his head and kissed her, meaning it to be reassuring, but he was again taken aback by the effect she had on him. He took a deep breath. "You have every right to ask, and every right to know. It's just..." He paused and ran his hands through his hair. "I thought it would be easy, telling you about all this. It's all history, done and over, way in the past. But it turns out it's not—either easy, or in the past. You've already made me think again about my relationship with my family, and agree to go meet them for the first time in years. I'm starting to re-evaluate how I treated Clare. None of it paints me in a very good light and any minute now you're going to ask me why Lesley and I split up."

Leonie nodded as he paused and then continued, "And I thought I was the injured party there, utterly in the right, and I strongly suspect you're going to make me look at it differently."

Leonie smiled at him. "It doesn't have to be now, we've got forever. Tomorrow, next week, next year, never, whenever you want, there's no hurry."

"No," he said. "I'll tell you about Lesley now. I said I would and it will only get harder. The others can wait, but you should know about Lesley."

He guided her over to a bench and they sat down. Leonie looked at him expectantly, but he didn't know how to start. Eventually he just came out with it. "I made her pregnant. We were careful, but not careful enough."

"You have a child?" Leonie's eyes were wide, her skin paler than usual.

"You look so shocked. No, I don't. Lesley had an abortion." He could sense Leonie shrinking away from him, retreating into herself, even if her body barely moved. Somehow, every issue in his past seemed to touch a raw nerve for her, but he had to carry on. "That wasn't what we split up over, at least not directly. If I'd known I would have told her it was her right to make the final decision. What drove us apart was that she didn't tell me. I didn't even know she was pregnant until after she'd had the abortion. I'd suspected, and asked her and she'd denied it. After that I couldn't trust her, and she'd clearly not been able to trust me and that pretty much destroyed everything."

"What happened to Lesley?" Leonie sounded concerned—it was just like her to want to know the outcome for everyone involved in an issue.

"She moved to a different college and hospital to continue her training – her choice – and became an excellent doctor. She's very well respected in her field. She got married a few years back, that's all I know."

"Would it have made a difference if she'd told you first?"

"I don't know. How can I know? To the eventual outcome, maybe not. I would have offered to marry her, support her and the child, and any other children, of course, but if she'd still wanted an abortion, I'd have supported her through that, too. Or if she hadn't wanted the child I would have raised them. The difference would have been that we'd still have trusted each other."

Prospero studied Leonie carefully as she took all this in. She still seemed withdrawn, remote and he didn't know what raw nerve he'd touched. He wasn't aware of anything particular that she'd told him, but abortion was always an emotive issue. She slid her hand into his and spoke quietly.

"It must have been very hard for both of you."

He nodded, but he was more concerned about her. "Are you okay? It's not easy to hear, either."

She looked into his eyes and hers were so full of sadness and fear. "So many unwanted children," she whispered.

He wrapped his arms around her, desperately wanting to make her feel better, loved and wanted. That would be what had upset her; she had to have felt unwanted all her life. Probably her mother would have contemplated aborting her. He'd only known her for a few months, weeks really, and he couldn't imagine a world without her in it. He held her close until he felt her body start to relax again and then eased back a little.

"I think we're both a little shaken up by all this, don't you?" he said gently.

She nodded so he continued, "Let's just enjoy the walk back shall we? Save our questions for another time?"

She nodded again, but he felt her shrink against him, just a tiny amount but he noticed it.

"What is it? Don't you want to go back?" he asked. He had a moment of inspiration. "Are you worried that you're going to be in trouble?"

Another nod. He realised that when she was worried or stressed, she struggled to find words and reverted to simple body and sign language. He could reassure her on this at least. "You're not in any sort of trouble, not for running away—"

She interrupted, finding the words for this at least. "I wasn't running away," she insisted again. "I was just...leaving."

"Well then, not for leaving, nor for agreeing to marry me. For some reason Lord Gabriel is very much in favour of that."

"Why?" Leonie was curious and puzzled, as was he.

"I don't know. He always has his reasons for everything, but you don't find out unless he chooses to tell."

She accepted that and moved on, "How soon can we be married, be together?"

"Is that what's worrying you? I don't know, I'm sorry." He had his arm round her now as they walked and he held her a little closer. "I don't want to be apart either, but there are so many different customs in different Houses. When Melanie married here it took several months to organise. Where I grew up, a couple would be handfasted within a week or so of deciding to marry. That wouldn't be a big event at all, then they'd have up to a year and a day living together, and either they'd marry within that time, or they'd separate. During that year they'd probably live with one of their families, and both families would help them set up their own place."

"Amongst the Traders, you'd be preparing for your marriage from your early teens, even before you had any idea who," Leonie volunteered. "So by the time a couple decide to marry they'd have pretty much what they needed, and the wedding itself would take place in a week or two."

"Seems like we're both used to something much quicker than is likely here," Prospero agreed. "Did you prepare for your marriage while you were with the Traders?"

Leonie shook her head. "I didn't need to. No one would marry an *Osti*." She used the Trader word for outsider, and then had to translate for him. "Someone who doesn't belong, who isn't one of them."

He ached for the rejection she had suffered. "Well, I'm going to marry you, just as soon as we can. You belong to me, I belong to you, and we belong here."

They had reached one of the little wicket gates that gave access to the back of the House grounds. Prospero took his arm from round Leonie to place his palm on the sensor plate.

"This gate's close to the secluded area so it will only open for those in the Order," he explained.

Leonie looked slightly guilty. "Well, like that, yes."

He was curious. "You know another way?"

She looked even more guilty. "I just sort of feel for it with my mind and tell it to open."

"I'm beginning to understand how you got into the shopping centre. Are there any locks that would hold against you?"

"I haven't found any," she confessed.

He laughed but was also puzzled. "So why were you so worried early on about being a prisoner, if we couldn't have held you anyway?"

"It isn't locks that hold you, it's people. You have to get past them, too."

Comprehension dawned for him. "It isn't being held, is it? It's being chased that frightens you. That ties in with your nightmares, too. You're being chased." Now he was filled with remorse. "And I came after you, so many times. I must have made things worse."

"No, you came and found me, like you promised. It's not the same thing."

"Isn't it?" he asked, but she just shook her head. He badly wanted to ask what she was afraid of at the end of the chase, what she thought would happen if she was caught, but he could sense that this was not the right time. Instead, he chose to change the subject and lighten the mood.

"Come on," he said, taking her hand again. "I left hours ago to find you. Gabriel will think we've eloped together."

That made her smile, if not laugh, and together they walked across the campus towards Lord Gabriel's office. Andrew joined them as they crossed the next courtyard.

"I take it congratulations are in order?" he asked them, smiling.

Prospero tightened his arm around Leonie, and they both nodded, Leonie a little more slowly than Prospero.

Andrew's face became more serious. "Leonie, you will be asked if you are sure this is what you want. If he gave you a free and fair choice."

"I did!" Prospero said vehemently, but Leonie answered Andrew anyway.

"I had a choice. He said I could walk away and he wouldn't chase me."

"Did he now?" Andrew's eyes flicked towards Prospero. "You need to be very careful of exactly what he says."

Leonie turned to Prospero. "Would you have let me walk away?"

He looked at the ground for a moment, scuffing his foot slightly, knowing Andrew was right.

"I wouldn't have chased you," he confessed hesitantly, "but I would have followed you, tracked you down, made sure you were safe and warm and fed and provided for. I wouldn't have chased you, exactly. I just wouldn't have let you get away from me."

Leonie stared at him for a moment, and then, to his surprise, burst out laughing.

"I love to hear you laugh," he said, not sure what was going on but relieved at her reaction. "It doesn't happen often enough."

He pulled her closer against him, and she turned towards

Andrew. "I believed I had a free choice," she said. "And that's what matters. Thank you for the warning."

Andrew left them to make their way to where Lord Gabriel was waiting for them in his office.

Leonie

As we approached Lord Gabriel's office I hung back a little, slowing down and dropping slightly behind Perry. Did I really want to do this? It was still only mid-morning, but I felt like I'd lived a lifetime already today. I suppose in a way I had, or possibly two. I had taken Perry through my memories – not day-to-day detail, but the key events – and he still loved and wanted me. He hadn't quite worked out why I couldn't tell him how I felt but he'd seemed so confident that it didn't matter. In that place and moment of confidence and security and love I had agreed to marry him. Now that was battling with my uncertainty as to how Lord Gabriel would react.

I felt emotionally drained by everything I had shared, and emotionally stuffed by what I'd learnt about Perry.

Really, I wanted to curl up somewhere dark and quiet and digest it all. I had this nagging feeling that there was something I'd missed, something that Perry had sort of told me but that I hadn't quite cottoned on to. Andrew had just told me that I needed to be careful about exactly what Perry said. That was in the context of chasing after me, and Perry's face had been a picture when he realised he'd been caught out. I couldn't help but laugh. I was sure there was somewhere else that this applied, too, but instead of taking time to work it out, I now had to face Lord Gabriel.

But I didn't have to do this alone any longer. As well as holding Perry's hand I reached out and curled my mind into his. He smiled at me and put his arm around me.

"It's all going to be fine," he said, and together we walked into the office.

Chapter 5

Monday morning

Gabriel

Andrew had reported back to Gabriel that, if nothing else, Prospero and Leonie were together and safe. So Gabriel had recalled his search teams and sent those who had been up all night off to get some sleep. He hadn't followed his own advice; instead he had spent some time praying in the Monk's Chapel, before returning to his office and his desk.

Ellie was waiting for him there to offer advice, ready to solve his problems almost before he realised he had them. He stared at her, his mind blank, barely listening as she started educating him on marriage customs. Why did he need to know those in detail?

"Both Prospero and Leonie will be used to traditions which differ from ours," Ellie said. "Melanie's wedding took me months to arrange. Are you listening to me?"

"Of course I am," he said, resolving to do so. "You said weddings take months to arrange."

She glared at him. "I said Melanie's wedding did. They don't have to. We need to follow our traditions but I don't think we should take more than a couple of weeks. Having made a decision, we should just get on with it. It means the two of them can be together for whatever's going to happen in your visions, it'll cause less disruption in the long run, and it'll minimise the chances for rumour and scandal getting out."

"Seriously, Ellie?" he asked. "I mean I'm sure you and Brother Edward could put on a wedding in just a couple of days, but do they really need to be married that fast?"

Ellie nodded. "I think we need to be planning for a week on Saturday and I wish it could be sooner. Edward's well ahead in plans, thanks to you."

Gabriel nodded. It was a good job he'd started things off back in January when he'd showed Edward the jewellery sent by the Traders – matching betrothal and wedding rings. "So if you want it sooner, why nearly two weeks' delay?"

"We need to sort out somewhere for them to live." Ellie gave him a look he knew was full of meaning, but he couldn't work out what she was trying to convey.

"You have to remember, Gabe," she said. "You must remember the problems we had with him and Mel."

The interaction between sex and the energy used for the Gifts was neither widely known nor well understood. It didn't need to be; it only became an issue when such activity was between the very Gifted, those rare people with at least two, probably more, of the major Gifts. When such people came together in sex, unknowingly and unwittingly, with as little control as within a nightmare, and aided by the power of their Gifts, they would broadcast their feelings widely, which often had embarrassing consequences for susceptible people nearby. The campus was, of course, prepared for the situation; the Shields over the accommodation for Gifted students were configured to dampen and contain such broadcasting, but these adapted Shields were both expensive and difficult to manage. And Prospero and Melanie had not restricted their activities to the student accommodation.

Gabriel put his head in his hands. "So what do we do, Ellie?" he asked. "I can't deal with that level of disruption again. And you've just told me they need to be married quickly."

She just grinned at him. "Don't I always solve your

problems?" she asked, rhetorically. "There's a suite of rooms on the top floor over there." She gestured out of his office window to the building opposite, across the main courtyard. "They're just being used as storage now, but once, long ago, they were accommodation."

That made sense. Many of the rooms, buildings and courtyards that formed the campus had changed their purpose over the years, some more than once. Now the central courtyard contained the dining hall and kitchens, formal reception rooms, offices, storerooms and some public rooms of the House, such as the House library.

Ellie carried on, "And, what's more, they have plumbing, and they have wiring for the enhanced Shields. And Brother Richard says if I clear out what's there, he can have them ready in about a week."

Gabriel almost laughed at the triumphant look on her face. "Ellie," he said. "What would I do without you?"

"You wouldn't manage, Gabe," she said with a grin. "You just wouldn't manage." The grin left her face. "For now, you'd better reinforce the idea of no sex before marriage and then keep them off campus, under Shields or separate as much as possible. Send them off on a picnic today, or something like that."

At least when Leonie and Prospero arrived at his office later that morning, Gabriel felt he was somewhat prepared and able to direct the interview the way he wanted it to go.

Leonie

Actually, and almost annoyingly, Perry was right about our meeting with Lord Gabriel. Knowing that it was the only fair thing to do, I opened my mouth to try to tell Lord Gabriel all about my past, but the words just wouldn't come out.

He smiled at me, seeming to understand. "Have you told Prospero?" he asked.

I nodded.

"Then you don't have to tell me anything you're not ready to. All I want to know is if you agree to this marriage of your own free choice?"

That I could answer easily. "Yes," I told him.

After that he seemed perfectly happy. In fact, he appeared to have started planning for our wedding already.

"I'm well aware of the marriage customs of your birth House," he said to Perry. "And of the Traders." Now he smiled at me. "But right now, you are both part of my House and we will follow the customs of this House. That means a formal betrothal, which is a promise to marry at some future date, followed by a wedding. There is to be no consummation of this relationship between the betrothal and the wedding. You understand?"

He looked hard at Perry. I suppose that was because betrothal could be considered similar to the handfasting that Perry had mentioned to me and that certainly involved a couple making love prior to the formal wedding. Then Lord Gabriel looked at me.

"However," he said, "there's a lot to be said for the Trader policy of a quick wedding in a small and close community. I'm not going to have the pair of you disrupting the peace and stability of this campus for weeks."

He wasn't either. His plan was that Perry would spend the next day in prayer and fasting, and be released from his monastic vows the morning after that, at a service which would be followed by our formal betrothal. Then we would be married barely ten days later, the day before most students would return from the Easter break between quarter sessions. Lord Gabriel said that was the fastest things could be arranged; while Perry was occupied tomorrow I would be involved with Edward and Pedro and Lady Eleanor, starting to sort out details. I felt a little overwhelmed by that but both Lord Gabriel and Perry reassured me it wouldn't be that bad. Then Lord Gabriel looked between us both.

"And I need a little bit of time to manage this news," he said. "It'll be a lot easier if you aren't around. So, Leonie, Pedro has sorted out a picnic for you both, if you'd pop down and fetch it please, while I just have a word with Prospero about one or two other things. Then both of you get off campus for the rest of the day. You can come back for or after the evening meal, whichever suits you."

When I left Lord Gabriel's office, I turned the corner and walked straight into Andrew.

"Sorry," he said. "I didn't mean to startle you, I just wanted to make sure you were alright with all this."

I looked at him, puzzled. I knew how he felt about Perry, how he loved him—everyone did except Perry himself. It was one of those open secrets that nobody talked about because Andrew had chosen not to act on it and they all respected that.

"You mean that Perry's okay?" I asked him.

"No, I mean you," he insisted, turning round to walk alongside me towards the kitchen. "I know Perry better than anyone. I know how charming and persuasive he can be. I want to make sure you are doing this because you want to, not because you've been swept along by his charm and enthusiasm. You don't have to do this, you're still one of us, we'll still make sure you have everything you need."

"It's what I want most," I confessed to him. "For me, anyway. But for Perry? How can it be best? It takes him away from here, from the Order, from where he belongs. And I'm hurting you too. That's part of why I left. I want this but how can I let you and Perry pay the price?"

"Oh, Leonie," he said, his voice coming out on a deep sigh.

For the first time ever, he put his arms round me and hugged me. I felt a wave of sympathy from him for the confusion I was in.

"Because I love him, I want what's best for Perry," he said. "And that's you not me. He's going to leave the Order anyway and I'm not. I've always known he'd leave one day and I'm okay with that. But outside the Order he'll need help—he needs someone to keep him grounded. You marrying him isn't hurting anyone, it's what Perry wants and needs. But I don't want that to be at your expense, you to be coerced into it if it isn't what you want."

"It is what I want," I repeated. "But…"

He just waited while I got the words together in my mind. I remembered what Perry had said about Andrew being able to just be, to sit or to listen or whatever was needed. Somehow, there were things I could say to Andrew that I couldn't say to Perry.

"Everyone I've loved has died or left. What if that happens to Perry?"

"Oh, Leonie," he said again. "Perry'd be no great loss, you know. He's impulsive, competitive, arrogant, proud, stubborn, argumentative, acts without thinking, always convinced he's right especially when he's not." He pulled such a funny face as he said it all.

I couldn't help laughing again.

"That's better," he said. "Now, seriously, if anything did happen to Perry, you won't be alone, I promise you that. You've got a family here, and we'll always be here for you, no matter what."

I knew Andrew meant it, and that made me feel an awful lot better. We'd reached the kitchen door, which reminded me what I was supposed to be doing. Pedro had a picnic all packed up and a wicked grin on his face. He didn't say anything, but I suspected that meant Lord Gabriel was already way behind the rumour mill in managing any news.

Chapter 6

Leonie

Perry and I went up into the wood and the hills. It was only a mile or two away, but there was a secluded little lake where hardly anyone went. Someone had to have known it and loved it once, because there was a shelter that was still pretty weatherproof and decking that stretched out over the lake. It was old, but sound so we sat on the edge, dangling our feet in the water while we ate. Pedro had put in a couple of glasses and a bottle of wine which made Perry raise his eyebrows, but then he looked at the bottle and smiled before turning it round to show me it was non-alcoholic.

"Pedro knows me well," he said.

I hadn't realised before today's revelations that I'd never seen him drink wine, even though it was sometimes served at meals.

"Is wine a problem?" I asked him.

He shrugged. "Probably not. I hope not. I don't think I got that far. But I haven't risked it, ever since. And even the communion wine is non-alcoholic, here. There are others for whom it definitely is a problem."

I looked at him in curiosity.

He grinned back. "No," he said. "I'm not telling you who. That's their secret, not mine."

I leaned comfortably against him. "Anyway," I said. "Communion, what's all that about?"

That amused him. "Am I your personal fount of all knowledge?" he asked with a laugh.

"Absolutely," I said, but it came out with a yawn which made him laugh again. I suppose I hadn't slept that much last night.

"Will you stay awake long enough for me to tell you?" he asked.

"If you make it interesting enough," I told him but there was another yawn in there too.

We moved so that we'd both be comfortable if either, or both, of us fell asleep. I guessed Perry hadn't got much sleep last night either. He'd have to make his explanation very interesting. His arms were around me and his fingers twisted idly in my hair; I wasn't going to stay awake long whatever he said.

"It's got lots of names," he started. "Communion, the Lord's Supper, Mass, Eucharist. And a number of different ways of celebrating it. But they all refer to the same event." He ran his fingers down my neck and along my arm. "I like the name Communion best," he said. "Because we do it together, as part of a community."

I liked the feeling of belonging that that inferred.

"Jesus and his friends were in Jerusalem for the Passover festival," he said.

I twisted a little to look at him. "I know about that," I said. "Pedro told me. They were celebrating God freeing their people from slavery a long time before. And they had a meal together and shared bread and wine."

"That's right," Perry agreed. "He told them the bread was his body, broken for them and the wine his blood, shed for them for their forgiveness. Jesus was referring to his death, where he was going take our punishment for what we've done wrong, to atone for us so we can be good enough for God."

I nodded. "I can understand that now, but I don't see how Jesus' friends could have done so because he was still there with them, whole, alive."

"No, perhaps not," Perry agreed. "But he told them that every time they did this, they were to remember him."

"That seems pretty clear to me," I said. "So when you eat and drink, you remember that Jesus died for you."

"Simple, isn't it?" Perry asked with a smile. "Really the differences in how it is celebrated are about interpretation."

"Such as?" I asked, wanting to know, but having to stifle a yawn. I settled back more comfortably against Perry, and he threaded his fingers back into my hair.

"Well," he said. "Was sharing the bread and wine part of the annual festival or part of a weekly ritual? Was it a habit of friends sharing a meal or a way of remembering your dead? It could have been any of them, so what does that mean for us? How often should we celebrate it? Was it something everyone was used to already or something totally new?"

"Well, I don't know," I said.

Perry laughed. "And some people think that the bread and wine actually become Jesus' body and blood. Others say they just represent that."

"Eww," I said. "Representation. Definitely. I don't care what anyone else thinks."

Perry agreed with me. "And as for the rest," he said. "I don't think it matters. The important thing is like you said, to remember that Jesus died for us, for our forgiveness. For all of us, all believers, all over the world, linked as one family, one body." He took a deep breath. "And it's a choice and a promise. 'I will be your God, if you will be my people'," he quoted. "Our choice and God's promise."

Very sleepily I asked him if I could join in.

"Yes," he said. "If you love and serve Jesus, and acknowledge him as your Lord, then here, with us, you can."

***

When I woke, Perry was asleep, curled around me protectively. I didn't want to disturb him, and anyway I was very comfortable, so I lay still and reflected on what he'd been telling me. The last thing I remembered was that somewhere in my sleepy and rather confused head, I'd worked out that Jesus was the one person it was safe for me to love. He couldn't die and leave me because he already had died and not left. That made me feel warm, safe and wanted all the way through.

Perry stirred slightly so I slipped out of his arms and lay along the edge of the decking, dipping my toes and fingers in the lake.

Prospero

Prospero went from asleep to awake in a moment, woken by the knowledge that Leonie was no longer in his arms.

Where is she? Has she run away again? Did I really find her? Was it just a dream?

His eyes shot open and she was the first thing he saw, lying along the decking, dangling her fingers in the lake. He closed his eyes in relief, waiting for his racing heart to slow, but keeping his mind's eye always on the glowing yellow dot that meant a happy Leonie. When he opened his eyes again she hadn't moved. She reminded him of someone but he couldn't place who and didn't struggle to try. Instead, he held still and watched her. She had agreed to marry him and he knew she wouldn't break a promise but all the same he didn't expect it to be easy to get as far as the wedding, much less afterwards. He was very wary of doing, or saying, or telling her anything which might scare her into running again. And there was one thing he was certain would do just that. Andrew had nagged him about it telepathically when they had met him on their return to the campus before seeing Lord Gabriel.

"Have you told her about him yet?" he'd asked.

"No," Prospero had replied shortly.

"You have to. You have to tell her. It's only fair that she knows."

"I know, I know. I will. Just…not yet."

"If you don't tell her soon, I will. She needs to know what she's getting into."

The things that Andrew had said after that to Leonie – warning her to be very careful about hidden meanings in what Prospero was saying – had made it quite clear to Prospero that Andrew would carry out that threat. It had been tough enough sharing what he already had with Leonie. Even if many of the events of his life were public knowledge, it had been a long time since he'd told anyone how he'd felt about them and why they'd happened.

He was delighted that they would be married in such a short time. Could he possibly wait to tell her about *him* until then? No, Andrew would tell her before that. And anyway, leaving the Order the day after tomorrow – so soon – would bring it all back into play immediately. He shuddered at the thought of what he would have to face. Actually, in many ways he was looking forward to tomorrow's day of prayer and fasting to have an opportunity to work through, with God, all that was ahead of him.

But for now all those things could wait. He had the rest of today with Leonie, and he smiled to himself with pleasure. He called out to her quietly, not wanting to startle her. "There's no one around. You can swim if you want to. I won't look."

She rolled over slowly to look at him. "I don't mind you looking. Anyway, won't you swim too?"

Now his smile was for her. "No," he said. "It's something else I won't risk. You have no idea how much I want you. If I look, or join you…"

He left the sentence unfinished, afraid that he lacked enough control even to talk about what he anticipated would happen. Leonie continued rolling, moving fluidly until she was sitting by his feet. She looked up at him, a small crease appearing between her brows as she puzzled out what he meant, and then smoothing as hope lit up her eyes.

"Truly?" she asked hesitantly.

He ached for all the times she'd found herself rejected, cast out, unwanted. "Truly," he confirmed and then, despite his worries about control, he kissed her.

This time, she was the one who broke the kiss, returning to her curious, enthusiastic self and bouncing to her feet as she asked, "Then can we go up to the Lookout Rock?"

"Of course," he said, getting to his feet. "Is that what you call it?"

He knew the place she meant. Further along – perhaps ten to fifteen minutes walking – the hill above this lake ended abruptly in a sharp cliff edge, a relic of a long past landslide or earthquake. There was a solid rock on which they could walk almost to the edge and see for miles across the landscape below. Lookout Rock was a good name for it and it probably had been used as such in the past.

They ate the rest of their picnic there, before wandering back to the campus through the dusk and twilight. The fading light didn't bother him and it was full dark before they got back. Just before they reached the boundary of the wood, Perry brought them to a stop and pulled Leonie towards him. He took her face between his hands, gently.

"I'll be in the chapel tomorrow so I won't see you and you won't be able to reach me," he said. "But don't worry. I haven't disappeared and I won't change my mind. I'll be there in the Abbey, the next day, waiting for you."

She nodded, understanding.

He went on, "I know you're worried about the things you have to do tomorrow but you'll be fine with Edward and Lady Eleanor. It'll just be about the wedding itself and what you want to happen. There's nothing you can do, no decision you can make that will be wrong, so don't fret about it."

She still looked concerned, the crease appearing again between her brows, so he wrapped his arms round her in a reassuring hug, and bent to kiss her once more. When they both stopped to draw breath, Perry smiled at Leonie, pleased to see her looking a lot less concerned.

"That'll have to keep us going for a day or so," he said. "But don't worry, we'll make up for it after that!"

Still holding hands, they left the privacy of the woods and crossed onto the campus itself. Perry was in time for the final service of the day, which he joined, sliding quietly into place at the last minute beside Andrew as he had done so many times before.

Andrew raised his eyebrows in mute question, but said nothing, clearly seeing all that he needed to from Prospero's quiet smile.

Chapter 7

Monday Afternoon

Gabriel

Despite Eleanor's organisational skills and solutions to his problems, by Monday afternoon Gabriel was once more sitting with his head in his hands thinking back over the morning.

He'd been happy enough that Leonie hadn't been coerced or even persuaded against her will, but he'd needed to talk to Prospero about his family issues. Prospero had totally thrown him with one small piece of information.

"Leonie showed me much of her past," he'd said hesitantly. "And the aunt that looked after her as a small child looked remarkably like Augusta Lindum. I remember seeing some of the pictures at the time."

Gabriel had panicked. He knew he had. This had to be kept secret. If Leonie was Augusta's niece she was both dangerous and in danger. And the action he had taken... No, he'd had no other choice. He sat quietly, knowing that once more he was way out of his depth.

With hindsight, it was so obvious. An unknown, unclaimed, red-headed Chisholm girl, eighteen years old, born on 29th February. A Chisholm girl with what he now knew were deep, dark, Lindum eyes. His only excuse was that no one else had picked it up either. No one had been looking for her or expected it; they'd all believed her long dead. Katya had called his jewel a rare merge. A child born with both Chisholm and Lindum parents was certainly that – the Houses had been vicious enemies as far back as anyone could remember. But he'd seen her in his visions as a single ruby so that didn't make sense. Then it came to him; the stone and colour which traditionally represented Lindum were ruby and red, but those of Chisholm were diamond and white. If you merged a diamond and a ruby then perhaps all you thought you saw was the ruby.

When he had first come across Leonie and understood that his actions would lead to her death, she'd been an orphan, a stray with no connections. Then he had discovered her connection with the Traders and had had to consider whether that made a difference to his actions. He had decided then that it didn't, that he couldn't let it. Now he'd discovered her additional links to the two greatest Houses and had to consider again whether this impacted on what he should do. Status and family were irrelevant, he told himself. The right action was the right thing to do no matter what.

Recognising that matters were beyond his ability to cope alone, he called both Ellie and Benjamin to what he tried hard not to consider a council of war. They arrived promptly and watched him, puzzled and concerned as he shut his office door, switched on the full range of Shields and added a few electronic gadgets that would ensure they were not overheard.

"Do you remember Helena of Lindum?" he asked them. "Lord Leon's granddaughter? His son Alfred's daughter?"

Ellie nodded. Of course she'd remember. She'd always been a romantic at heart.

"She fell in love with and got pregnant by one of the Chisholm twins," she said. "Probably Jaim, because Edmund was recently married. Then Lindum killed Jaim, Helena died in childbirth, and her sister Augusta grabbed the baby and disappeared. Only, about four years later, Augusta and the child were found dead in a remote cottage somewhere."

Just like Ellie to stick with the love-story element. Gabriel nodded. "With Alfred dying young, Helena would have been Leon's heir, but her actions were treason. His advisers wanted her executed immediately when they found out about the pregnancy. Leon wanted to find a solution that let her live. And the baby, too, once it was born. They were still arguing over it when Helena gave birth – and died anyway."

"I agree with him morally," Benjamin said. "But it wouldn't have been very sensible strategically. They'd have been a focus for any malcontents, and for Chisholm. For anyone who wanted to attack Lindum, really."

Gabriel nodded in agreement. "Anyway, Leon's heir is now Anthony, Helena's brother. Except that Helena was never formally charged, or disinherited which means that, if her child lived, she would be Leon's heir."

"So?" asked Benjamin, shrugging. "The child died later, with Augusta; it's irrelevant."

Gabriel shook his head, looking between them. "Leonie has been showing Prospero her memories. In them he saw her aunt. And he recognised her as Augusta Lindum. Which means that somehow, our Leonie is the child."

Benjamin was unconcerned. "He must be wrong. It's a long time back and he'd be just a child, a farm boy. What would he know about it?"

But Ellie looked up and Gabriel could see the light dawning in her eyes as she thought about it.

"Not long ago," she said, "you told me that, before he came here, Prospero was House Tennant's heir. He'd have been in his early teens, with Lord Neville, in the thick of it. He'd know all about it."

Gabriel nodded slowly. "One of the heirs, rather than the only heir, but yes, I think we can trust his identification."

Now both Ellie and Benjamin stared at him, eyes wide in horror as the full ramifications of his news broke on them.

Benjamin found his voice again first. "So, we have the heir to Lindum, fathered by a Chisholm and therefore able to challenge for that House, adopted to our House, and you're marrying her to the heir to House Tennant? And she's pretty much a Trader princess?"

"I think that sums it up," Gabriel said, leaning back in his chair, finding himself feeling almost flippant with relief at sharing this problem. "Once we let them marry, we've tied together the two Greatest Houses, being the blood enemies that are Chisholm and Lindum, Tennant which is the largest Sanctuary House and ourselves, the biggest Religious House. And the Traders. Followed by the probable death of both parties."

Benjamin shook his head. "No wonder you're having visions and dreams. Who else knows all this? Does she know? Or Prospero? I had no idea he was heir to House Tennant."

"I don't think Leonie has a clue about any of it. Anyone could work out the Chisholm link from her hair, but the rest? No one would suspect the Lindum connection. None of us spotted it. Only the Traders know how they value her. And Prospero and House Tennant – well, that was one of the pressures that caused his problems back then. Resolving that now is still up in the air, under discussion between me and his High Lord."

Ellie spoke, "But he could tell Leonie the Lindum connection and explain what it means?"

Gabriel looked a little shamefaced. "No," he confessed. "Neither of us thought he could keep it from her, so I blocked his memory of it."

"Gabriel, how could you?" Ellie was more than shocked.

"He consented. And I needed time to think, Ellie. I was desperate. I didn't know what else to do," he pleaded.

"It can be undone," said Benjamin calmly. "I think it's more important to know for sure that Leonie is who you think she is." The others looked at him as he went on. "So far you've only got Prospero's identification of something he saw in her memories – remind me to have words with him about doing something like that outside controlled conditions by the way – based on his own memory of a picture he must have seen fourteen years ago. The circumstantial evidence may be compelling, but it's hardly conclusive."

"So what do you suggest?" Ellie asked him.

"It's easy enough to prove one way or another," he told her. "Lord Leon made Helena's DNA profile readily available when the baby was abducted, to disprove claimants. And while Lord William has refused to make his sons' profiles available, his own is. If I analyse Leonie's profile it will show clearly enough whether or not she's Helena's child and whether or not she's fathered by a Chisholm. And both Prospero and Leonie should have medicals before their wedding. We'll do that after the betrothal service day after tomorrow. I'll get a sample then and I'll have a result for you that evening."

"And if she is?" asked Gabriel. "What, and for that matter when, do I tell Lord Leon?"

Leon would not thank him for resurrecting the contention around the inheritance of his House, but could Gabriel keep this from him? On the other hand, if, as he anticipated, his actions were sending Leonie to her death, did it matter?

They discussed the options for some time, concluding at last that Lord Leon needed to be told if, and only if, Leonie proved to be his missing heir but that he should be told however limited her prospects for the future might be. That would mean a personal meeting which would take some arranging; the matter was too confidential and far too controversial to trust to telephony. Gabriel agreed with Eleanor that the marriage of Prospero and Leonie should take place quickly but really, if Leonie was heir to House Lindum he should have Lord Leon's approval first. Once more he felt God's leading was requiring him to take actions which would seem unreasonable from an external or worldly point of view.

"I still don't think we should wait, for all kinds of reasons," Eleanor said. "Besides, they'll be betrothed before you know the answer. Lindum to Tennant is a good match from both sides. Lord Leon isn't going to be particularly upset if we present him with that as a fait accompli. And anyway, House Tennant and Lord Neville? What does he feel about the marriage?"

"In principle, Neville is happy to strengthen ties will us and the Traders through marriage but I'm speaking to him in detail tomorrow," Gabriel said. "When Prospero joined the Order and became part of this House, Neville only agreed on condition he reverted to House Tennant if, and as soon as, he left the Order. And that returns him to being one of Neville's heirs which, as I said, was one of the pressures that caused his problems in the first place. I've been trying to negotiate a deal with Neville, but my only real bargaining point is not to release Prospero, although Prospero can also refuse to return to Neville's territory. Where the Chisholm, Lindum issue fits into that I'm not sure but as a Sanctuary House, Neville can't support one over the other, so he's probably neutral to it."

"But you need to resolve all that tomorrow, to release Prospero, which will be before you can speak to Leon," Ellie worked out. "So you can't tell Neville anyway."

"This is getting so tangled," Gabriel said. "Sometimes I wish we could just get on with serving our Lord God and stay out of the political side."

Ellie smiled at him sympathetically. "We can't, though, can we? We're called to serve in this world and that means every aspect, even the tangled messy stuff."

Benjamin agreed. "But the other tangled messy bit we have to sort out is just what Leonie and Prospero get to know."

"No more than they do now," was Ellie's verdict. "I admit I was shocked at what you did, Gabe, blocking Prospero's memory, but I've come to think it right, at least until we know for sure about Leonie. And even then, I think we need to speak to Lord Leon before we unsettle the pair of them."

Again Benjamin agreed, which was going a long way towards unsettling Lord Gabriel. One of the things he appreciated about having both Ellie and Ben as his advisors was that they tended to look at things from radically different viewpoints. For them to agree might confirm he was taking the right action, but experience suggested that usually meant significant trouble ahead. Still, that was probably a given anyway.

"Leave them in ignorance," Benjamin advised. "It won't make any difference to Prospero, and, as for Leonie, it's pretty foolish to unsettle any teenage adept until you have to."

Chapter 8

Tuesday

Leonie

"I know it's not public knowledge yet," Pedro said across the worktop where we were kneading bread. "But I'm really pleased about your news. Congratulations!"

I lost my rhythm and stopped working, blushing in confusion, not knowing what to say.

"Don't worry," he reassured me. "That's all I'll say about it for now. Come on, we need to get this bread done."

The morning routine was soothing and relaxing even if we did work hard. By the time Lady Eleanor came to find me after breakfast, I was feeling more capable of facing whatever was to come.

"This isn't what today is about," she said as I followed her out of the kitchen. "But we can go round this way and I just want to show you something first."

She took me up to an area I'd not visited before, on the top floor of one of the main buildings, not that far from my room. There was a lot going on there; Brother Richard appeared to be directing renovations of some sort and there was all sorts of banging and sawing and hammering going on. Brother Richard turned towards us.

"Come to have a look?" he asked.

I looked at Lady Eleanor in bewilderment.

She smiled. "You and Prospero are going to need somewhere to live," she said. "Many years ago this used to be an apartment for some of the High Lord's family. We're putting it back to how it was for you."

I was utterly speechless. Brother Richard didn't seem to notice. He started gesturing around and explaining the space; I'd never seen him so enthusiastic. "This will be the main living area," he said. "There's plumbing for a small kitchen which we'll put at that end. Over there will be your bedroom with a bathroom off it. And here there's space for another bedroom and plumbing already in place for a separate bathroom. Or you could use the second bedroom as a place to study."

Lady Eleanor seemed to understand that I was incapable of saying anything. "We just popped up for a quick look," she said. "We're due to go and see Edward now. Thanks, Richard."

I managed to thank him too and then we headed back down towards the stores and Edward's workroom. Lady Eleanor turned back to look at me over her shoulder. "Did you find that all a bit much?" she asked, frowning slightly.

I nodded. "So much work, so much space," I said, trying – and failing – to express my feelings.

"It's part of my role to decide on and arrange accommodation for those living in the House, rather than the Order," she said. "I've decided that this is the best option for you and Prospero. So this is all about what I choose to do."

Put like that, I felt much better about it. I expected that was why she'd said it.

She carried on, "It will need decorating and furnishing. Would you like to do that?" She had to have read the answer in my face. "Or Edward would really enjoy setting it up and then you could change anything later as you grow used to it?"

I sighed in relief. For me, that was a much better idea.

"Okay, then," she said. "We'll do that. But if you see anything you like, or have any ideas on what you want, just tell Edward or me and we'll get them included."

We arrived at Edward's cavernous storerooms and workspace. Despite my nerves, I couldn't help but smile at Edward and he grinned back at me. He had an amazing ability to weave magic into my clothes as he made them. I looked beautiful in them and yet I knew I was nothing special. I wondered what he would come up with this time.

"Right," he said, rubbing his hands together with glee. "A wedding dress. Now, I've got some gorgeous fabric here that I've been saving for just the right event."

He was right about the fabric. I thought it was white at first, and the base weave was, but it was shot through with metallic threads in all colours. When it moved it rippled with colour like a rainbow. My main role was to stand and be measured, have fabric draped over me and agree with all of Edward's suggestions. I could manage that so Lady Eleanor left us to it.

We were all day about it, having lunch together as we worked. It wasn't just the wedding dress. Edward seemed to feel I needed practically a whole new wardrobe. Some of the items he thought would be a good idea – well, I was surprised a monk even knew that they existed, much less how to make them. He just grinned and, I think, got some enjoyment out of my discomfiture.

"You're not the first bride I've dressed," he said, his hands full of lace and ribbons.

He'd also got any number of ideas about decorating and furnishing the apartment. He chattered away about them as he worked, and from time to time he broke off what he was doing to fetch something to show me. Done like that I started to feel more comfortable with it, and even confident enough to make a few suggestions. The time passed quickly and I was surprised to find how late it was when Lady Eleanor returned to collect me, just as the bells rang for the afternoon service.

Edward smiled at me. "Time for me to be off," he said. "But we've done all we can for now. Come back at the beginning of next week and I'll check the fittings."

As he left, Lady Eleanor turned to me. "Gabriel's said he'd like you to sit with him at this evening's meal. In the meantime, would you like to see your rooms again, get a feel for them whilst it's quiet and there's no one else there?"

I decided that I would; one way or another I was going to have to get used to them so I might as well start now. There'd been a lot of progress during the day. All the walls were in place, and the doors and a fair bit of wiring and plumbing. I could see which room was going to be where and how it all fitted together. Funnily enough, the fact that they seemed to have done so much in such a short time made me feel better. If they could get this far in as little as a day, then perhaps what they were doing wasn't as much as I thought it was. That might have been a pretty convoluted logic but it helped me. Lady Eleanor let me wander round for a bit, looking out of the windows, working out what would be where and getting used to the space.

"I need to talk to you about what is happening tomorrow," she said quietly.

I turned to look at her as she continued, "After breakfast there's a service to release Prospero from his vows, followed by your formal betrothal."

I kind of knew that, but it hadn't really sunk in.

"You won't have to do very much," she told me. "You'll just stand with Prospero, and Gabriel will ask you both a couple of questions. Prospero first, then you so you'll know what to do and what to say. Then Gabriel will present you both with betrothal rings and that will be that."

She looked at me to see if I understood. I took a deep breath and decided I could manage all that, especially as Perry would be right there with me. She carried on, "After the service, both you and Prospero will need to have medicals."

An icy knot of fear started in my stomach, rising up into my chest. It must have shown in my face.

"It will be fine," Lady Eleanor said. "It's a formality, just a check before you get married. Benjamin will do yours himself and Andrew will do Prospero's."

I thought I'd have preferred it the other way round but I didn't get a chance to say so.

"It'll be in Benjamin's office, not the clinic or anywhere like that. I know you've been to the offices before, so you will be fine."

That took several deep breaths but again I decided I could manage, just about. After all, I liked Benjamin and he'd always been nice to me.

"Anything else?" I asked with a weak attempt at humour. There was; I should have known. There was always something else.

"In the afternoon, we'll need to discuss the actual wedding service."

Too much. Definitely too much. I sat down on the floor so that I didn't have to concentrate on standing up while I took it all in. Despite all the dust and dirt, Lady Eleanor sat down beside me.

"I'm sorry," she said sympathetically. "We're trying to fit what would normally take weeks or months into just a few days. I don't suppose you've ever been to a wedding like this before, have you?"

I shook my head. "Just Trader ones," I whispered. "The whole caravan gathers, you make promises to each other, and then there's a party, like any other rest day."

"It's not very different," she said. "Everyone in the House or Order will know about it and gather. But unlike a travelling caravan we have the option of inviting those from outside. And they need a little bit of notice. Is there anyone you'd like to come? Tobias and Leah, or any other Settlers maybe? You don't need to say now, just think about it."

I nodded slowly as, to my surprise, a glimmer of pleasure seeped into my mind. I hadn't thought that maybe I could share this with people I knew outside the campus.

"The other thing to think about," she continued, "is where you might like to gather. It's normally the Abbey but it doesn't have to be. It could be outside in one of the courtyards."

I closed my eyes and Lady Eleanor actually put her arm round me and stroked my back which was surprisingly soothing as I tried to get myself back together again.

Come on. You can do this. Everyone is just trying to make it good for you. And at the end of it you'll be married to Perry. You can do it. You can.

I opened my eyes and said, "I'm okay now. I'll be fine. Thank you for all you are doing to arrange this."

Lady Eleanor smiled at me. She looked relieved that I was okay with it. "You're more than welcome," she said. "I'm enjoying it."

Well, I wouldn't have gone that far for myself, but each to

their own.

"I think we'd better be getting along to the evening meal," she continued. "It wouldn't do to be late."

***

Lord Gabriel waved me to the seat next to him. Several of those around him were taking up his attention with conversation and issues so although he talked to me a little about inconsequential matters, I was able to take the time to compose myself further as I ate. Towards the end of the meal he turned to me and smiled.

"Have you had a busy day?" he asked.

I looked back at him. "You are being very generous. I don't quite understand why?" The words had just come out; I hadn't meant to be so bold.

I expected a frown, but Lord Gabriel went on smiling. "You are my ward, my daughter, and Prospero is a valued member of my House," he said. "Am I not allowed to be generous?"

I nodded but somehow I couldn't leave it. "I am grateful, but it is more than we need."

He agreed, "Yes, it is. Shall we say that I am trying to make up for the past?"

My mouth ran away with me – again. "My past or yours?"

I tried to apologise instantly, but Lord Gabriel was still smiling.

"Prospero was right about you. You are very perceptive. Don't hesitate to say what you think, I find it refreshing. Make sure you say what you think to Prospero, too, he has a tendency to hide from hard truths."

Actually, I knew that already, although I wouldn't have worded it like that.

Lord Gabriel carried on, his voice curious, "What makes you think it might be my past?"

Now I was in for it, but I still tried to answer what I thought. After all, he'd just told me to. "The past can't be changed. Making up for it suggests feelings of guilt. You are not responsible for what happened to me in the past so that suggests your past." I looked him in the eye, took a deep breath and added, "Or my future."

He raised his eyebrows in surprise. "Very shrewd," he said. "Could I perhaps be feeling guilty on behalf of my fellow humans who have mistreated you?"

I shook my head. He continued, "No? Then let us say that I have a role for you in the future that requires that you are used to living in a way that is appropriate for the daughter of a High Lord."

I had to check. "One that includes Prospero? Often children are married off in exchange for land or support."

He replied gently, "Don't worry, child. I wouldn't have agreed to your marriage otherwise. I won't keep you from him."

That brought back to the surface something that had been troubling me all day. It had been buried below everything that had been happening but now it bubbled up and would not be denied. "Until now I've seen him here and there, not every day, and I've been fine. Today I miss him so much, I didn't know I would."

Again his voice was gentle. "Now you've acknowledged that you belong together. It makes a difference. Go to him, child, you know where he is. I don't mean to make you suffer."

"Go where he is?"

I couldn't believe that—I knew he was in the Monks' Chapel and I wasn't allowed there.

"Yes. Tell him I'll see him in my office in about half an hour. You can stay with him till then."

I stammered my thanks, pushed my chair back, then ran before he could change his mind.

The Monks' Chapel was in one arm of the Abbey. It was considered part of the secluded area, although there were no locked doors between it and the public area, like there were elsewhere. I supposed there were no physical barriers to the monks' area of the Abbey either, but everyone respected those boundaries. Except me, perhaps. Hiding up in the gallery over the monks' area like I'd done last week wasn't really respecting their boundaries even if I'd got away with it. I entered the Abbey through the side door from the courtyard, which was never locked, ran the length of the public area, through the screen to the private area, up the Monks' Stairs and then down to the chapel. I stopped suddenly at the entrance, not wanting to intrude.

Perry was there, kneeling at the altar, praying. His head was shaved and he looked like he fitted there, like he belonged. He couldn't possibly have seen me but without looking round he held his arm out, and I slipped across the room and knelt beside him, his arm around my shoulders. I'd always felt safe in church, and being there next to Perry I felt so secure, so comforted and at peace after my difficult day that I was happy to stay there.

After a while Perry sat back on his heels, stood up, and we moved over to one of the benches where he had a Bible, notebook and some water. I couldn't read the notes he'd made; his handwriting was appalling. He held me close as we sat down.

"You're not supposed to be here," he said.

"I am," I told him. I might have been slightly smug. "Lord Gabriel sent me. He said to tell you to come to his office in about, it'll be about twenty minutes now. He said I could stay till then."

"He let you come here?"

I nodded. "How did you know it was me?"

That made him smile. "Who else would it be?" he said simply. "I was praying for you and you were there. Besides I heard your footsteps. Anyone from the Order would have come straight down the stairs. No one else would have run through the Abbey except in an emergency, and if it had been an emergency, they wouldn't have stopped at the door. And no one else would have been barefoot."

I looked at my feet in some surprise to find they were indeed bare. "But I was wearing shoes earlier..."

"I expect you kicked them off when you started running through the Abbey. We'll find them later."

"I was running before that," I confessed. "Ever since I left the dining hall. I wanted to get here before Lord Gabriel changed his mind."

He laughed and held me closer. "He wouldn't have done that. And your shoes will turn up somewhere." His eyes were teasing now. "Did you miss me that much that you had to run?"

"I did," I whispered and reached up to touch and stroke his shaved head.

"It'll grow again," he said.

It was growing already. He might have been clean shaven early this morning but now, no more than twelve hours later, there was a fine shadow of dark stubble across both his head and his chin.

"I wasn't expecting this... I did know, you told me once before, I just didn't think..."

He reached up, pressing my hand against his head for a moment before lifting it down into his lap. "What your touch does to me..." he said. "I can't think straight."

His touch left me feeling dizzy with a desire I understood only in theory. I still couldn't quite believe that my touch could have the same effect on him, with all his experience. I would have pulled my hand right back but he twined his fingers through mine and held it firmly in his.

"Have you been alright with all you had to do today?" he asked me.

I nodded. "It was okay. Some of it was even fun."

He smiled. "Tell me about it?"

This time I shook my head. "Later, tomorrow, not now."

It didn't seem to be the time or place to go into all that had happened. Somehow, sitting here, my worries seemed so small and inconsequential, and there didn't seem to be any need to fret Perry with them. Perry understood and we sat together quietly for a while. I felt so secure and at peace, and to me Perry also felt peaceful, more so than I'd ever known. I commented on it, and he agreed and tried to explain.

"I realise now that even before you turned up, God was trying to tell me to be ready to move on, only I wasn't listening. And then, since that first nightmare you had, before Christmas, you have mesmerised me. I've been torn between my service to God, here in the Order, and my growing feelings for you. How could it possibly be right to leave a life of worship and service for human desire? Last week, down by the river when you'd hurt your foot..."

He paused as we both looked down at my bare foot, the bruising still visible but faded to green and yellow, then he continued.

"That was when I knew, right or wrong, I couldn't make any other choice than to be with you. All the services over Easter just confirmed to me it was time to move on, to leave the Order, especially the one on Thursday night. And then you agreed to marry me."

He paused again, smiling at me, and freeing his fingers from mine to stroke my hair and face.

"But even then, although I knew this was what God wanted, I felt conflicted between service and desire, between God's leading and my own hopes and fears. I've needed today to understand that I can serve God wherever I am, it doesn't have to be as a monk, it just has to be doing what he tells me, whether that grants my hopes or requires me to face my fears. Or both. And sometimes, like now, what he tells me to do is what I also deeply desire. That sounds very simple, and I knew these things, but I never really understood them before today. So, now there is no conflict, and yes, I am far more at peace with God and with myself than I have been in the whole time you've known me."

There didn't seem to be anything to say in response to that, so I twisted my fingers back into his and we sat once more in peaceful silence.

"I mentioned Thursday night, didn't I?" Perry asked. "That's a very private service just for the Order. You're probably not supposed to know about it, though it's not really secret, just private."

I had to confess; Perry had been so honest with me, and anyway I didn't want to have any secrets from him.

"I do know, though. I saw it."

Perry's face was a picture. "If anyone could it would be you, but how could you possibly have done that?"

I tried to explain; I told him how I'd come into the Abbey to think, like I sometimes went to the Old Chapel, to work things out because the Shields cancelled the background hum of the community that I could hear as a telepath. I told him about my favourite places within the Abbey including the chapel opposite the one we were in and how when I was desperate to sleep I would sometimes curl up under the altar table there where I couldn't be seen. That upset him, not because I slept there – he didn't have a problem with that – but because I'd felt I had to, to be able to sleep. And I told him about my favourite place, hidden up in the gallery, overlooking the monks' area and how I'd been there on Thursday night, not knowing that there was another service about to take place. He shook his head in wonder.

"I can understand how you ended up there unintentionally. What I can't understand is that no one spotted you because that's the one service the Shields are turned off for. We might not have been able to see you physically, but someone would have sensed your presence as soon as the Shield was turned off. I would have seen you."

"But I was spotted. Lord Gabriel came in first and he knew I was there and he told me to stay. And he showed me how to shield myself even though I knew anyway."

He nodded. "That makes sense, and I don't suppose we'd have noticed that use of power amongst everything else that was going on. But, letting you stay, that makes me wonder what he's up to?"

I shrugged. I'd wondered the same, which was what had led to me challenging him about my future earlier, but it hadn't got me a concrete answer.

Perry smiled. "Never mind. I expect he'll tell us when we need to know."

Our time was pretty much up by then, with Perry being due at Lord Gabriel's office.

"We'll retrace your steps as we go," Perry said. "And see if we can find your shoes."

Just as Perry had thought, I'd kicked them off at the Abbey door. I bent over to put them back on, and as I straightened up Perry slipped his arms round me and kissed me.

"Should we have done that?" I whispered, very conscious both of where we were and that Perry was still a monk, for a few more hours at least.

"Why ever not?" he asked grinning. "God certainly knows and I expect everyone else does too by now."

He was right about that; he might have spent the day cloistered in the chapel, and I'd spent it hidden away with Edward, but all the same the news had spread through House and monastery like wildfire.

"Besides," Perry added, eyes gleaming, "when we are formally betrothed tomorrow, I intend to do just that, over there"—he pointed to the centre of the Abbey—"in full view of everyone."

I blushed, I know I did, I felt the heat rising in my cheeks, but he just laughed and said that we'd better head off to Lord Gabriel's office. I left him there and headed down to the kitchens to check on the baking preparations for tomorrow morning. I'd started the day with bread making and found it soothing; now I would end it the same way and hope for the same effect.

Chapter 9

Gabriel

Gabriel shuffled the papers back and forth on his desk without taking in anything written on them, his mind occupied with Leonie.

He had watched her run out of the dining hall with some amusement. He rarely had much to do with the younger students though he remained aware of them and any issues. Normally by the time he became more involved they were older and wanting to join his House or Order. As a result they were enthusiastic and eager to please, so he found Leonie's frankness both unusual and refreshing, as he'd told her. Challenging, too—she'd been very sharp picking up on both his feelings of guilt and that they related to her future. Very much afraid that she had no future, he knew he was being over-indulgent in the present. He didn't think he'd done wrong in letting her stay on Thursday evening, nor in letting her go to Prospero in the Monks' Chapel, but he was well aware others would differ with him on the matter.

Some of his words came back to haunt him.

"I don't mean to make you suffer."

He did, though, didn't he? He had a fair idea of what was ahead—she would suffer, and it was his actions and choices that were precipitating it. It was all very well being certain that he was doing what God required, but that didn't absolve him of responsibility for the pain and suffering it would cause. He had chosen a path for this couple and he had to take responsibility for the consequences. He was pretty certain they would have chosen the same path, if they knew what he knew, but he still struggled with keeping them in ignorance of what was to come. Whatever decision they might make, they weren't being given the choice.

Despite his own uncertainties, he was sure that they needed to know nothing more until after they were married. They needed to be able to rely on the fact that their relationship was genuine and of their own free will. Which it was. He might have set up the situation, facilitated it, but they had at least made those choices themselves.

As he had told Ellie and Benjamin that he would, Gabriel had spoken to Lord Neville that morning about options and choices that might be, or become, available to Prospero. He thought back over part of that conversation now.

"It's a good strategic marriage for you," he'd said to Lord Neville. "Whatever her background, she's my ward and a Trader princess. And it's more than that; I'm just unable to tell you."

"I don't have a problem with the marriage. He can marry who he chooses. I'll not make that mistake again," Lord Neville had replied. "It's what you're asking with respect to Prospero and the future of my House. There are family issues too. I don't think I can release him."

"You have a more than capable heir in the form of Lilyrose. Just tell me she's your preferred heir with Brin second and I'll settle for that. You can't use Prospero anyway unless he chooses to return to your territory."

Neville had been silent for a moment so Gabriel had continued, "Besides, look, Neville, there's something big coming up. I don't know what, but it's major and it's almost certain my daughter will die."

"You and your predictions," Neville had said, but his voice had been sympathetic. He had too much prior knowledge and experience to dismiss Gabriel's prophecies and he knew the pain of losing both a child and a wife. "What happens to Prospero then?"

"I don't know. There's a possibility he could die too. Or he might retreat back to the monastery."

"You'd take him back?"

"In a moment, if it protected him from the destructive pressures he was under before. But I'd like him to have the opportunity to be reconciled with you and with Mary first."

Neville had sighed heavily. "Very well then. He'll be welcome back here safe in the knowledge that he's third in line. Will that do?"

That would do very well indeed, and Gabriel had thanked Neville before their conversation had turned to other matters.

At the very least that would buy time for reconciliation. Now, just half an hour after watching Leonie leave the dining hall, he had Prospero to deal with directly. Given the happy look on Prospero's face as he arrived, he was clearly a beneficiary of Gabriel's over-indulgence, too. But then, he probably didn't have much of a future either, did he?

"So," he said, after greeting Prospero and inviting him to sit. "What have you learned?"

Prospero took a deep breath. "I have been hiding behind my service to God within the Order," he said slowly. "I told myself I could only serve God here, in the monastery, and it was that which meant I couldn't be what my parents or my High Lord wanted – that it was God's choice not mine. But something Leonie said yesterday made me think differently. I caused the rift with my family by choosing to be a doctor. It wasn't to do with serving God. Knowing that, I can't hide in the Order any longer, and so I'm free to leave to serve God elsewhere. And having realised that, I can hear what he is telling me to do once more and so I know that I'm doing the right thing and all the conflict I've been feeling has disappeared."

Gabriel nodded. Perhaps this was going to be easier than he had feared. "You've taken your time, but you've got there in the end," he said. Then he grinned. "Or more accurately, given that you're leaving, at the end."

"It would always have been at the end, wouldn't it?" Prospero confirmed. "Because as soon as I worked this out, I was free to leave, which I wasn't before. I know now that you've been trying to get me to understand this for years. I just wasn't able to hear it before."

Gabriel sat back in his chair. "I must say, I'm very impressed at Leonie's ability to achieve in days what we have failed to do in years."

Prospero just grinned at him, a little sheepishly he thought.

He carried on, "There are a number of things we need to sort out. Firstly, there's the matter of your House allegiance. Once you are released from the Order, you revert to House Tennant with all the consequences. And you can only avoid those consequences by never returning there."

"I know. And whilst I would rather remain part of this House, I have to return there to resolve other things. So, I will have to meet with him and negotiate what I can. If I have to resume as one of his heirs, then I have to, although I'm worried that it wouldn't be easy for Leonie."

Gabriel was pleased that Prospero was prepared to face up to this issue. "It won't be as bad as you fear," he said. "I've already spoken to Lord Neville. He's agreed to your marriage and he's agreed to place you as his third choice of heir and he's happy for you to continue living and working here if you wish, as long as you spend part of each year there. I don't think there should be any real problem. His preferred heir is Lilyrose."

Prospero's astonishment was clear in his voice. "Lilyrose? But she's just a child." He paused. "She isn't, is she? She's a grown woman now, older than Leonie." Belatedly he added, "Thank you for negotiating that. It's far better than I hoped."

"You're welcome. Now, what are you going to do about your relationship with your parents?"

In Gabriel's opinion this was both the more serious and the more complicated issue. Tradition and compassion told him Prospero's parents should be at the wedding; his gut feeling told him they shouldn't and he was finding reconciling the two impossible. He was curious as to how Prospero would approach this.

"I need to see them, to sort this out face to face," Prospero said. "I've already suggested to Leonie that we'll go to visit them this summer."

"That's an excellent idea. You should consider taking the full quarter session to have a proper visit, with them and Lord Neville." Gabriel took a deep breath then plunged in, "Have you thought about inviting them to your wedding? The timescale is tight, but I'm sure we could arrange something."

Prospero was hesitant in his response. "I've thought about it, and I think not, but I'm not sure if that's for the right reasons."

Gabriel watched him carefully. "What's your reasoning then?"

"Leonie has no family to be present. Everyone she's ever really cared about is either in the House or the Order, or unreachable, or they've died. She has some friends among the students, but they won't be back by then. If I don't invite my family it's the same for both of us, just those from here present. If I do, then my family starts to dominate, and I think that would be hard for her. And if my parents come, he will also come, and I will have to address all this then, and the time will be about my relationship with them, and I think it should be about the relationship between me and Leonie. And I will be torn between Leonie and my family."

Silent relief that the decision had been taken away from him flooded through Gabriel. "I think to some extent you are avoiding this, and that you're underestimating Leonie, but I agree with your conclusion," he said. "However, you need to contact your parents as a matter of priority, and explain all this to them. I know you can't telephone them. You'll have to write to them as quickly as you can to be sure the letter arrives in time."

Prospero nodded. "Leonie needs to be on the intensive watch list."

"Is that a professional opinion or a personal one?"

The intensive watch list was maintained in the control centre to alert the night-watch team to those who were particularly at risk of suffering nightmares and sleepwalking – not the normal risk of any Gifted person, but exceptional risk or likelihood brought on by specific circumstances.

Prospero considered that. "Actually, it's both. All the things that have happened over the last few days would put her at risk anyway. On top of that, things we've talked about, things I thought were in my past but that she needed to know, they all relate to some difficult issue for her. And sharing her past with me when she's kept it secret from everyone for so long, that's got to have an impact too. I think she's building up for a major incident before the week is out."

"You are being entirely open with her? Have you told her about your position with regard to House Tennant?"

"Yes, I'm being open with her. No secrets, no more hiding. Just...not everything at once. I've told her my family situation, just not that it relates to the Great House."

Gabriel sighed. "I agree you shouldn't overwhelm her but make sure that 'not everything at once' doesn't turn into avoidance. She does need to know about House Tennant, that's only fair. She's already on the watch list, I consider her a high risk, too."

Gabriel debated telling Prospero that he considered him a high risk as well, given the dramatic changes in his own life, and that he was also on the watch list. In the end he decided against it, thinking that raising the issue might make it more likely. After all, what was one small lie of omission in all that was going on? He dismissed Prospero, with instructions that he was to stay in the restricted area of the monastery until the service the following morning.

Chapter 10

Wednesday morning

Pedro

Pedro wandered into his office and across to his desk. It was the first thing he did every morning, to check the day's menus. At the edge of his vision, a slight movement caught his attention and he jumped.

Have we got mice? Surely not?

Alan kept telling him he should find any nest and kill all inhabitants. Pedro couldn't bring himself to do that; if they ever did have mice he caught them humanely and released them far away. How could he possibly destroy a *nest*? He turned towards the bed.

"Leonie," he exclaimed. "What are you doing here?"

She shook her head at him and curled up more tightly into the corner, pulling the blankets around and over herself and flinching away from him. Already certain about her background, and very familiar with the behaviour of such children, he placed food and drink close and left her undisturbed whilst he sent a messenger for Lord Gabriel.

"She's a nestling," he explained when Lord Gabriel arrived. "Or at least she was, once. A feral child, from a pack, a nest. Something is scaring her and she's coming as close as she can to hiding out in her nest."

Lord Gabriel nodded. "How long have you known she was a nestling?"

"Since the first time I met her, before Christmas," Pedro told him. "It's not something I'd miss, given everything. I just tried to make sure she thought of here as somewhere safe to hide out. I guess it worked, because at least she hasn't disappeared."

Gabriel agreed. "What do you think is upsetting her? What do we need to do to help her?"

Pedro thought for a moment. "Belonging, being part of a family, is what every nestling wants. In her eyes, today Prospero is choosing to leave that behind for her. I should think that's way outside anything she could cope with. She certainly won't think she's worth it. I imagine Prospero would be able to reassure her?"

"That's not an option, not this morning. No, I think this one's down to you."

"Me?" exclaimed Pedro, flabbergasted. "I can't. I don't know what to do."

"Well, if you don't, none of us are going to be any good," Gabriel told him. "Alan can handle the kitchen and I'll send Ellie to you after breakfast."

With that, he left. Pedro summoned up his courage and went to sit in the office near Leonie. He took time to pray before speaking, but he still didn't really have any plans when the words just came out of his mouth. "What's worrying you?" he asked quietly. "What's the matter?"

Leonie looked at him with deeply troubled eyes. "I can't do it," she whispered. "I can't do this. I can't let him leave where he belongs. He's done it before. I can't make him do it again, not for me. But I can't stop it. I don't know what to do."

"No," Pedro agreed. "You can't stop it. This is his choice to make, not yours."

"But he's doing it because of me, so it's my fault. I should stop him."

"No," he said, thinking hard. "You've got it the wrong way

round. He's leaving the Order because that's what God is telling him to do. He'll do that anyway. But because he's leaving it, he's then free to marry you. It isn't marrying you that's causing him to leave."

He could almost see Leonie's brain working as she considered this. "But he's still leaving where he belongs," she stated.

"Perhaps it's better to think of it as moving on to the next place he belongs," he suggested. "Neither of you are actually leaving. You'll both still be here, belonging in the same place, doing much the same things, and most importantly, with the same people, who care about both of you."

Leonie relaxed as they talked, unwinding from the blankets to sit cross-legged on the edge of the bed.

He continued. "Prospero's going to do this anyway but today isn't going to be easy for him. You being there is what will make it better for him. Do you think you can manage that?"

"Will you be there?" Leonie's voice was still little more than a whisper.

"Of course I'll be there," he said, relieved that he seemed to have persuaded her. "I think of you like my daughter, and Prospero's my Brother. I wouldn't be anywhere else. I'll have to sit with the others, but Lady Eleanor will be there and sit with you. Is that a deal?"

Slowly, Leonie nodded, and he thought he almost saw a smile pass across her face. He smiled back anyway.

"Now, how about some breakfast?" he asked. "Suppose I rustle us up some pancakes?"

Prospero

When Prospero entered the Abbey with the other monks, the first thing he did was to scan the rest of the building for Leonie. He was immensely relieved to see her there, sitting with Lady Eleanor, but immediately concerned over how scared she looked. On Monday night he'd looked for her presence with his mind just before the Shields had been switched on and had been pleased to see that she was asleep. Last night he'd done the same; that time she'd been awake but had seemed calm and content. Benjamin had told him about the planned medicals and he'd expected her to be worried by it, so last night he'd been relieved that she'd seemed calm.

He'd wanted to check on her this morning, too, expecting that his actions in leaving the Order were likely to upset her. He hadn't had the chance. Gabriel had required him to remain within the restricted and still shielded area, both for breakfast – as many of the Brothers did anyway – and then until this service. He had spent the time in prayer and meditation – again as required by Lord Gabriel – but it had taken all the spiritual discipline he had learned over the last few years to concentrate on this instead of worrying about Leonie. He'd been aware of Gabriel's departure, but not what it was about. He'd suspected Leonie was involved, which worried him more, but he knew that even if this was the case Gabriel would not tell him, not this morning. Now he found himself trying to work out what could have happened, but at least she was there, where he could see her.

The service passed in something of a blur for him. He used his musical training to focus on the hymns. He managed to concentrate when he was actively taking part, giving all the right responses to the questions Gabriel asked him about leaving the Order. But between those, when anyone else was speaking or reading, his eyes and thoughts drifted towards Leonie. Why was she so upset? What had happened earlier? Was she finding the service too much? And then the first part was over and he walked towards Leonie. He crouched down beside where she was sitting, taking in her tear-streaked face.

"Perry, I'm sorry," she whispered, leaning towards him. "I didn't think…"

He reached out and stroked her cheek. "It's okay, sweetheart," he said gently. "The good bit starts here."

"It does?" She seemed hesitant, uncertain.

He nodded, taking her hands and pulling her to her feet as he stood up himself. "Yes, it does. Come on."

He led her back to the centre of the Abbey, keeping one arm round her to comfort and support her. To his surprise the monks and nuns had left their normal area and were now gathered around the place where Gabriel awaited them.

"Still part of us," said Gabriel as they reached him, though Perry wasn't sure whether that was for his benefit or Leonie's.

Andrew leaned forward and whispered something in Leonie's ear; he didn't hear what but it made her smile. She pulled herself together, standing free of his support although she kept hold of his hand. Together they turned to face Lord Gabriel who smiled at them as he began to speak.

"Prospero Michael of House Tennant and House St Peter, do you promise yourself in future marriage to Leonie, of House St Peter?"

"I do." Of course he did.

"Do you make this promise of your own free will and from your own desire and not at the behest or compulsion of any other person?"

"I do."

Gabriel turned towards Leonie. "Leonie of House St Peter, do you promise yourself in future marriage to Prospero Michael, of House Tennant and House St Peter?"

Prospero held his breath awaiting her answer.

Her voice was quiet, but clear. "I do."

"Do you make this promise of your own free will and from your own desire and not at the behest or compulsion of any other person?"

"I do."

Lord Gabriel gestured to Brother Edward who placed a pair of intertwined rings in his hand.

"Then as a symbol of your promise before God, I give you these rings, formed from one source, joined as one body, as you will be when you fulfil your promise."

He twisted the rings to separate them and slid the smaller onto Leonie's finger and the larger onto Prospero's. He smiled at them both again. "Congratulations on your betrothal."

Just as he had told Leonie he intended to, Prospero inclined his head to hers and kissed her. She responded instinctively, then blushed and, once more overcome by all that had taken place, buried her face in his shoulder. He understood and held her close against the shelter of his body as the monks, nuns and the rest of the congregation dispersed.

Benjamin hung back a moment. "It's been an unsettling morning," he said. "Sit a while and recover. Find me whenever you're ready, there's no hurry at all."

Finally alone together in the Abbey, Perry coaxed Leonie

over to a seat and sat down keeping his arm around her.

She looked up at him. "I didn't mean to... I didn't want to... You shouldn't have left them for me."

"I didn't," he told her. "We both still belong here, to this House, to these people. Leaving the Order was my choice, because it was time. Marrying you is a wonderful bonus as a result, but it's not why I did it."

She nodded slowly. "That's what Pedro said."

"Did he?" Perry asked, not really bothered, simply enjoying the feeling of Leonie relaxing against him. "See, sometimes even Pedro talks sense."

Leonie

With Perry's arms around me, held close against his body, feeling his warmth, I finally started to relax. I felt like I was able to breath easily again. Working in the kitchens last night had been soothing; I'd eventually gone to bed feeling calm and able to cope with what today would bring. But I'd woken in the night, panicking. Not a nightmare, not the Them; I was awake and worrying about all that had been and what was to come.

Worries are so much worse in the night. Things that can be dismissed during the day come back to fret and haunt. Ideas that are ludicrous in the light suddenly seem real and probable. And daft notions and solutions seem to make sense and be logical.

But once more I'd found myself torn between not being able to leave – I'd promised to marry Perry so I couldn't leave – and not being able to stay – it would cause too much harm to Perry. And again I hadn't known what to do or where to go. I hadn't been able to run away; I hadn't been able to break my promise. I'd needed to find somewhere safe, someone who would help me stop Perry. I hadn't been able to go to the Abbey. In my befuddled night-time brain I hadn't been able to seek safety in the place that I was trying to take Perry from. In the end I'd headed for the other place I thought of as safe and soothing, the kitchen.

I'd curled into the corner of the bed in Pedro's office to wait for morning. I'd woken at Pedro's approach and for a moment I'd thought I was back in the nest. Then I'd realised that of course, he'd been a nestling too.

Now, sitting in the Abbey with Perry, I wondered how I'd missed that before.

This morning, Pedro had simply sat with me in his office. Slowly and quietly, he'd started talking to me and he made sense. He'd told me I had to let Perry make his own choices and live with the consequences. But what really helped was Pedro telling me I was part of his family.

I wriggled even closer to Perry, revelling in the warmth and security his body brought me. Now he was my family.

Once I'd made it to the Abbey I'd only had eyes for Perry. I'd watched him all the way through. What he'd done had seemed so wrong, leaving the place where he belonged. The words of the service had been harsh, about being cast out, leaving security and family behind. He'd done that once before, to come here and now he was doing it again and I knew I was the cause. I hadn't been able to help the tears on my cheeks although I'd tried to brush them away.

Perry had appeared beside me, pulled me close and led me back to the centre of the Abbey. Lord Gabriel had said something but Andrew had leaned over and whispered in my ear.

"Not losing him, gaining you," he'd said.

Andrew had an amazing ability to be in the right place and

say the right thing at the right time. It had given me the strength to face Lord Gabriel and do what needed to be done next. Then Perry had kissed me and everything else had disappeared. Until someone had made a noise – probably Chloe cheering, it would have been just like her – and I had remembered where we were and what we were doing and who was watching and I had blushed from head to toe. I'd hidden my face in Perry's shoulder but felt him vibrating with amusement even as he had protected me while everyone left.

And now it was just us and we were sitting quietly in the Abbey. Our hands entwined, I studied our rings. They were beautiful, a matching pair designed and carved in Trader style. If they weren't being worn they fit together, the smaller inside the larger, but connected. I'd seen similar before and I wondered where these came from. But then another question came to mind and I turned to Perry.

"I didn't know you were called Michael?" I said.

He smiled at me. "Once you start asking questions, I know you're feeling better," he said. "I expect there are a lot of little things we don't know about each other. I was called Michael after my father. Prospero is after one of his distant ancestors."

"And House Tennant?" I asked. "Is that where you were born? Lord Gabriel said House Tennant and House St Peter. I didn't think you could belong to two Houses."

"Ah," he said and his face sobered, the smile fading off it. "I'd rather forgotten that little detail. The agreement with my High Lord was that I belonged to House St Peter only for as long as I remained in the Order. Now I've left, technically I'm part of House Tennant again. I don't know why Lord Gabriel used House St Peter as well. Probably because I want to stay here and he wants us to stay. Or to show that I still belong here, no matter what."

"I like it here," I told him.

"You'd like House Tennant, too," he said with a half-smile, his eyes going out of focus for a moment as he was no doubt remembering it. Then his face sobered again. "Look, Leonie," he said. "There's another detail I haven't told you yet and I should have, and I'm sorry I haven't."

I looked at him in expectation. Right from the beginning, from the very first time I'd met him, there had been things, details that he hadn't told me that I could have done with knowing. I shouldn't have been surprised. He took a deep breath and tightened his arm around me.

"I told you that my uncle chose me as one of the group from which he'd pick his heirs. What I didn't tell you then was that my uncle is the High Lord of House Tennant."

It took a few moments for that to sink in and then I exploded out of his arms, backing away from him. It was a good thing we were in the Abbey with its Shields because if I'd been able to I'd have gone for him with more than just my voice.

"You didn't tell me? You thought that was just a detail? You thought it wouldn't matter? That it wouldn't bother me?" I could hear my voice getting shriller.

He stood up and stepped very slowly towards me with his hands out, as I backed away, looking for the exits. "No," he said. "I knew it would upset you. That's why I didn't tell you."

"You waited until after the service? *After* we promised to marry? Not *before*? Were you trying to trap me?" I continued backing away, feeling for anything I could use.

He followed cautiously. "No, never. I wouldn't trick you. Honestly. I just couldn't find the right time."

"When were you planning to tell me, then? What did you think I would do?" I wasn't done yelling at him yet. My hand closed around a book, and I lifted it up, ready to throw.

"I thought you'd run away again," he said simply. "You've no idea how terrified I was when you disappeared on Sunday night. I couldn't face that again."

The raw fear in his voice cut into me, an almost physical pain stabbing my heart, stopping me in my tracks. I'd been looking for the exits to do just that. I dropped the book. My temper and anger disappeared in the light of his obvious pain. I couldn't understand that I had the power to make him hurt like this. Before, I'd been trying to protect him by leaving; now I could see that I would hurt him. I stood still, my arms by my sides, and the tears started rolling down my cheeks again. He stepped closer and put his arms round me, pulling me against his chest.

"I'm sorry," he said. "I'm so sorry. I should have told you, I know I should. Don't cry. I love you."

That didn't help. How I could feel so safe with him, wrapped in his arms, and yet know that being with him would put me in the path of all these things I feared? But I had no choice; or rather, I'd already made my choice and now it was time for me to live with the consequences. I freed my arms from where they were trapped between us and lifted them up to put around his neck. I looked straight into his eyes.

"It's okay," I said. "I don't like it, but I'll be okay. In the end. I'll be okay."

The fear faded from his eyes and they lit up as a smile spread across his face. "I love you," he said again. Suddenly, he bent down a little and swept me up into his arms.

I squealed, taken by surprise.

"We're not going to see Benjamin until I'm absolutely certain you're okay," he said. "So we might as well go sit somewhere more comfortable and a little more private in case anyone comes in."

He chose the side chapel, where the seats were definitely more comfortable especially if there were two of you sitting together. He didn't put me down until we got there, when he sat down and pulled me onto his lap. He held me close against him, but I pulled away a little; I had more questions to ask.

"Is there anything else you haven't told me? Or that I need to know?" I asked him. "I promise to listen and not run away or get mad if there is. But you have to promise not to keep stuff from me."

"I promise," he said. "With all my heart." Then he shook his head. "There isn't anything else that I know I haven't told you. But there might be things that come up as I remember them. Or that I don't realise you don't know. There's a little more about House Tennant if you're ready."

"Go on then," I told him.

"My uncle picked me as one of a group of three from which he'll eventually pick his heir. Lord Gabriel has got him to agree that he'll consider me third, only if the others aren't possible. And I can avoid it by never going back to the territory of House Tennant." He paused. "Only I want to go back, to see my family and to take you there. I think not going back would be running away from it all."

I agreed with him. "I want to go, too, and meet your family. Who are the other two heirs?"

"His daughter, Lilyrose and our cousin, Brin. Gabriel says Lilyrose will make a very capable heir, so I shouldn't worry."

I was curious as to why Lilyrose wasn't automatically her father's heir, so Perry spent some time explaining how different Houses had different patterns of inheritance. Some were passed down through the eldest child, others specified eldest daughter or son. Some, like House Tennant, picked the heir from a limited group, such as all the children or grandchildren or descendants of the current or a previous Lord. The qualifications for that group might vary considerably from House to House and might or might not include those born outside formal marriage. For some Houses, anyone could challenge by right of battle, for others the current Lord alone picked their heir, and others a group of senior advisers voted. Some had strange and complex rules to cover all possible circumstances. It all seemed very complicated to me but Perry said it wasn't, it was just different in different Houses.

For House St Peter the qualification was to be a member of the Order and the heir was chosen by the current High Lord. For House Tennant, you had to be a grandchild of the previous High Lord – or a great grandchild of the one before that if there weren't many grandchildren – and the current High Lord had the final say in his or her heir. I worked through all that and what it meant.

"Perry," I said. "That means you went from being an heir for House Tennant to eligible as an heir for House St Peter and now back to House Tennant again. I don't understand. Why is one okay and the other not? Why is it different?"

He looked at me, astounded. "I never realised that. I'm not entirely sure it is different. I just didn't think about it here." He grinned at me. "You keep making me look at things differently. I'm not sure I can keep up!"

I had one more question. "What's your uncle's name? You've never said."

He sighed and answered slowly. "It's Neville, Lord Neville." He looked at me and carried on, "Do you know, I've never actually said his name out loud since l left House Tennant."

"Name it and tame it," I said to myself but it must have been out loud because Perry asked what I meant and now it was my turn to explain. It's a Trader saying that if you name what you fear then you're on the way to dealing with it. It doesn't really mean name it literally, but if you acknowledge it and face up to it you can start to deal with it and some of the fear eases. I might have been trying to run away physically but I was pretty sure that Perry had a habit of running away inside his head. I assumed that was what Lord Gabriel had meant yesterday about not facing up to hard truths.

Chapter 11

Leonie

Although I was in no hurry to go and see Benjamin, I thought we'd probably kept him waiting long enough. Perry was more relaxed about it but I wanted to get this over with so we headed off towards Benjamin's office in the hospital building.

"Perry," I said as we walked. "Where are you supposed to live now? You can't stay in the monastery, can you? And the rooms Lady Eleanor has chosen for us aren't ready."

"Has she picked rooms for us? What are they like?"

Typical. Avoiding the question was definitely one of Perry's skills.

"Big," I said with feeling. "And only half finished."

He grinned at me, both amused and acknowledging my feelings about all that was being provided. "I could sneak into your room?" he suggested with a wicked smile.

"But seriously, Perry?" I said, getting a little frustrated. Much as I would love him to sneak into my room and sleep there, I couldn't see that going down well with anyone else. It did cross my mind that it probably wouldn't be the first time that Perry had sneaked into someone else's room and got away with it but I thought we'd be bound to get caught.

"Seriously," he said. "There's hospital staff accommodation round the courtyard next to the hospital. Groups of rooms that share a lounge and kitchen. I'll be fine there for a few nights, it won't be for long." He looked at me. "Do you want to see it? We can go round that way."

I did, so we detoured. Perry led me into a large living space, with sofas and arm chairs, and a decent sized kitchen area towards the back. A number of doors opened onto the living space and Perry directed me across to one, pushing the door open.

"This one's mine," he said, "and Edward's already put my things in it."

The room was basic – bed, chair, desk, cupboards, access to a bathroom – but comfortable. Edward might have moved Perry's things in, but there didn't seem to be much there. I supposed Perry really didn't have very much of his own. I felt a lot better having seen where he was going to be.

We didn't stay long and when we reached Benjamin's office, Andrew was already there, leaning on a desk in the main office, chatting casually with Benjamin. Benjamin greeted us with a smile and gestured for me to go into his office. As I did so, he stopped Perry.

"Not you," he said. "Just Leonie. You're to go with Andrew for your own medical."

Perry started protesting of course, so I turned back. "I'll be fine," I told him. "You go with Andrew."

It was true; I would be fine however nervous I was. I knew his staff had him down as a disciplinarian and a strict taskmaster but I'd always found Brother Benjamin to be polite, courteous and respectful. If I had to sum him up in one word, I'd have called him gentle.

In the end Perry went, though I had to reassure him again and he protested to Andrew all the way down the corridor.

Brother Benjamin shut the door and indicated some comfortable chairs to one side rather than his desk.

"I will need to examine you and do some tests," he said, "but I'd like to start by talking." He passed me a small gadget.

"But first take this."

I looked at it in bewilderment and then back at him.

"It's a controller," he told me. "You can use it to switch the Shields for this room on or off. It's up to you what we have on. Whatever you feel comfortable with."

I noticed that it was set only for the Defender Shield to be on, so no one could reach us or disturb us, but we could use what gifts we liked. I left it at that and Benjamin nodded approvingly. I wondered if it had been some sort of a test.

"Right," he said. "Now, do you understand why I have excluded Prospero?"

I did and I said so. "He'd try to take over, answering for me and looking at the results of your tests."

Benjamin smiled. "That's about it," he agreed. "However, it doesn't mean you have to be alone. If there is anyone you'd like with you we can fetch them, or if you'd like me to get a female member of staff to sit with us, or find a female doctor to do this, that would also be fine."

I shook my head. "This is okay."

I trusted Benjamin, but even if I hadn't I wouldn't have asked for anyone else to be there. The only person I'd want would be Perry and we'd already ruled him out. Had it been a dangerous situation – and I was sure it wasn't – anyone he suggested, male or female, would likely be on his side and if it came to it that would be two for me to deal with rather than one. Benjamin seemed happy enough to leave it as just us.

"You should know," he said, "that anything you say to me is confidential. I will share what you say only if it affects your safety or wellbeing or the House's security and then only with

Lord Gabriel. Is that okay?"

I thought about that and decided that it was okay. I wanted to belong here and that meant I had to trust Lord Gabriel.

Benjamin had a notepad and he started asking me questions, about what I knew of my parents (nothing), my background (nothing), and what my life had been like as a child. Picking my words with care, I told him what he needed to know, becoming more relaxed about it as time went on.

Part way through he said, "I know that you've spent time with the Traders because I've seen your bracelet. Another time, I'd love to talk about some of what you've learnt from Katya. I believe she was Headwoman for your caravan?"

I nodded, and he went on, "But from what you've told me, and certain things I've noticed because I'm a doctor, I think you were also a slave child and then a nestling? Is that right?"

I stared at him in horror, no longer relaxed and unable to answer.

Does everyone know?

He continued, "Only those with the right training would spot it and it's fine if that's the case. There are other ex-slaves and ex-nestlings around here. But it is important for medical reasons. It tells me what sort of thing your body has had to deal with as you grew up."

Slowly I nodded. He made a note before going on to something else, and bit by bit I relaxed again. Then, as we had to, we reached the point where things became more practical and Benjamin moved on to examinations and tests. He listened to my heart and my chest then moved his stethoscope round to my back. He asked to look at the whole of my back; I guessed he could see the scars from where I'd been beaten and where I'd been injured by the hunters before I'd found the Traders. After that he tested my blood pressure, checked my reflexes and took various samples. I endured it, with my eyes closed at some points when I felt it necessary.

At long last he said he was done.

"But," he then said.

Why is there always a 'but'?

"Because of the things that have happened to you, I would like to do a scan to ensure the damage isn't deeper than we know or can see. How do you feel about that?"

I had two questions. "What does it involve? And can Perry be there?"

He smiled at me, although it didn't reach his eyes. "No, Prospero can't be there. If there's someone else in the room with you, it affects the results, so the only place for him would be the control room."

Yeah, that's not going to work.

"He'd be a right pain there, wouldn't he?" I asked, trying to summon up a grin myself.

Now Benjamin's smile reached his eyes. "Yes, he would. But honestly, it won't be that bad. It'll only take a few minutes. You'll have to lie still and the machine will rotate around you in a spiral. It'll never cover more than half of you at any point."

"Are there windows?"

"There's plenty of daylight, but the windows are just below the ceiling. You can't see out of them. But you can have headphones with relaxing music if you'd like."

I took a deep breath and decided once again that I trusted

Benjamin. "Okay, let's do it," I said.

Andrew

Perry had muttered all the way down the corridor and into a vacant examination room.

"She needs me. Whatever she says, she's scared. She needs someone there for her. She shouldn't be alone. Why won't he let me be there with her?"

Andrew just let him froth until he got it out of his system. In some ways it made his life easier. Perry was never the easiest of patients and usually objected strongly to any form of examination. Fretting about Leonie occupied him sufficiently that for once he was quite cooperative. Andrew took his time with the examination, aware that Benjamin would need longer with Leonie.

As he worked, he ignored Perry's continued mutterings and thought about the day so far. To be fair, it hadn't been an easy day for Perry. Leaving the Order... Andrew tried not to shudder; that had to feel very odd indeed. And Perry had taken it well. Okay, he'd been a little distracted, but overall he'd been calm and disciplined. Andrew had been impressed. Leonie'd been impressive too. Calming Perry like that and sending him off for his medical. That'd been more effective that anything Andrew had managed in the past.

He realised that Perry had stopped muttering. Andrew grinned at him, "Safe to take your blood pressure now, do you think?"

Perry grinned back, amused, acknowledging that he'd been fairly unreasonable. Andrew took that as a good sign and went ahead with the measurement. He nearly destroyed this hard won calm just a moment or two later, though. He knew the risk he was taking, sure the answer would be no, but he felt compelled to ask.

"Have you told her yet? About House Tennant?"

To Andrew's surprise, what he got was a smug smile.

"Yes, I have. I told you I would."

"And how did she take it?"

The smile dropped. "Not so well, to start with. She nearly bolted." The smile came back, complete with smug tone. "Now she's okay with it."

Andrew simply raised his eyebrows, disbelievingly.

"Honest," Perry insisted. "She is okay with it. She's here, isn't she?"

Andrew couldn't deny that. Relieved at the outcome and not wanting to cause any further disruption, he indicated they should return to Benjamin's office. His heart dropped when he saw the door was open; surely that could only mean they weren't in there? Perry dived into the room then charged out again, looking all round as if he'd spot Leonie hiding somewhere.

"They aren't there. She's not here. Where are they?"

Benjamin's assistant interrupted. "You're to wait in the office. They won't be long."

Perry turned on him. "Where are they? Where've they gone? What's wrong?"

Andrew grabbed Perry's arm. "He won't tell you. You know that. Come on, take a deep breath. She's safe with Benjamin, whatever. They'll be back soon."

"She'll be frightened. She doesn't like hospitals. He'll be scaring her."

"No, he won't. Benjamin won't make her do anything without her agreement. She's as safe with him as she would be anywhere."

Glancing over Perry's shoulder, Andrew spotted Benjamin and Leonie coming back down the corridor. With relief, he pushed Perry round so he could see them too. Perry stepped forward rapidly to meet Leonie, reaching out to touch her, his hands stroking down her arms as he reassured himself she was okay. Leonie smiled up into Perry's worried face, reaching up to touch his cheek.

"I'm fine," she said quietly. "We went for a scan. It was all fine."

Perry rested his forehead against hers, his voice just as quiet. "I was worried when you weren't here."

"I won't leave," she said so softly it was clearly intended only for Perry.

Andrew was almost sure the words were unnecessary, that they were touching minds too. They straightened up as one to stand side by side, Perry keeping one arm around Leonie as they both turned towards Benjamin.

"I decided on a scan to be on the safe side," Benjamin said. "But everything looks fine to me. I'll see you both, let's say, ten tomorrow morning, to go through the test results." He looked at Leonie, almost grinning at her, an expression Andrew was not used to seeing on Benjamin's face. "That is, if you are okay with Prospero being there for that?"

Leonie grinned back and nodded.

"Fine," Benjamin continued. "Right, you can all go. You should make it back to the dining hall in time for lunch."

On the way, Perry questioned Leonie about her examination, but her limited medical knowledge combined with the fact that Benjamin hadn't really told her very much about the tests or their purpose conspired to prevent him finding out anything useful.

Arriving a little late for lunch, they ended up sharing a table with Chloe, Nick and Aidan. Leonie slid eagerly into the chair next to Chloe and it was clear that Perry wasn't going to sit anywhere but next to Leonie. Andrew found himself beside Aidan.

"I thought you were leaving on Monday?" Andrew asked Aidan.

Aidan shook his head. "I'm staying for the next three months, to cover for someone's sabbatical. I prefer teaching to translating, anyway."

Perry looked up. "What about your wife and child?"

Aidan shrugged. "They're visiting her mother. They'll be gone most of the time I'm here. Now, Chloe says you'll be married in less than two weeks. Why so soon?"

Perry glanced at Leonie before answering. "Because Lord Gabriel says so? Does there need to be another reason?"

"I guess not," agreed Aidan. "In that case..." He raised his glass towards Perry and Leonie. "To the joining of House St Peter and House Tennant." Then he tilted his glass towards Leonie. "And to the Traders and House Chisholm, of course," he added.

Andrew thought he saw a flash of confusion cross Leonie's face, followed by one of concern across Perry's, both so fleeting he couldn't be sure. Had no one had ever told her she could be linked to House Chisholm? He reached out to Perry.

"Does she know? About House Chisholm?"

"Turns out not. I'll tell her after this."

It wasn't long before they had all finished eating. Nick, Aidan and Chloe dispersed to their various tasks and duties. Andrew was about to get up and leave himself, but Leonie's gaze was fixed on Perry, and she spoke before Andrew could move. He stayed and watched, concerned that he might disturb them by moving, and telling himself it was in case either of them needed him.

"House Chisholm?" Leonie said, her voice quiet but firm. "Tell me now."

"Are you going to get mad?" Perry asked her, equally quiet, but with a hint of amusement in his voice. "Because if so, I'd rather go outside where I have space to defend myself."

"You're safe enough. As long as you tell me. Now."

Andrew was amused, though he tried to hide it. They were well matched. He could safely leave them to each other's care. Perry grinned at Leonie. Only someone who knew him as well as Andrew would be able to tell he was nervous of her reaction.

"I really thought you'd know," he said. "Anyone with hair the colour of yours is almost certainly descended from the ruling family of House Chisholm. They aren't exactly known for their chastity so there are any number of descendants around. The High Lord will pick his heir from any of those descendants, though he usually sticks to the legitimate ones, and any descendant, legitimate or not, can challenge for the House if they wish."

Leonie looked at him in what Andrew took for horror. "Does everyone know?"

Perry was reassuring. "It's something that's fairly common knowledge. It doesn't matter to anyone."

Leonie just sighed and shook her head. He slipped an arm round her and held her close. That brought a smile back to her face.

"I'm okay," she told him. "There's just so much that I keep finding out that I don't know."

"What matters is that we have each other," he said. "The rest we'll work out."

Andrew slipped away sure they'd never even notice that he'd left.

Chapter 12

Leonie

"Come on," Perry said as he stood up from the table. "We're supposed to be meeting with Gabriel and Eleanor."

Smiling, he stretched his hand towards me. I took it and followed him out into one of the courtyards. He stopped there, and pulled me closer, wrapping both arms around me.

"Are you sure you're okay?" he asked.

I nodded, a little surprised to find it was true. There was something about Aidan that made me feel uncomfortable but I couldn't tell Perry that because I knew they'd been friends. And that reference to House Chisholm – and Perry's explanation – had put me right on edge. But they were things I had to deal with. And I could handle them. Strangely, since I'd realised in the Abbey that I'd made my choice and now needed to live with the consequences I was finding some of these things easier to manage.

"I'm fine," I said. I reached up to slide my hands into his hair and brought his lips down to touch mine. They were warm and soft. His touch sent sparks flying through my body and I forgot everything else.

He pulled away and grinned at me. "We're going to be late," he said, grabbing my hand and tugging me along to where we were meeting.

Brother Joseph was there as well as Lord Gabriel and Lady Eleanor. They were all gathered round a piano on the far side of the room, Joseph sitting at the keyboard. Perry dragged me over to join them.

"You get to choose the music you want at your wedding," Brother Joseph said with a grin.

I glanced at Perry in panic. I knew nothing about music, just some of the songs Traders sing. Perry was looking at Joseph, his eyes lit up, his delight obvious. Perry was in the choir, of course, and a soloist. Relieved, I realised I could leave the music to him. But Joseph looked at me. "I think you might recognise this one," he said as he started playing it.

I did. It was the music – a dance – that was always played at the end of Trader weddings after the bride and groom had made their promises to each other.

"We could have that?" I asked Perry hopefully.

He nodded but it was Brother Joseph who spoke. "I thought it might be a good piece for when you are leaving the Abbey after the service."

We agreed on that but I left the other music choices to him and Perry.

I turned to Lady Eleanor and rather hesitantly asked, "You said that it didn't have to be in the Abbey?"

She nodded. "That's right. It's the biggest space but it could be anywhere on the campus that's big enough for those coming."

I looked between her, Perry and Lord Gabriel and then very daringly just came out with it. "Could it be in the Old Chapel? Would that be alright?"

Everyone answered at once. Perry said that he'd like that too, Lord Gabriel and Lady Eleanor both said it would be fine, but in different words and Brother Joseph said it would be no problem for the music. I guessed that settled that.

The other thing Lady Eleanor wanted to sort out was who to invite. I'd been thinking about that and I had a bit of a list. It included Emmi from the café and her husband and cousin who also worked there. Then there were Tobias and Leah from the Settlers and some of their family. And I wanted to include the people who owned the bakery where I'd worked in the past – where I'd hidden out on Sunday – and a few others from around the town. I wasn't sure if these were all suitable but between them, the others seemed to know of everyone I'd suggested and were quite happy to invite them. Perry added a few more people he knew, and of course everyone from the House and the monastery would be there.

There was one group rather conspicuous by their absence – Perry's family. I debated with myself whether to bring the subject up or not. Then I decided that there was no way Lady Eleanor wouldn't have thought of this, which meant there was something going on or some decision already made that I didn't know about. Instead, I decided to ask Perry as soon as we were alone. Was this something he was keeping from me?

Once all was agreed, Lord Gabriel looked at me, his eyes studying my face, and then meeting mine. When he did that, I thought he could see right through me, knowing everything I'd done and was thinking. "I think you've had enough for today," he said. "Both of you, go find something else to do, relax. We'll see you at the evening meal."

I didn't need telling twice although Perry was a little slower. Lady Eleanor suggested that I take Perry to see our apartment, perhaps later when there was no one else around there. For now, though, we escaped to the Old Chapel.

As ever, I ran my hands along the memorial stones, the smooth cold stone interrupted by the engravings. Strange to think that in not much more than a week we'd be getting married here. I liked the sense of history, the feeling of continuity that gave me. With thoughts freewheeling through my mind, I turned towards Perry and the one currently at the top just came out.

"Pedro was a nestling," I said.

"Was he?" Perry's voice was curious but not particularly surprised.

"Didn't you know?"

"No, he's been here a lot longer than I have. How did you find out?"

"I just realised, this morning."

He came and put his arms round me. "What happened this morning? Something upset you badly, didn't it? Before the service?"

I nodded, brave in the safety of his arms. "What I was asking you to do, to leave where you belonged. I felt so guilty. In the night, I couldn't stop it and I couldn't leave. I hid in the kitchen and Pedro found me. That's when I realised. About him, I mean."

He stroked my hair and face very gently. "You didn't ask me to do it. God told me to. There's no reason for you to feel guilty."

"I did though. And then the service, you walking away, leaving all that... It made it worse."

"The service isn't about walking away. It's about being sent out to fulfil a role elsewhere, knowing that your family is behind you, always there for you, always ready to welcome you back. I'll find you the words, so you can read it and see. You probably found it all difficult to take in, at the time."

Now he grinned at me. "Fancy a distraction?" he asked. "I said I'd show you teleporting. Want to learn now? Just little things, mind. Not people."

I agreed eagerly. No way would I turn down an

opportunity to learn something new, and a distraction was just what I needed. We walked down to the river where Perry chose a number of small twigs, leaves and stones. We sat together on the bank, him behind me, his legs and arms round me.

How am I supposed to concentrate with his touch surrounding me?

Perry looked over my shoulder, his head beside mine and reached to spread the small items out in front of us.

"Now," he said. "You have to feel for the item with your mind, so it seems your mind is wrapped around it. Then visualise where you want it to land, and just move it there."

That seemed straightforward enough. I pulled my thoughts together, focusing hard on the twigs and leaves rather than on Perry. We linked minds again, our earlier link having broken when we'd gone into the Old Chapel, and I watched him do it a couple of times, the leaf disappearing and then reappearing a short distance away. Then it was my turn. I reached for a leaf, wrapping threads of thought around it, and chose a spot to move it to, a little closer to the river. Now for the tricky part. Perry had twisted his mind like *that*, so if I did *this*... The leaf moved.

"I did it! I did it." I twisted round to look at Perry in delight.

"You did," he said. "Now do it again."

I turned back and moved a twig, and then a couple of pebbles, before Perry called a halt.

"It takes a lot of energy," he said. "I'm ready for a drink and a snack. How about you? Emmi's café or shall we go and sneak something off Pedro?"

I chose Emmi's café. It wasn't far to walk and I thought it

would be quieter and more anonymous than going back onto campus. I might have been wrong to think it would be quieter although the café wasn't particularly busy. Emmi greeted us from the counter.

"You two again," she said. "You look better than last time," she told me and then turned to Perry. "And what are you doing out of uniform?"

He looked at me, grinning wickedly, and so I just took his hand and put our hands together on the counter. Emmi wasn't a Trader or a Settler, but I knew she'd know Trader jewellery when she saw it. She squealed at us and it was definitely a sound of approval. Then she was calling for her husband, Ells, and her cousin, Liann and we were caught up in a whirlwind of hugs and congratulations.

"I can smell burning," Liann said suddenly and she and Ells disappeared sharpish. Emmi laughed and pushed us towards a quiet table in the corner by the window. "I'll bring you drinks and cake on the house," she said.

She sat down with us when she brought them. "Tell all," she demanded.

Perry did, briefly, and added that all three of them were invited to the wedding. Emmi immediately started making plans to close up the café for our wedding day. Then Ells called her over to serve someone and I remembered something I'd meant to ask Perry.

"Your family," I said. "What about them and being invited to our wedding? Why is nobody mentioning it?" A small suspicion crossed my mind. "Have they even been told?"

He looked down at the table and fiddled with his plate, before answering me. "They're not that easy to contact. I have to write to them and there's not been that much of a chance yet."

I supposed that was true.

He went on, "There isn't really time for them to get the letter, decide to come, make arrangements and get here. Then there are my brothers and their girlfriends and who comes and who doesn't. And then how do I not invite my uncle? And if he comes, as a High Lord, with an entourage, it all starts to get a bit out of hand."

Rather more than a bit, I thought, starting to have some sympathy with his point of view.

He looked up at me. "And if they are here, then I have to deal with them and all the issues with them, right then. And I don't want that to distract from our wedding."

I didn't either; it just felt kind of wrong that his parents wouldn't be there.

"You will write and tell them, though, won't you?" I asked him.

He nodded. "Either tonight or tomorrow morning." He grinned at me. "It'll probably take me both to get the letter right."

I had another idea. "Sometimes, when someone in a Trader wedding has close family in another caravan that isn't there, they have a second wedding and party when they meet up with that caravan. Could we have a second wedding or something when we visit your parents, so your family can be there?"

Now he smiled at me, relieved. "I think that's a great idea. I'd like to do that."

He went on to tell me about Lord Gabriel's suggestion that we take an extended visit there over the summer. I wasn't sure whether that was something that made me feel excited or terrified, but I knew it was something I wanted to do either way. By now we'd finished our drinks so, after waving goodbye to Emmi (still overexcited about our news), we headed back to the campus to look at progress on our rooms.

***

The rooms weren't quite empty; Edward was just leaving. He looked Perry up and down.

"You need new clothes," he said. "Plus, I need to sort out your wedding outfit. Come and see me tomorrow, straight after breakfast."

With that, he was off. Perry pulled a face at me. He clearly didn't like the idea of being fitted out for new clothes any more than he'd liked the idea of a medical examination. I just laughed.

"If I have to do it, you have to do it," I said.

They'd made a lot of progress on our rooms again; the space was making sense, and I could see that it would soon be ready for Edward to furnish and decorate. I quite enjoyed showing Perry where everything was, and he was properly appreciative. As we looked around the room that would be our bedroom he had this wicked look on his face again. Then he pulled me into his arms.

"I think," he said, "I think that we need to dedicate this room properly." He slid one hand into my hair, twisting his fingers into the curls. Slowly, he ran his other hand down my spine, until it rested hot and electric, against the small of my back. Then he brushed his lips from my forehead, down my nose, tantalising me until he reached my mouth. Once again I melted into him, the rest of the world disappearing as I concentrated on the sensations he was making ripple through my body. Right then, I would have gone along with anything he suggested, whatever

Lord Gabriel's restrictions.

We were interrupted by a knock on the outer door, and Lady Eleanor came in looking for us. "There you are," she said as we both tried not to look guilty. "I thought I'd find you here. What do you think of the progress?"

We chatted about it for a while, but then it was time for all of us to make our way to the evening meal. By the end of that, I found myself yawning. I hadn't had much sleep last night and an awful lot had happened since then.

"You need an early night and a good night's sleep," Perry said. "And you've got an early shift tomorrow. And I've got a letter to write. Come on."

However much I was yawning, I felt it was still too early to go to sleep. We ended up in the House library, sitting together, me reading, him starting to write his letter.

"If you start to fall asleep on me, I'm marching you straight off to bed," Perry told me, with a wicked grin.

A little later he did just that. We stopped outside my room, my back to the door. He placed his hands either side of my head, leaning into me as I blinked sleepily at him. Then his mouth claimed mine, and the craving that ran through me drove all thoughts of sleep from my head. The door opened behind me and I almost fell inside.

"Goodnight," Perry said, grinning at me, and just shut the door behind me. I leaned on it for a moment, getting my breath back.

How am I ever going to wait until we're married?

Chapter 13

Wednesday evening

Perry

Perry took a seat in the small lounge area near Leonie's rooms planning to keep his mind's eye on her until he was sure she was sleeping peacefully. He still expected her to react to the events of the past few days with a major nightmare and he intended to be close when it happened.

He knew he was being over protective – unduly possessive Andrew called it – but he couldn't help it. From his perspective, Leonie had run away from him on Sunday night, had tried again on Monday morning when he'd found her, been terrified enough last night to try to stop their wedding, and she had thought about running this morning when he'd told her about his uncle. Finding her missing from Benjamin's office had been close to the last straw for him. Logically, he knew she had promised to marry him and she'd said she wouldn't run away and he believed that she would keep her word. It was just that emotionally he hadn't quite caught up with the logic.

As he sat there, his mind drifted back over the day, ignoring the traumatic elements to concentrate on his time with Leonie. He couldn't wait until he didn't have to leave her at her door. He had very nearly got carried away earlier in what would become their bedroom; Lady Eleanor's interruption had been opportune. She'd spoken to him telepathically as they'd left the apartment.

"There will be a modified Containment Shield as soon as possible."

He had looked back at her quickly in consternation as her meaning had dawned on him but fortunately Leonie hadn't noticed.

"I had forgotten," he'd replied the same way.

Actually, even in the past most of the time he hadn't had to remember as his partners had rarely been anything like as Gifted as he was. Really, the only one had been Melanie and, as she was Eleanor's daughter, he certainly wasn't going to mention her. It was embarrassing enough that it was Eleanor who had sensed and interrupted him and Leonie.

"I rather thought you had. Gabriel usually has good reason for his restrictions."

That was true enough, but for the next week or so Perry was going to have to be very careful to control his feelings or at least his actions. Right now, Leonie was asleep and he was struggling with this letter he had to write. He picked up his things and headed towards Lord Gabriel's office for some advice.

Benjamin walked into the office only moments after Perry himself had got there.

"I have those reports you wanted," Benjamin said quietly to Gabriel. "I can come back later?"

"No," said Gabriel. "Come on in. If it's about Prospero and Leonie you can share the general health highlights with both of us. I'm sure Prospero will welcome the distraction."

Benjamin did so, looking first at Perry. "Well, your health is fine, which is no surprise. As for Leonie, she's remarkably healthy all things considered. There are signs of past malnutrition but she's clearly eating much better now."

Gabriel interrupted, with a sidelong glance at Perry. "I imagine that's to do with the team that's been watching her for the last few months to make sure she eats properly."

Perry experienced a moment of guilt.

How does Gabriel manage to know everything?

"I didn't know you knew," he said.

"Oh yes. I know you're the ringleader, but I could name most of your conspirators too. It might be easier to name those who aren't involved. Including Pedro was a master stroke. As was Chloe."

"I didn't recruit Chloe—she added herself."

She would have been a master stroke, if only he'd thought of it. She had made ensuring Leonie ate properly so much easier. Benjamin didn't hide his amusement. "I'm still going to put her on a supplement, a broad spectrum of vitamins, minerals, to make up for past shortfalls."

Perry nodded. He should have thought of that.

Benjamin continued, "Turning to other matters, she's not, and never has been, sexually active..."

"I knew that," Perry interrupted, somehow needing to show how well he knew Leonie.

Gabriel didn't look up and Benjamin ignored the interruption. "But she has been badly beaten in the past."

"I knew that too," Perry insisted.

Benjamin indicated a medical scan showing the damage and scarring particularly across her back. Perry winced.

"I thought you knew," said Gabriel.

"I knew. I hadn't seen. It's different," Perry told him.

"There are scars from old bites there, too," Benjamin said. "Dog bites by the look of them."

"She was hunted," Perry said shortly.

Benjamin moved on. "There's something else to consider," he said. "I don't know what your plans are but right now I wouldn't think she's strong enough to maintain a pregnancy. I'd advise waiting a year or two."

Perry looked at him blankly, all other thoughts wiped from his mind. "I'd never thought about it," he said slowly. "Children. We can have children. I hadn't thought."

He stood up. He needed space. He had to think this through. He needed Leonie. "I have to go," he said. "Excuse me."

Gabriel

Gabriel watched Prospero leave, then went over to the outer office and asked Chloe to find Brother Andrew and send him in. On his way back he shut the doors and turned on all the Shields and protective devices he had. Benjamin looked at him, concerned.

"Did I say the wrong thing? I don't think she is strong enough, but I also couldn't countenance adding an unborn or new-born child to our mix."

"It would be unborn. Everything is getting closer, much closer. I can feel it." Gabriel worked hard at keeping sheer panic out of his voice. Thinking that the crucial moment was close was keeping him awake at night, his body flooded with fear-generated adrenaline.

"So what was it?" Benjamin asked, his calm voice reassuring Gabriel and reducing his incipient panic. "Leonie's already taken care of contraception. Could children be an issue for them?"

"Possibly," Gabriel replied. "But nothing that need affect

what you do or your advice to them. They'll work it out should it be necessary." He dismissed the thought with a wave. "There's something more, isn't there?"

Benjamin nodded. "The scans showed a small tracker implanted, just under that area of scarring. From what we can tell, it's a model perhaps fourteen or fifteen years old and still active. It sends location, that's all. I could deactivate it without any invasive surgery, or we could remove it, but I'd rather not operate until I have more of her blood type in stock. It's a rare type."

"It would be." Gabriel considered the tracker. "I came to suspect something like this. Well before Christmas, I had a report from the watch team of an odd signal they couldn't trace. Now it makes sense." He thought a bit longer. "Leave it active for now, and don't tell anyone else. Whoever put it there is either no longer an issue, or they already know where she is and aren't taking any action, and haven't for years. If we deactivate it, they'll know that we've found it and that we know, and that might cause them to react. I don't want to precipitate anything."

Benjamin nodded. "I've completed the DNA analysis. She's very definitely Helena's child." He paused while Gabriel took that in. "And yes, she's fathered by a Chisholm, which is hardly a surprise, given her hair. But why would someone be tracking her? And more importantly, who? She must have been a small child when it was implanted and they are very expensive. Is she really so valuable?"

"I suspect she is, as a weapon or a hostage or a bargaining chip depending on who holds her." Gabriel sighed. "As for who, we've always been led to believe the death of Augusta and the child were due to natural causes – illness and malnutrition. But now we know someone removed Leonie and replaced her with another child's body. That person knows Leonie's alive. Was Augusta actually killed rather than dying naturally? Was it even

Augusta?"

"And why implant a tracker and then leave a valuable child as a slave orphan? That doesn't make sense either," Benjamin said.

"No," said Gabriel slowly. "It doesn't. But I'm just beginning to get the glimmer of an idea. It doesn't answer who, but it might tell us how. Let me think. I'll share it with you and Ellie when I get my thoughts more in order."

There was a knock on the door and Andrew put his head round it. "You sent for me, Father?"

At least Gabriel could safely pass one of his problems to someone else, for now. "Yes," he said. "Prospero has just realised that he and Leonie could have children. I need you to find him and do what you can. I would rather not risk him having nightmares again."

Andrew nodded, with a slight slump of his shoulders, which emphasised to Gabriel just what a task he might be handing over. He studied Andrew again, and decided to give him what help he could.

"I am Leonie's guardian," he said, firmly. "If there is anything – perhaps otherwise confidential – that you know that you need to tell Prospero to resolve or ease this, you have my permission to do so." With a slight wave of his hand, he sent Andrew on his way.

Andrew

Andrew went searching, wondering just how Gabriel seemed to manage to know everything, even those things he couldn't possibly know. It took him more than an hour to find Perry, though when he did he realised that his location should have been obvious. Perry was in the hospital, sitting in the neonatal unit just watching the babies. The senior duty nurse caught Andrew as he approached.

"He's been sitting there for more than half an hour. He's just been sitting, not doing or saying anything. Is he okay?" she asked.

Andrew reassured her, "He'll be fine. Don't worry, I'll deal with it."

He sat down beside Perry and simply waited.

Perry turned to him. "Children," he said. "I can have children. Leonie and I can have children." His voice was full of wonder.

Andrew smiled at him, relieved that, after everything in the past, at least he wanted children. "Yes, you can, just perhaps not immediately."

"No, I want Leonie to myself for a while first. And she needs to complete her studies. And I know she's not strong enough yet, I'm not stupid. It's just the thought never crossed my mind."

"And of all the things that have been happening over the last few days, this is the one that has knocked you for six?" Andrew was amused.

"It never crossed my mind," Perry repeated. "I was used to the fact that I'd never have children. In some ways I saw it as my penance for what happened with Lesley. And now it's all opened up before me."

"Idiot," said Andrew affectionately. Much as he loved him, sometimes Perry could be so slow. Together they headed towards staff accommodation.

"I need to think about contraception," Perry said. "We've

only a few days until the wedding."

"You need to find Leonie and talk to her about it," Andrew told him. He did not want to go down this track, not knowing what he knew.

"I went there first, but I could tell she was asleep as soon as I was close. No way am I going to wake her when she's actually asleep. I need to sort this; I'm not going to take any risks. I don't even know if she wants children."

Andrew was silent, unable to think of any answer he could honestly give.

"Andrew? What do you know that I don't?" Perry asked, his voice full of suspicion.

"Lots of things?" Andrew responded hopefully.

"About Leonie?"

Andrew tried again. "You need to talk to her, not me."

"Andrew, she's not here. What is it?"

"Have you never heard of patient confidentiality?"

"I could find her notes."

"That's not ethical, and it wouldn't help," Andrew bluffed.

"Andrew!" Perry was getting frustrated and it showed clearly in his tone. He came to a sudden stop and turned towards Andrew. He took a half step closer. "You. Know. Something." He punctuated his words by poking Andrew in the chest with his finger. Andrew batted his hand down.

"You do know something," Perry continued. "If you didn't you'd just say so, but you're avoiding the question."

Andrew looked at him in despair. "You don't get it, do you?

Even now, you don't get it. You still don't understand how she feels about you, and how long she's felt like that." He shook his head then carried on before Perry could defend himself. "She can't say no to you, she's never even wanted to. Way back she realised that if you'd made the slightest move she'd have gone along willingly, eagerly. She didn't understand then that you wouldn't. She was trying to protect herself from herself."

"You knew I wouldn't but you must have still prescribed for her." There was an edge of anger and jealousy growing in Perry's voice.

Andrew turned away from him and continued down the corridor. "She'd have gone somewhere else." He flung the words back over his shoulder. "Better it was me, able to keep an eye on her."

Perry strode after him, his jealousy turning into angry denial. "And she said no fast enough when I asked her to marry me. She ran away."

"She didn't say no, though, did she? You are getting married. And I'm betting that she never actually said no. I reckon she decided that it wouldn't be good for you, so she tried to leave so it couldn't happen, and I don't think she could manage even that. And if she did say anything, she'd have been listing other people's objections so that it would be someone else who stopped it, because she couldn't. She didn't want to say no, she wasn't able to, but she felt she had to for your sake."

That was so close to what had happened that Perry was silent, his jealousy and anger draining away. They had reached the staff accommodation and Perry sank into one of the lounge chairs, resting his head in his hands for a few moments. He looked up. "And does she want children? I suppose you know that, too?" he snapped.

"I don't suppose you'd settle for waiting and asking her yourself?" Andrew asked, with no real expectation that this would happen.

"Not if you know, no I wouldn't."

"Very well then. Yes, she wants children. Specifically, she wants your children, but not unless she's in a position to care and provide for them properly."

"I'd provide for my kids! And their mother!" Perry was indignant.

"The conversation between us wasn't in the context of you being free to provide for her," Andrew replied drily.

The last of Perry's anger dissipated and he returned his head to his hands. "I'm sorry, Andrew. I'm glad she saw you. Thanks for being there for her."

"That's okay. Want me to stop here with you tonight?" Andrew was very concerned that the next thing he'd have to deal with would be Perry having a nightmare.

Perry shook his head. "No, I'll be fine. I'm on the watch list, aren't I?"

Andrew nodded. "Yes. You have been for several days."

"I suppose that's fair. I'd have put me on it, if I'd thought. But I'll be fine tonight." He carried on, "I'm sorry I made you break patient confidentiality. I shouldn't have done that."

Andrew grinned back. "You didn't. Gabriel's actually her guardian, remember. He told me to tell you, if I needed to."

Perry picked up the nearest cushion to throw at him, laughing. Andrew ducked and headed for the door, still laughing himself, and confident now that Perry would be fine, at least overnight.

"See you tomorrow!"

Chapter 14

Thursday morning

Perry

Perry went looking for Leonie as soon as he woke early the next morning. He found her in the kitchens with Pedro, preparing breakfast. He smiled and reached for her, but spoke to Pedro. "Can I borrow Leonie for a few minutes, please? There's something we need to talk about."

Pedro, who was always a sucker for romance, agreed readily. "Take your time, I can manage here."

Perry took Leonie's hand and pulled her after him. "Come on," he said.

She followed him, half running as she picked up on his excitement, and he led them through the courtyards to a quiet spot by the river.

"What is it?" she asked eagerly.

But suddenly he didn't know how to start and the words tumbled over themselves. "Last night, talking to Gabriel, I hadn't realised... Leonie, we can have children!"

She smiled at him happily and reached to stroke his cheek. "Yes, of course. Is that what you're excited about?"

He nodded. "What with Lesley, and then the Order, I'd assumed I would never have children, I'd got used to it. I didn't realise how much this would mean to me." His worries flared again for a moment. Had he got this wrong? "You do want children too, don't you? I don't mean immediately, but at some point?"

She wrapped her arms around him and kissed him in a

way that left no doubt in his mind, her lips warm on his, her hands stroking up his back and into his hair. "Of course I want children, your children."

He could feel a slight smile on her face, almost a laugh on her breath, as they kissed. How could he have doubted her?

After a few moments he, drew back. "I didn't mean immediately. I'd like you to myself for a while first, just us. And it would be sensible for you to finish your studies." She nodded in agreement, and he continued, "That means we need to think about contraception."

She shrugged. "That's all taken care of. Andrew organised it for me a while back. I didn't want to take any risks and I knew I couldn't trust me," she said.

"I wouldn't have put you in any danger." He needed to tell her, needed her to know he'd look after her.

"Andrew told me that, and I know it now. I didn't know it then; I couldn't take the risk."

"And if anything had happened, I would have taken care of you, provided for you and our child."

She looked down at the ground, sheepishly. "I wouldn't have told you. I'd just have left."

He lifted her chin so that she was looking at him again and smiled at her. "I'd have come after you anyway. I promised I'd always find you, remember. I'd have kept that promise. I always will, no matter what."

She nodded, and he continued, "I want you to promise me something, okay? Any child you have will be my child. I want you to promise you'll tell me the moment you realise you're pregnant, agreed?"

She nodded again, frowning a little. "Of course. I wouldn't keep that from you now. It would just have been then; I thought it would be easier, better for you if you never knew. Otherwise it would have forced you away from where you belonged."

He tried to correct himself, still overwhelmed by the concept. "I didn't mean I thought you'd hide it from me, it's just if it happens, when it happens, I don't want to miss out on a minute of it."

His excitement was still infectious. Leonie moulded her body against his. "Let's not wait too long?" she whispered.

"Deal," he agreed as his lips touched hers.

As they walked back to the kitchens, Perry voiced a thought that was starting to trouble him. "You said you'd have run away to protect me from the consequences of my actions. Do you think that was what Lesley was trying to do?"

Leonie

'Do you think that was what Lesley was trying to do?'

How am I supposed to answer that?

Of course she'd been trying to protect him, but it wasn't going to make him feel any better if I told him so. On the other hand, Lord Gabriel had been quite clear that I should make Perry face up to things. I shrugged as I tried to decide what to say. "I don't know. I should think it's probable. She had to face some sort of consequence whatever, but if she didn't tell you anything, then perhaps you didn't."

"But it was my actions as much as hers. I should have had to face the consequences. That's only fair."

I agreed with him in principle but I didn't think he'd taken her feelings into account. "Well, yes. But what's fair and what's right and what you do for someone you love aren't always the same."

He stopped and turned towards me as he thought about that and a smile flitted across his face. "I told you that you'd make me think differently about what happened with Lesley. I wasn't very fair to her at all."

That was true enough but I was more concerned about how he felt in the here and now rather than her in the past.

He carried on, "I've made a mess of practically every relationship so far, haven't I?"

That was true too; I could see what Lady Eleanor had meant about him having been very messed up. I needed to reassure him and I reached up to hold his head in my hands, stroking his hair. "They were all a long time ago. You're a different person now."

He nodded. "I promise to try and do better for us, if you'll help me."

I brought his head down to mine to kiss him in agreement and as we did so the Abbey bells rang for the early service. Perry's mind and body leaned towards them, almost longingly, just for a moment. It was okay; I'd felt what he felt. It wasn't that he wanted to return to what he had been or regretted his choices. It was that worship gave him a foundation, reassurance, security, something that made him complete.

"Go on," I said. "It might not be quite like what it was but you'll feel better for it. I'll see you later."

He kissed me again, quickly. "I love you," he said then went without argument while I returned to the kitchen to continue the breakfast preparations.

I didn't see him at breakfast – I was working in the back of the kitchen and I ate there – but I knew he was around, I could feel him. He came to find me later, mildly disgruntled and muttering about Edward and fittings and new clothes, but much more balanced and content within himself. I was feeling much more balanced myself; I think it was to do with realising that I'd made my choice and now the thing to do was to live with the consequences and deal with those as they came along, and that I didn't have to do that alone. I felt quite calm and unconcerned as we headed towards Benjamin's office. Benjamin confirmed that there was nothing wrong with Perry's health and then said that I was in pretty good shape too, all things considered. He wanted me to eat more – which led to a smug look from Perry – put on a bit of weight and to take a vitamin supplement. He said that he was a little concerned about the blanks in my memories. Not about there being blanks so much as about what might be behind them. They were different from Perry's blanks because there were a fair few people who could witness to those things Perry couldn't remember directly for himself. Perry's blanks were about self-inflicted damage – that wiped the smug look off his face – whereas mine were about protecting me from remembering trauma. He was very clear that there was to be no investigation of them without his knowledge and approval.

I didn't mind any of that; the problems came when he started talking about having children. He thought I wasn't strong enough yet and we should wait a year or two. Even that I didn't have any problem with. I'd agreed with Perry earlier when he'd suggested we should have time together first and I should finish my studies. And we needed to get used to being married to each other, work out where we were going to be longer term and what we were going to do. But I had to ask, I had to know, what would happen if I accidentally got pregnant sooner.

Both Benjamin and Perry were vague to start with but

eventually it became clear. Firstly, they would contemplate abortion if my life was at stake and secondly, it wouldn't be my decision as to what they did. The first I understood the logic of, even if I found it difficult emotionally. The second sent me into a tailspin.

This is my body, I should decide.

Or Perry, I'd trust him if I wasn't in a position to decide for myself, if say, I was unconscious. But no, until I was twenty-one it was Lord Gabriel as my guardian who had the final say. It wasn't that I didn't trust him to make what he believed was the right decision; it was that he had the right to make that decision and it might not be the one I would make. I had nowhere to run, nowhere to go. I curled up tight, hiding deep in my head, alone.

Then Perry was there in my head too coming after me faster than I could retreat. His mind wrapped around mine, reassuring, soothing, comforting, with me. I remembered that I no longer had to be alone, no longer had to fight on my own. If anything happened, Perry would be there, fighting just as hard for me as I would for myself, and just as hard for our unborn child. I stopped hiding and found he was kneeling on the floor in front of me, his arms round me, his head resting against mine as he talked to me, telling me it would be okay.

I've had enough. I can trust Perry.

I rested my head on his shoulder, closed my eyes and just stopped.

Perry

Desperately, Perry tried to reach Leonie any way he could. "Leonie, your child would be my child too. Don't you know I would do everything in my power to save you both?"

He was inside her mind and he felt her respond to something – his touch or his words, he didn't know which. Her eyes cleared for a moment and then she closed them and relaxed against him. It felt like she'd given up fighting and he remembered the last time she seemed to have given up like this. That had been after a nightmare when she had felt there was nowhere left to go, no one left to trust. But at that moment she had trusted him and it had marked a significant development in their relationship. He could only hope that this too was a result of her trust in him and not a sign of despair. All he could do was hold her close and pray.

After a minute or two she lifted her head from his shoulder and framed his face with her hands while she looked into his worried eyes.

"It's okay," she said softly. "I'm okay. I just forgot that I'm not alone."

It took Perry a little longer to be convinced, his eyes searching hers, his mind seeking the reassurance of hers, but then he smiled and sat back beside her.

Benjamin watched Leonie closely for a moment, and then, appearing to make his mind up, he reached into a drawer and put a small bottle on the table in front of them.

"Two doses," he said to Leonie. "No more than two doses. It's the inhibitor drug. Two nights sleep uninterrupted by the fear of nightmares between now and the wedding. You can choose when to take them."

She hesitated, but thanked him and then pocketed the bottle before they left. Perry was still concerned about Leonie and he knew he didn't have long before he had to report for work. Instead of leaving the hospital he took her up a floor and outside to a secluded part of the roof garden. This particular spot was formed by the angle between two walls and hidden away from the more normal routes. Even in winter it was something of a sun trap and was used to grow those plants which generally liked a hotter climate than was normal in this area. Leonie was both distracted and fascinated by the plants, all earlier stress apparently forgotten. Perry leaned against the wall and watched her for a while, answering her queries about the plants until he became more aware of time passing.

"Come here," he called. "Please?"

She came straight over, flowing into his arms.

He stroked her face. "You were so upset before. I know you were. I could feel it. You wanted to run away. And then you gave up, I felt that, too. And now you seem fine. I want to understand," he pleaded.

She struggled to find a way to explain. "I didn't give up," she said. "I just realised that I didn't have to fight."

"Because we would look after you?" he asked, still puzzled. It didn't seem a complete answer.

"Not them. You," she told him. "I've always been the only one I could rely on to fight for me. Even when there were people who cared for me, they always had other things to think about." She hesitated. "Like Lord Gabriel has to consider what is best for the whole House, not just what is best for me. And what's best for the House might not be what's best for me, so there's only me that can fight for that."

He understood that. "Sometimes the good for the many outweighs the good for the one."

"Yes," she agreed. "And I thought there could only be me to fight for what was best for me and my child and then I realised that you would, too. That I wasn't alone and I didn't have to fight because you were there. I didn't give up, I just stopped."

He wrapped his arms round her pinning her against him. "I'll always be there for you and I'll always fight for you," he whispered. He pulled away slightly and grinned. "Only right now I'm supposed to be at work. Do you want to come and see where I'll be? It'll mean seeing the ward."

She'd felt better yesterday when he'd shown her where he would be living for the next few days; he thought maybe something similar would help today, even if she was normally unwilling to visit that part of the hospital. To his surprise, she came with him, gripping his hand for reassurance. She didn't stay long, but he was able to show her round a little before escorting her down to the main exit and kissing her goodbye – for now.

Chapter 15

Friday

Leonie

Despite the business of organising a wedding, once or twice, Perry and I managed an hour or two free at the same time and escaped the campus grounds altogether. The day after we saw Benjamin we headed down to the river and climbed out to sit on one of the big boulders in the middle. I leant back against Perry and listened to the water rippling past.

"You are writing to your parents, aren't you?" I asked him.

"I've finished it," he said. "Lord Gabriel took it this morning to send to them. It was a lot harder to write than I expected and I expected it to be hard."

"But you have done it?" I insisted.

"Yes, I've done it," he reassured me. "Do you want to know what I wrote?"

I shook my head. "Only if you want to. You don't have to tell me what you write to your parents." I looked at him for a moment. "You're not going to be the sort of husband who wants to read my letters are you?" I asked in mock horror.

That made him smile. "No," he said. "You can write what you like. As for what I've written, I'm not sure I could tell you anyway. In the end I just decided to write it straight out, what happened and what's going to happen and why we aren't waiting. I put in your suggestion, though, that we go and visit them and we have another service of some kind when we're there. I like the idea of that."

I was just relieved that he had actually written, though I hoped it had been in his best handwriting or it wouldn't have mattered what he'd put as no one would be able to read it. I could see that he might have kept putting writing off as being too hard. It was going to be hard enough for me meeting his family anyway, without being blamed for keeping them from the wedding, which I thought could easily happen. I dropped the subject and we simply enjoyed the rest of our time together.

***

Sunday

It felt very strange to sit with Perry in the Sunday morning service. Before, he'd have been with the monks and I'd have found somewhere quiet to sit, perhaps with Lady Eleanor, or Tobias and Leah and the Settlers, or with others I knew from the town. I guessed it was pretty strange for Perry, too. He'd gone from four services a day to really only Sunday, though I knew he'd been to at least one service each day this week. He seemed to be finding it hard to let go of the framework he'd lived with for years. Not that he regretted leaving, I was quite sure about that, it was just very different for him now and it would take some getting used to.

As we stood up for one of the hymns, I slipped my hand into his and held on for reassurance. He looked down and smiled and I wished I could have twisted my mind into his too, but the Abbey Shields stopped me.

Lady Eleanor was on my other side and once the service was over she put her hand on my back. "Come on," she said. "We've got some invitations to give out."

She guided me over to Leah and Tobias, but I kept hold of Perry and dragged him with us. Only then I had to let go because Leah hugged me, and Tobias was congratulating Perry, and other people started to join our group. Being the centre of attention made me feel nervous and twitchy. I tried to stick close to Perry and Lady Eleanor had to have noticed.

154

"Are you supposed to be on duty in the kitchen?" she whispered in my ear.

I nodded.

"Go on then," she said, indicating the side door just behind me which led into the campus courtyard.

I grabbed Perry's hand and we escaped rapidly, running across the courtyard, until we reached the safety of the main buildings.

Perry pushed me up against the wall in the shelter of the doorway and kissed me, his hands running down my back, sending shivers of pleasure down my spine as he pulled me close against him.

"You're a bad influence on me," he said smiling. "Never have I run from church before!"

Well, I didn't think I had either. Usually I ran towards them to find somewhere to hide out.

We didn't have much time together. "I really am supposed to be in the kitchen," I said.

"Don't worry," said Perry. "I've got a shift in the hospital in ten minutes anyway. But I think we're both free tomorrow afternoon. Why don't we take a picnic down to the lake?"

I nodded my agreement and stole another kiss before running off to my duties.

***

The rest of my day passed in a haze of work though I did get a chance to sit quietly in the library for an hour or so, thinking. Just a week ago we'd been celebrating Easter, the place had been packed with people, Perry had still been a monk, and I'd been torn with indecision about what to do. Now it was quiet, with guests gone and students not yet returned, Perry had left the Order and we were to be married in just a few days – by next Sunday we would be married. I was no longer torn with indecision, not exactly, because I'd made my choice. But I was still fretting over and worried by the consequences, especially for Perry; I'd lost so many people I loved. My head told me I was being silly; my heart wouldn't listen.

And yet at Easter I had felt such joy; now I realised that I still felt that joy, bubbling along inside me. I'd just been so busy with all that had been happening that I'd not taken any real notice of it. I let it rise up and take over, enjoying it, diminishing all my worries, putting them to one side, at least for now.

I headed for bed early that evening deciding I had to be in need of a good night's sleep. I looked at Benjamin's bottle of medicine but decided not to take it. My mind already felt sluggish and however good that inhibitor was, I always felt a bit slow the morning after taking it.

***

The Them appeared, hovering round my bed, looming over me, their faces hidden in the shadows of their hoods, their arms stretching slowly towards me.

I should have taken that inhibitor. Too late now.

I sat up sharply, grabbed a pillow and swung it in an arc around me. Each of the Them dissolved as it touched them, reforming behind it a moment later. I swung again, and dived through the momentary gap, heading for the door. Perry, I had to reach Perry. I couldn't see him. Had he left me? Was I alone again? No, he was over there. There was a wall between us, thick, tall and solid. I sent a blast of power towards the wall but I was too far away. It didn't do enough damage, didn't destroy it and now the

Them were following me, getting closer again. I leapt forwards, out of their reach and suddenly I was at the foot of the wall. It was even taller than I'd thought but I had to get through. Perry was on the other side. He needed me and I needed him. I gathered the power again and this time the wall disintegrated. One more leap and I'd nearly reached Perry but now a line of the Them appeared between me and him. I grabbed two daggers and tossed one over the heads of the Them towards Perry.

"Help me!" I called then turned to fight the Them.

With a spear in one hand and a dagger in the other I lunged forward, stabbing with the spear to make them duck and fade, then throwing the dagger at them as they reformed. However often I threw the dagger, it reappeared in my hand. The Them backed off, a gap forming in their line, and I could see Perry. He'd lost his dagger and now the Them turned, moving to surround him. "Perry," I shouted, as I threw a ball of energy to distract the Them.

Sunday night/early Monday morning

Perry

A flash of multi-coloured energy hit Perry's mind, jerking him fully awake just as he had wound down enough for sleep. He had barely worked out where he was – the lounge outside his room – when Leonie appeared in front of him, teleporting from goodness knew where.

Teleporting! She shouldn't be teleporting. She doesn't have the training to teleport people.

Even as he thought that he realised she was in the middle of a nightmare and not controlling her actions. Her skin was flushed and tendrils of hair stuck to her face with sweat.

Her eyes focused on him for a moment. "Perry," she gasped. "Help me!"

Before he could respond, her eyes glazed over again as the nightmare returned. Things started moving around him as she reacted to whatever she thought was going on, but he ducked towards her, wrapped his arms around her and used his abilities to dampen and restrain her actions. The nightmare eased almost as soon as he touched her, her body relaxing against him. The objects she'd been throwing telekinetically either continued their flight path or simply dropped; he couldn't catch them all so he concentrated on ensuring nothing hit the pair of them. She was burning hot, he noticed, and she hadn't woken, the nightmare had simply eased. He tried waking her, but with no effect, so, concerned that this was more than a normal incident, he laid her down on the sofa while he went to get his medical bag and call for help.

It took him only seconds to realise that was a big mistake. The nightmare returned with a vengeance before he was halfway across the room and this time she was attacking him too, or at least actively trying to prevent him getting close. The watch team should have arrived long before this and he wondered what was keeping them, what damage she might have done before reaching him. Even as he was thinking this, he followed his training, trying both to distract and overload her to create a weakness he could exploit. It was harder than he'd ever faced before and then he was the one distracted as the lounge door opened to Gabriel and Benjamin. He ducked to avoid something which shattered on the wall behind him. Then he yelled out, "Distract her!"

Gabriel grabbed two cushions and threw them straight at Leonie. What her mind thought they were Perry didn't know, but she attacked them, blowing them apart as they reached her. In the confusion the falling feathers caused, Perry raced towards Leonie, wrapping her once more in his arms, and now able to dampen down her abilities at close quarters. Again, she relaxed against him, and there was a sudden silence, though this time Gabriel and Benjamin caught most of the flying objects.

"Well, that was an entertaining sight," said Benjamin. "You being beaten by a slip of a girl."

Perry glared at him. "Where on earth is the watch team?" he asked. "She's burning up and I can't wake her."

Benjamin went from joking to professional in a moment. "Lie her down on the sofa and I'll take a look," he suggested.

Perry shook his head. "No, that was the mistake I made. She just teleported in here. When I got hold of her the nightmare stopped, but I left her on the sofa to fetch something, and that's when it all started again. It's not stopped even now, I can feel that I'm holding it at bay, but if I let go it's all going to happen again."

"In that case, please don't let go!" interjected Gabriel.

Instead, Perry scooped Leonie up into his arms and sat down, rather suddenly, on one of the few pieces of furniture still remaining upright. Benjamin stepped closer. "You okay?" he asked even as he checked Leonie's temperature and pulse.

Perry nodded. "She's stretching me to the limits of my abilities already. What's going to happen as she gets stronger?" He felt Gabriel's mind buttressing his. "Thank you," he added.

Gabriel spoke quietly, "It may not be that bad. Girls mature faster; she could be reaching or even at the peak of her strength already. And I think that once you are married she'll settle, calm down anyway. That's one of the reasons I think it should be so soon."

Benjamin spoke again, "More immediately, I don't want you to let go of her either, but the only place where you can acceptably stay with her tonight is the hospital, and I'm worried about that temperature and the fact that we can't wake her. I'd like to admit her."

Perry agreed, "She hates hospitals, but I think you're right. The Shields are better there, too." He nodded towards one of the bedrooms. "There's a dressing gown on the back of that door that we can wrap her in. I don't think we should risk her getting chilled."

Benjamin went to fetch it, and together they wrapped it around Leonie.

Gabriel also agreed. "Can you carry her?" he asked.

Perry nodded. "She hardly weighs anything."

Gabriel continued, "I'll come with you, give any necessary consents, then go and find out what happened to the watch team."

The main door to the lounge opened, crashing against the wall. Half a dozen members of the watch team poured through, eyes scanning the room to assess the problem. Perry thought he heard Benjamin say "About time!" – a sentiment with which he agreed totally.

"What happened?" Gabriel asked mildly as the team leader – Philip – came to a stop in front of him.

Philip answered, "The first surge, when she teleported into the control room, the power she was using, it blew some of our equipment. When she disappeared we couldn't tell where she'd gone. With it starting in the control room it looked like something in every shielded area. It wasn't until the third surge we could tell where to come. There was an awful lot of power around."

"Anyone hurt?"

Philip shook his head. "A couple of people with headaches

from the power overload, nothing serious." He glanced towards Leonie. "What about her?"

"We'll admit her to the hospital, but she'll be fine," Benjamin answered. "No one else is hurt."

"Very well," confirmed Gabriel, taking charge. "You can return to the control centre. Get a clean-up team in here and let me have the usual report."

Perry stood up and headed towards the hospital, Leonie in his arms and Benjamin right beside him. Gabriel followed closely.

"Has she taken that inhibitor I gave her?" Benjamin asked.

Perry shrugged. "I don't know. She hasn't told me if she has. It doesn't look like it, does it?"

They agreed that she should be given a dose of the drug to temporarily inhibit her powers a little and ease the nightmare, and even that the dosage should be higher than normal, but that was as far as it went. Benjamin wanted to add a sedative to ensure she slept, whilst Perry wanted a stimulant to ensure she woke properly and broke the nightmare. Perry thought her temperature might be caused by a low-grade infection and wanted antibiotics; Benjamin thought it was due to the nightmare and would ease as that eased, especially as Perry couldn't offer any evidence as to her state of health. They agreed quite happily to give her the inhibitor and allow half an hour or so for it to take effect before adding any other medication.

Ignoring the normal admissions procedures, they took her straight to the ward set aside for those whose problems related to their Gifts – the same ward that Perry had shown Leonie only the other day. Benjamin indicated a vacant room, opening the door and switching on the lights and the full set of Shields.

"You take her in there, we'll sort the most essential

paperwork, and I'll be back with the medication," he said then went to find what he needed.

Perry placed Leonie on the bed, and sat on the edge himself so that she was half leaning against him, his arm round her, and her head on his shoulder, eyes closed. They were still sitting like that when Benjamin returned with the medication they'd agreed on. As Benjamin drew up the injection, Perry folded back the dressing gown Leonie was wrapped in and held her more closely, both his arms wrapped around her but her arm held firmly in case she reacted to the jab. He needn't have worried; she opened her eyes but barely flinched as Benjamin cleaned her skin and administered the dose. Benjamin looked up in relief, having been equally worried about some sort of adverse reaction.

"I'm going to insert an IV, too," he said. "I don't want to risk her getting dehydrated."

Perry nodded and deftly adjusted the way he was holding Leonie so that her arm was free for Benjamin to work. Leonie had closed her eyes once more, but again barely flinched as Benjamin inserted the needle and then the cannula. He connected and hung the bag of fluid.

"Nearly done," he said reassuringly, which caused Leonie to open her eyes and look at him.

She screamed in terror, pushing Perry away, both arms flailing at him. She grabbed for the drip, ripping it out of her arm as she lunged for the end of the bed and the door. The Shields started to whine as they struggled to contain the energy she was trying to access. Quick as she was, her reactions were slowed by the fever and her confusion at not being able to use her abilities freely.

Despite a slow start, Perry was both quicker and stronger, and moments later he held her firmly against him, shaking and crying, but quiet, not struggling, with both of her arms tucked between them. Very gently he rocked her, stroking her hair and murmuring to her.

Benjamin watched them for a moment. "I think we'll pass on the IV," he conceded. "And despite everything, I'm going to switch the Dampener Shield off. I think sensing it is causing her to panic and making things worse."

Perry nodded without stopping what he was doing. As Benjamin left the room, Perry's voice moved from a murmur to very quiet singing, the words almost indistinguishable. Leonie's breathing and heartbeat slowed to a more normal rhythm. He was fairly certain she felt cooler, too, but found it difficult to be sure, given the effect holding her so closely was having on him. Eventually, she pulled back slightly and looked up at him.

"Perry?" she asked, her tone confused.

"Shush, sweetheart," he replied. "You've had a nightmare which gave you a fever, or the other way round, it doesn't matter. Everything is fine now. I'm here, you're safe." He held her closely for a little longer and then spoke again. "Sit here a moment, you've scratched your arm and I'm just going to get what I need to clean it."

Quiet and obedient for once, she watched him as he moved round the room collecting supplies. He sat back down beside her and gently cleaned and dressed the tear on her arm where she'd pulled the drip out.

"Do you remember doing this?" he asked.

Leonie shook her head. "All I remember," she replied slowly, "is needing to find you and the Them kept trying to stop me."

He smiled reassuringly. "Well, you did find me, and now

you are safe."

That prompted her to look at her surroundings. "Are we in the hospital?"

"Yes, we were worried about you. I thought this might be the best place to look after you properly so I brought you here. But don't worry, I'm going to stay right here with you. I won't leave you alone. You'll be quite safe."

"There's blood on your top."

It seemed a strange answer, but he took the change of subject as a sign she trusted that she was safe with him.

He smiled at her again. "Yes, your blood. From your arm. You were scared, so I held you close. I guess some got on my top." He finished the dressing. "There, that's done. Now, slide into the bed, you need to sleep."

He stood up to clear the excess supplies away, but Leonie held on to him, her hand tangled in the fabric of his tunic. "Don't go away!" she pleaded.

"I'm not going anywhere. I'm going to sit right here beside you and hold you until you go to sleep, and then I'm going to sit in that chair and watch you. Although I won't promise not to fall asleep myself!"

He suited his actions to his words, seating himself comfortably on the bed beside Leonie, who lay down contentedly, her head resting against him. Very soon she was asleep. Once he was sure he wouldn't disturb her, Perry disentangled himself and stood up, just as Benjamin returned to the room carrying a blanket.

"Asleep?" Benjamin asked.

"Yes, she woke and now she's sleeping naturally. She's a lot cooler, too. I don't think she needs any further treatment."

"Good. I assume you are planning to stay here?" Benjamin indicated the reclining chair to one side of the bed. "I brought you a blanket."

"I'm not planning on leaving, certainly. Thanks for the blanket."

"I've also brought a monitor." Benjamin indicated the small metallic disc in his hand. Light and unobtrusive, if stuck to a patient's skin with medical adhesive, it would transmit vital signs – heartbeat, breathing, temperature – to a screen at the central desk.

Perry shrugged. "It sounds like a good idea, but I think she may subconsciously see it as an intrusion, even in her sleep."

"Only one way to find out," said Benjamin, reaching over and placing it on Leonie just below her collarbone.

There was a quiet sigh from Leonie who remained asleep. A sharp pinging sounded as the monitor ricocheted off the wall. Perry bent over and picked up the now misshapen and molten lump of metal, trying not to laugh as he did so. "I think that answers that," he said, dropping the item into Benjamin's outstretched hand. "I guess that inhibitor's not as strong as we thought. Or perhaps it hasn't taken effect yet!"

Benjamin's own amusement came through in his tone. "You'll have to keep an eye on her then!" he said as he tossed the blanket at Perry before leaving the room.

Perry grinned and after making himself comfortable on the reclining chair was very soon asleep too.

Chapter 16

Monday morning

Leonie

I sat up, unsure of where I was but certain I was safe because I could sense Perry. As I glanced around the room it came back to me. I'd had a nightmare and Perry had brought me to the hospital. I smiled at the sight of him, asleep on a reclining chair beside the bed. If he was here, relaxed and asleep, I had nothing to worry about. Andrew was standing by the slightly open door. As he beckoned to me, I slid off the bed and went to join him.

"How are you feeling?" he asked me. "Do you know why you are here?"

"I'm fine," I said. "I had a nightmare. Perry said I had a fever but I feel okay now."

Andrew nodded. "That's right. Come over to the office and I'll check you over." He grinned at me. "I shouldn't really have let you out of bed, but I'm pretty sure you're fine and I didn't want to disturb Perry."

Nor did I.

Andrew put his hand on the small of my back and guided me into the office. Once he had examined me he asked if he could put one of the little monitor discs on me. It didn't bother me and if it made him happier I was fine with it. Then he suggested we went to find some breakfast.

"What about Perry?" I asked.

"Let's not disturb him. He needs to sleep. We'll leave him a note and someone will tell him where we are anyway. He can come find us."

I wasn't quite sure about leaving Perry, but I was hungry so I went along with Andrew. The café wasn't far from where we were. On the way he asked me gently if I knew what had caused my nightmare, if there was anything I thought likely to have led to it. I was pretty sure it was to do with worrying about losing Perry but I didn't know how to admit that.

"It's about Perry, isn't it?" Andrew asked. "Would it help to talk about it?"

I nodded. Andrew was easy to talk to and he always seemed to understand where I was coming from, perhaps because of how he felt about Perry.

"Okay," he said, thinking for a moment. "The canteen's not the best place, though, and it won't be long before Perry finds us. After we've eaten I'll send him off to fetch you some fresh clothes and things and we'll talk privately then."

He was right; it wasn't long before Perry joined us. We'd only just started our breakfasts when he slid into the seat next to me, put his arm round me and hugged me close.

"Feeling better?" he asked.

I guessed he could tell I was because he barely waited for an answer before turning to Andrew. "I thought you'd run off with my girl." He was smiling so it was obviously just part of their usual banter.

"That'd be a first," said Andrew. "Now, you running off with my girl, that happened often enough, just not the other way around."

I studied them both. This easy acknowledgement of their past misdemeanours was in keeping with the people that I knew. It was the fact that they had such pasts that didn't sit well with the people that they were today. People really could and did change.

Perry nicked a bit of my bacon before going off to find his own breakfast.

"I'll bring you some more," he told me, which he did, along with extra pancakes and syrup.

I ate them too. Andrew and Perry started talking about hospital related stuff, which I ignored to concentrate on eating, until Perry nudged me and spoke to me.

"When you've finished eating we'll go back to the ward and Andrew can discharge you and then we can still go on our afternoon out."

I looked up at Andrew after his promise earlier.

"Andrew's not going to discharge her, not that soon," he said, almost as an aside while he finished his toast.

"Why ever not?" Perry sounded both surprised and a little indignant.

"She's my patient now and the standard is a minimum of twelve hours' observation. You brought her in around one in the morning. If I think she's fine, I'll discharge her after lunch."

"You can discharge her earlier to my care. I'll look after her. She'll be fine." Perry was rather dismissive of Andrew's plans.

"Even if I could, that doesn't mean I will."

"Andrew, you're just being difficult. You know she'll be fine. I won't take her off campus until the twelve hours are up." Now Perry sounded more indignant than surprised.

"In that case it doesn't matter if she spends the time here."

I nudged Perry hard in the ribs. "Stop talking about me as if I wasn't here."

His eyes opened wide in astonishment as he turned towards me. "He was doing it too," he spluttered, gesturing at Andrew.

"You started it," I told him. I was pretty certain that wasn't true. Andrew had started it; it was just Perry doing it that had got me all wound up.

Andrew grinned at me from where Perry couldn't see him, a partner in mischief.

"Look," he said to Perry, "you go and fetch Leonie some fresh clothes, have a shower and get a change of clothes yourself and come back." He looked at me. "After that, if I'm happy with your condition, I'll discharge you to Perry's care, okay?"

Perry agreed with that in the end, although he grumbled and muttered about it on the way back to the ward. I was getting used to this; when he'd been persuaded round to something that was rather different from his original idea his grumblings and mutterings were part of the process by which he reconciled himself to it. They didn't really mean anything. I ignored them and slipped my hand into his. He smiled at me apologetically and put his arm round me.

"Sorry," he said. "I just worry about you. I feel better when you're with me."

I thought I heard Andrew mutter something like "overly possessive" but if Perry heard it he was currently acting too mature to respond.

Perry didn't leave straight away when we got back to the ward. Instead, he hung around watching while Andrew checked my temperature and blood pressure, getting in the way trying to see the results. In the end Andrew threatened him with having his own blood pressure checked unless he disappeared pretty sharpish.

Perry grinned at that but he did leave. "I won't be long," he said to me.

Andrew saw him to the door and down the corridor, probably to make sure he really did leave, before coming back to me.

"Now," he said. "For starters, why don't you tell me what you can remember about what happened in your nightmare?"

I told him all about it.

He took a deep breath before answering me very gently. "It sounds to me like you're still worried about something happening to Perry just because you love him."

I nodded, fidgeting, unable to look at him. I knew it wasn't logical but I couldn't help it.

"I can't say anything that will convince you otherwise," he said. "You're going to have to come to believe that – or not – for yourself. But I will tell you this again, and again, and as many times as you need to hear it. Whether or not anything happens to Perry, you will never be alone again. You've got a family now who loves and cares for you. We'll be there, no matter what."

Coming from Andrew, who I knew had lost all his birth family, that really meant something. I burst into tears. It must have been the after effects of last night. Andrew passed me a box of tissues.

"It's okay," he said. "Sometimes it can help to have a good cry."

He waited until I'd recovered a little before speaking again. "Besides," he said, pulling a face at me, "I've told you before, Perry'd be no great loss." He started on his usual litany of Perry's faults, none of which I could deny.

The face he was pulling made me laugh and I interrupted him. "Whatever he's like, he's still Perry. That's what matters."

"Yes," he said, smiling back at me. "It is." The smile left his face, and his brow creased. "You should tell Perry why you can't tell him you love him. He knows that you do, but he needs to understand this too, you know."

I nodded. "I know. I will."

Then I started yawning and I couldn't stop. Somehow the bed looked very attractive.

"It's okay," Andrew said. "You can go back to sleep, I'll deal with Perry. He can wait until you wake up. I'm not surprised you're tired, you used an incredible amount of energy last night and you didn't actually sleep very long."

I looked at him gratefully, got into the bed, curled up comfortably and closed my eyes.

Andrew

Andrew watched Leonie fall asleep. Poor kid, he thought. She'd experienced so much bad in her life that she was scared to believe the good, so much looking after others that she struggled to accept that she could be loved and looked after in her turn. Well, he'd be there for her from now on if she needed him and he'd do his best to make sure Perry looked after her properly. Then he had something of an epiphany; this girl was getting what he'd thought for many years that he wanted – namely Perry – and not only was he not jealous of her, he was also thinking of her needs ahead of Perry's.

On the way to the canteen he'd felt the waves of worry and

concern rolling off her. He'd offered a listening ear, the only thing he could think of that he could do to help, and she'd taken him up on it.

The subtle change in her nightmare was interesting. It suggested that her greatest fear had moved from being chased or caught and whatever that meant in her past to a fear of losing Perry, which tied up with what they'd talked about. And that in turn suggested that being married to Perry and sleeping with him would have a very beneficial effect in reducing her nightmares. Given last night's damage – greater than either Leonie or Perry knew –Andrew was beginning to understand why Gabriel might want the wedding very soon indeed.

He'd quite enjoyed winding Perry up and foiling his plans to get Leonie discharged immediately. They'd spoken telepathically as he'd shepherded Perry out of the ward earlier.

"Andrew, see if you can find out what's bothering her. There's still something about this whole marriage thing she's very scared of and she doesn't seem able to tell me."

"I'll do my best, but I'm not going to break any confidences."

"She wants me to know. I know that. I ought to be able to work it out from what she's shown me but I'm not quite there. I need help."

"I'll do what I can. Now get going."

He'd known the answer anyway. Leonie was terrified that if she acknowledged how she felt about Perry, let alone told him out loud, something very bad would happen. He knew it was superstition; she did too, intellectually, but should some terrible coincidence happen after she'd said it out loud, she wouldn't be able to cope with the guilt, however undeserved.

***

It was the best part of another hour before Perry returned, striding down the corridor to where Andrew was sitting at the main desk. He spoke before he reached it.

"Where's Leonie? How is she?"

"Asleep," Andrew answered, nodding towards the monitor display visible from the desk.

"Did you give her something?" Perry's voice was almost accusing.

"No, she's still worn out," Andrew said. "Physically and emotionally exhausted. She didn't sleep that much last night and she used a phenomenal amount of energy. She teleported twice; I didn't know she knew how."

"I taught her, the other day," Perry confessed. "But not people, just a few small objects. I didn't realise her nightmares would use it. I should have thought about that. How did you get a monitor on her anyway? She destroyed one last night."

"I asked her. You should try it some time."

Perry ignored the suggestion for what was uppermost in his mind. "Did you find out what might be upsetting her?"

"Yes, though it should be pretty obvious even for you. Think about what's happened to everyone she's cared about."

Perry's eyes lit up as he worked it out. "Now I get it. She thinks everyone she's loved has died, or left her. That makes total sense; she showed me that in her memories. Of course she can't tell me. And she must be terrified of what might happen."

"She doesn't need to be told that bad stuff won't happen," Andrew snapped. "She needs to know that if it does there are ways to cope with it, that she won't be alone."

"Okay, okay, I get it."

Andrew wasn't entirely convinced that Perry did get it, but there was little else he could do or say. Perry went to sit with Leonie until she woke, taking some reading and notes with him to work on.

Chapter 17

Leonie

The next time I woke Perry was there, sitting in the chair beside the bed reading. Almost without thinking I slid out of the bed and straight onto his lap, barely giving him a chance to put his book down. He wrapped his arms around me and held me close for a moment before speaking.

"Am I really that desperately important to you?"

I knew he needed reassurance; I owed him that. I knew he wanted me to say that I loved him, but I couldn't, however much I wanted to. For once the words came tumbling out instead of getting stuck.

"I didn't want you to be. I tried to ignore you. I didn't want you to die like everyone else. I tried to leave but I couldn't and then you found me and now it's too late and I'm sorry, Perry."

I looked up at him but I couldn't see him clearly as my eyes were unaccountably wet. He dried them gently with his thumbs and then I could see that he was smiling. I realised that every word I'd uttered in denial had actually been the reassurance and confirmation that he'd wanted.

"I understand," he said. "I'm terrified of losing you, too."

I had seen his fear of losing me before but I still found it unbelievable; he always seemed so strong, so brave, in charge of his feelings. Underneath, could he really be feeling the same fear that I did? I reached out to him to comfort him, but he took both my hands in his.

"Leonie, there have been some terrible coincidences and events in your life, but loving someone can't harm them. I'm in no more danger because you love me than I would be if you didn't."

He paused for a moment then carried on, "I have to ask you this. Do you still want to marry me? If this is all too much, too soon, too fast, we can slow it down, stop. You don't have to do anything you don't want to or anything you're afraid of."

"I do want to but I'm so scared. If anything happened to you I couldn't cope."

"You're the bravest person I know. I think you'd manage."

"I'm not brave. I'm scared."

Perry had an unduly high opinion of my abilities; I couldn't explain just how scared I was. I used to be fine, alone, but now, knowing something better, the very thought of losing him incapacitated me. I struggled to remember even to breathe.

He stroked my hair. "Brave isn't about not being scared. It's about being scared and carrying on and doing the right thing anyway. You've tried to run away from your fear several times, but you haven't been able to, you've come back to face up to it. That's brave. You're braver than me; I ran away and I hadn't even contemplated going back until you came along."

I shook my head slowly, unable to take it all on board.

How can he think that I am braver than he is?

"Will you go back now?" I asked.

"If you'll come with me."

I nodded. I could do that, at least.

He smiled and returned to what he had been saying. "I promise you, I don't plan to ever leave you, nor to die until we've spent many, many years growing old together, but if anything did happen to me, this time you would not be alone. There's any number of people here who love you and would be there for you."

That gave me something to grasp onto. "That's what Andrew said but..."

"Yes? What else did Andrew say?"

I started without thinking, "He said you would be..." And then stopped, not wanting to repeat the uncomplimentary things Andrew had said about Perry.

Perry laughed, no doubt understanding instantly. "Don't worry, it won't be anything he hasn't said to my face, probably many times."

Slightly reassured I carried on, "He said you'd be no great loss, that you were self-centred, conceited, competitive, arrogant, proud, stubborn, argumentative, always convinced you were right especially when you weren't."

He was still laughing, and his eyes and tone were teasing as he replied, "And did you defend me?"

In truth, I hadn't, but that wasn't the point. "What matters is that you're you, not what you are like!"

That amused him too, and he pulled me close again so that my head was on his shoulder and his arms were around me. "At least you know what you're letting yourself in for," he said. "Seriously, your love cannot harm me. Listen."

His voice took on an almost musical tone as he spoke, "'If I speak in the tongues of men or of angels, but do not have love, I am only a resounding gong or a clanging cymbal. If I have the gift of prophecy and can fathom all mysteries and all knowledge, and if I have a faith that can move mountains, but do not have love, I am nothing. If I give all I possess to the poor and give over my body to hardship that I may boast, but do not have love, I gain nothing. Love is patient, love is kind. It does not envy, it does not boast, it is not proud. It does not dishonour others, it is not self-seeking, it is not easily angered, it keeps no record of wrongs. Love does not delight in evil but rejoices with the truth. It always protects, always trusts, always hopes, always perseveres. Love never fails. But where there are prophecies, they will cease; where there are tongues, they will be stilled; where there is knowledge, it will pass away. For we know in part and we prophesy in part, but when completeness comes, what is in part disappears. When I was a child, I talked like a child, I thought like a child, I reasoned like a child. When I became a man, I put the ways of childhood behind me. For now we see only a reflection as in a mirror; then we shall see face to face. Now I know in part; then I shall know fully, even as I am fully known. And now these three remain: faith, hope and love. But the greatest of these is love.'"

"That sounds like poetry," I said in wonder.

"Yes, I suppose it does. It's from the Bible. Have you heard it before?"

I shook my head, but without moving it from his shoulder. "Not out loud. I think I've read it before but I'd like to read it again."

"Remind me later and I'll find the reference for you. You can mark it in your Bible."

I sat up on his lap. I had to try, I owed him that. "Perry, I..."

He placed his fingers on my lips stopping me. "Don't say it now, wait until it comes naturally. One day it'll happen and then we'll both know that you believe your love can't hurt me."

Relieved, I curled back into him. We sat like that for some time, peacefully together. Eventually, Andrew came in, bringing some lunch for all three of us. Despite my large breakfast I was starving again.

"That's perfectly normal," Andrew said. "Your body's trying to replenish all the energy you used last night. Most people can't summon the energy to teleport once, let alone twice. Just take it easy for a day or so and you'll be fine."

***

After we'd eaten, Andrew let us go and we did get our afternoon out although we didn't go as far as we might have done. I thought Perry was worried about me getting over tired; he'd been like that before when I'd had a bad nightmare. That didn't seem to be all he was worried about. We went down to the river near where it forms the lake at the edge of the campus and I sat on one of the large boulders looking out over the water. Perry didn't seem to be able to sit still but wandered back and forth along the bank. I waited and at last he came to stand beside me.

"Are you worried about after we are married? About the physical side? About making love?" he asked me, his voice hesitant.

That did surprise me. "No, should I be?"

I definitely wasn't. I might not ever have put into practice what I'd been taught with the Traders but I'd paid attention and I remembered it all.

He hurried to reassure me. "No, no, of course not." But then he turned and paced along the bank a few steps again.

"But you are, so why?" I asked him as he turned back towards me.

"It's been so long…" His voice was still hesitant and he was running his hands over his hair, still very short.

"Are you worried you've forgotten how? Because I'm pretty sure we can work it out between us."

That made him laugh, his shoulders relaxing as some of the tension left his body. "No, it's not that," he said. "I want it to be special for you. I used to be considered a good lover…"

I'd heard that, too. "So what's the problem? What's worrying you?" I slid off the boulder to stand in front of him, running my hands up his body to frame his face.

He put his arms round me and rested his forehead on mine. "Leonie, after all this time, and the way you make me feel, the thing I think it is most likely to be is quick. I don't want to hurt you but I'm afraid that I won't be able to control how I feel, what I do."

He didn't need to worry but I didn't know how to tell him that, at least not without long explanations that I really didn't feel up to right now. Instead, I stroked his head and spoke softly to him. "It will be alright, Perry. You won't hurt me. Trust me, it will be okay. We'll be together. That's all that matters."

I wasn't sure he was convinced but he relaxed a little against me and the moment developed into an embrace and then a kiss that nearly led to us resolving the issue then and there.

"See," he said, and his voice shook, as he pulled away a little. "Proves my point. That was nearly out of control."

"Proves my point," I told him. "We did stop."

"It's not the same," he claimed.

"You can't have it both ways," I said. "Either it is the same and we stopped and it proves my point, or it isn't the same, in which case you can't use it to prove your point."

That made him laugh again. "Alright," he said. "You win. For now!"

Well, that was a first. We were both laughing as we ambled

back towards the campus buildings. There was a whirring sound above us and I looked up, Perry following my gaze.

"That's the transcopter," he said, referring to the dark shape in the sky. "It's the rotors that make the noise."

I knew that. The vehicle had four sets of rotors with the main body hanging between them. As far as I knew this one was used to get very sick or badly injured people to the hospital quickly.

"Have you ever been in it?" I asked Perry.

"That one? Yes, a few times when I was training. Once or twice since, if they knew they'd need my particular skills. Mostly it has its own specialist team."

Perry's eyes were still on the sky but his tone reminded me of something Andrew had said. *'You need to be very careful of exactly what he says.'*

"That one? You've been in others?"

Perry looked down at me and then at the ground, not meeting my eyes, scuffing his toes and then running his hands across his hair. "Most High Lords have one. That one's really Lord Gabriel's, it's just that he never uses it. Lord Neville uses his quite a lot."

Yeah, that explains it.

But I was still curious. "Why only one each? And why just High Lords?"

Perry smiled at me. "They're very expensive and not nearly as much use as you'd think. It takes a lot of energy to lift that much weight, which means they need to carry a lot of battery storage, which in turn makes them heavier, and takes up cargo or passenger space. They're great for short hops but even the best can't fly for more than a couple of hours, if that, without needing a full recharge."

I nodded, understanding. "It must be amazing, though, how much you could see from up there."

"It is," Perry agreed and then he grinned again, light and mischief in his eyes. "Want me to see if I can wangle you a trip on one sometime?"

Now that was a very tempting offer.

Chapter 18

Thursday

Mary

Mary treasured the letters that arrived from Perry, her firstborn. When one arrived, she separated it from any other post and put it in her pocket to read later, privately. She considered them her own personal treat; she would clear the most essential chores then make a cup of tea and sit down alone to read the letter, before sharing it with anyone else, even her husband, Michael. Ted, who brought the post out to the farm, knew a little of this. If there was a letter with Perry's handwriting on the address he would make sure he put their farm as early as possible on his circuit so Mary had the letter in time for her mid-morning cup of tea.

Perry was a conscientious and frequent letter writer and Mary wrote back quickly. Ted smiled as he handed a new letter over. "One from your lad, here," he said and, as usual, Mary tucked it away in her pocket for later.

She was in the middle of baking a cake, and it was laundry day so it was after lunch before she found a private moment to sit down and read her letter. Her normal practice was to read it once quickly, to get the gist of any news, and then again more slowly, probably more than once, luxuriating in each word and sentence. Today she had barely skimmed the first page before she was out of her seat, running across the yard, waving the letter, and calling for her husband.

"Michael, Michael, he's coming home. He's coming home!"

Michael came out of the barn in a hurry to meet her. "Who? What? What's up?"

Her words came out almost too fast to make sense. "Perry,

it's Perry. He's coming home."

Michael pushed her towards the bench by the house. "Sit down. Slow down. Now tell me what it is."

Mary took a deep breath. "It's a letter from Perry. He's leaving the Order and he's getting married and he's coming home."

Michael shook his head in disbelief as he took the letter from her to read for himself. Three of their sons, Matt, Sam and Jonny, who were all working about the yard, came over to see what was going on. Michael read the letter slowly and carefully.

"You're right. He's left the Order and he's getting married." He looked up. "He's getting married in just a couple of days."

Mary dismissed that. "But he's coming home, right?"

"It says they'd like to. Just for a visit, not for good. From July until September, if that's okay with us."

"Of course it's okay. I have to write back and tell him straight away. We'll have to plan what we need to do to get ready, what they need, where they can sleep..."

Michael slipped an arm round his wife. "Slow down, there's plenty of time. Why don't we walk down to see Pastor Thomas? He has a telephone and just this once we could use it, telephone House St Peter, maybe even speak to Perry?"

Mary shook her head. "No, not right now. I need to take it in, read the letter again and think a bit. Maybe tomorrow."

Michael had accepted Mary's decision but later he told her he'd spoken to Pastor Thomas himself and made plans for a telephone conversation the next morning.

***

Friday morning

Michael

Michael had found the telephone conversation itself highly pleasurable. Perhaps he could persuade Mary they needed a phone of their own? He'd talked to Perry himself, of course, delighted to be speaking with his eldest son again. But most of the conversation had been between Perry and Mary. Mary was ecstatic, full of plans. Michael couldn't remember when he'd last seen her so happy.

He was more concerned about the impact on the rest of his family. Well, on one member in particular. Jonny was too young to remember Perry well and so not really interested in what was going on. The twins – Jack and Eddie – were self-contained. They had each other and, as normal, were just mildly amused at what was happening around them. Sam was his usual calm, steady self, but Matt, Matt was definitely wound up by the situation.

After Michael got back from the telephone conversation with Perry, he found Matt in the barn, unnecessarily restacking the hay bales with an angry energy. Michael leaned against the wall and watched as Matt moved the bales from one side to the other, throwing them hard and fast at the wall, stacking them roughly. If only all his farm help worked this hard and this fast all the time, he thought as he tried to find something positive in the situation. He waited until Matt turned towards him.

The feelings that Matt had been bottling up poured out of him. "I love him. I want to see him again, of course I do. He's my brother and I missed him. I still miss him, so badly. But he ran away, he left us, he left all this. And now he's just going to waltz back in like nothing's happened and take it all away."

Michael shook his head, understanding Matt's passionate love for the farm he had worked on for so many years. "He's not going to inherit the farm," he said softly. "He's not even asking for any support from it. Nor have I offered it."

"But Ma is so happy, so excited. She's making so many plans." Matt gestured wildly towards the house.

Michael smiled slightly. "At the moment, all your mother can think is that she's going to see Perry again. She can't allow herself to consider that he will also leave again. But he made it very clear in both his letter and our conversation that this is no more than a visit. He has no intention of coming back here longer term."

Matt subsided a little although he looked disbelieving. "He could change his mind at any time."

"Anyone can, though I am certain he won't. And it's my decision too. When they come we will talk about how to remove that uncertainty for you. In the meantime, can you trust that I have your wellbeing at heart too? Try and enjoy the good bits of Perry returning without worrying about the future?"

Matt sighed heavily but it was clear he could see the thrust of his father's argument. "I'll try," he said.

Chapter 19

Friday morning

Andrew

Immediately after the first service of Friday morning, Gabriel drew Andrew to one side. "From now until the wedding," he said, "just a little more than twenty-four hours, I want you to focus on getting Prospero there. You are excused all other duties except your medical ones and you have my permission to do whatever it takes, just stick with him and get him there."

Andrew nodded his acceptance; indeed, given an order from Gabriel he had little choice. He'd spotted Perry in the main body of the Abbey during the first service. No doubt he'd have headed for the dining room next. As expected, he found Perry having breakfast and slid into the seat beside him to eat his own meal.

Perry grinned at him. "Do you remember this is where we first met?" he asked.

"That was a long time ago. This isn't going to be a day full of reminiscing, is it?" Andrew responded, pretending to be horrified.

Perry laughed. "Probably not. I've got to go and see Edward about clothes next."

"I'll come with you," Andrew volunteered.

Perry just shrugged. "Fine by me."

***

Edward looked them both up and down and sighed. "Honestly," he said, "does nobody think there's any value in dressing well?"

Andrew tried not to laugh, aware that Perry was having the same problem. Dressing well was hardly an issue for any of the monks, Edward included.

Edward just shook his head. "Come on," he said to Perry. "I need to check the fit on your outfit for tomorrow."

Andrew followed them. "I just want to know whether you've chosen blue for House St Peter or green for House Tennant," he said.

Perry glanced back at him. "I didn't get a choice," he said darkly.

"That's because you have no idea at all," Edward said.

Perry's outfit turned out to be dark trousers with a white, long-sleeved undershirt in recognition of his time as a monk. It was the design of the overtunic that impressed Andrew. Edward had chosen a blue silk, the signature colour of House St Peter, but when the light caught it there were hints and ripples of green. The subtle embroidery round the hems and collar also combined the cross key logo of St Peter with the fort logo of Tennant.

"Very clever," Andrew acknowledged.

"Hedging his bets," Perry said.

Edward just laughed, pronouncing himself satisfied with the fit. "There's suitable clothing for your new life in your new rooms," he told Perry. "But no going to check on it. You're not allowed in there until after your wedding. And don't worry about moving your things in, I'll take care of whatever is necessary."

Andrew and Perry were on the point of leaving when a messenger shot into the workroom.

"You're to go to Lord Gabriel's office, now," the messenger said to Perry, slightly out of breath. "There's a phone call for you and he says it's your parents."

With one quick look at Andrew, Perry was out of the door in a flash, running for Lord Gabriel's office. Andrew followed, hard on his heels. Perry's parents didn't use the telephone.

Please let this not be bad news. Please let them be okay with the wedding.

Perry raced through the outer office, before skidding to a halt as he just missed crashing into Lord Gabriel himself.

"In there," Lord Gabriel said, tilting his head. "Use the phone in my office."

Perry did as instructed, and Lord Gabriel shut the door behind him before turning to Andrew. "All will be fine," he said quietly. "You don't need to worry. Just wait and do whatever seems necessary, afterwards." He turned towards Chloe, who was blatantly watching from her desk. "Get Andrew a coffee, please, while he waits. No, better make that camomile tea." Then, with another glance at Andrew, he left.

Chloe brought the tea across to Andrew, and he inadvertently wrinkled his nose at the scent.

"You don't like camomile tea, do you?" she asked with a hint of a smile on her face.

"No," he said shortly. But there was no way he would disobey Lord Gabriel, at least not on this, so he took a sip and tried not to grimace.

"Why is this all so dramatic? Are you going to tell me what's going on here?" Chloe asked.

"No," he said again.

Chloe just smiled and walked back to her desk. Her silent

and good-natured acceptance of his answer raised far more feelings of guilt than any pleadings would have done.

"They haven't talked in years," he said. "Even though they write, regularly, Prospero feels too guilty about how he hurt them to visit them and they have a thing about not using the telephone."

"And will they object to his marriage?"

Andrew shook his head. "I shouldn't think so. It's just...his family and his High Lord have conflicting expectations of him."

Chloe grinned. "I expect Leonie will sort them all out."

Despite himself, Andrew laughed. Of course Leonie would sort them out. He could leave it to her. She might look delicate and non-threatening, but he was quite sure she'd fight anyone tooth and nail – possibly literally – for what was best for Perry. And what was more, why was he worrying about Perry anyway? Weren't they all doing Perry a disservice, thinking that now he had left the safety of the Order he would revert to past behaviour patterns? Andrew thought back to a conversation he'd had with Lady Eleanor a couple of months ago. Perry had changed, grown and developed in the last few years; they needed to treat him as such and give him the credit he was due.

Lost in his thoughts, Andrew jumped when Perry burst out of Lord Gabriel's office, the door banging against the wall, his face beaming with happiness.

"I have to tell Leonie," he said.

"Kitchen," Chloe answered, and Perry disappeared.

Andrew stood up and took his mug over to Chloe's desk. "I'd better go too. Thanks for the tea."

She glanced into the mug. "You didn't finish it. What will Lord Gabriel say?"

He grinned. "As I recall, the order was to you, to make me a drink. Nothing about me having to drink it."

She laughed, and waved him away. "Be off with you, I won't tell."

Andrew trailed Perry to the kitchen. Despite not being a skilled perceptor, if he was within about five hundred metres of Perry, he could always tell where he was, even if he couldn't perceive anyone else. Now he realised he could always tell where Leonie was, too.

Leonie

Perry charged into the kitchen where I was working, picked me up and spun me round and kissed me. That level of excitement was dangerous in a kitchen with flames and sharp knives. Pedro tilted his head towards the door – *it's a good thing he's such a softy* – so I guided Perry out of the back of the kitchen and through the herb garden. It took me a while to work out what he was on about, his words tumbling over each other.

"Slow down a bit," I said. "What is it?"

"I spoke to them, I heard their voices, they spoke to me. My parents, we spoke on the telephone."

I hadn't expected that to happen. Perry had told me telephones were a symbol that his mother had rejected in making her choice of life partner and walking away from her family ties. There seemed to be something of a history of walking away from family here.

"Wow," I said. "They were happy? It went well? They don't mind?"

"Yes, yes, they're really happy for us." He picked me up

and spun me round again.

I was caught up in his euphoria and wanted to celebrate with him. It felt he'd had a huge weight lifted off him that he'd not even known he was carrying.

"What about the wedding? They don't mind missing that?"

"No, they're fine with that. You solved that problem. If we have a second service when we go there, they'll think of tomorrow as a handfasting ceremony and that one as the real thing."

"But we will still be properly married, here?" I asked Perry, suddenly concerned.

"Oh, yes," he said, reassuringly, picking me up and spinning me round yet again. "Definitely. And I can't wait."

Andrew found us not long after that so I left the two of them and hurried back to my work in the kitchen. I suspected Andrew was in for a challenging afternoon keeping Perry's feet on the ground – they both had clinic duty later.

***

I tried to keep a touch on Perry's mind all afternoon, but from time to time Shields got in the way. We were supposed to be meeting at the Old Chapel for a final rehearsal in the early evening, but he hadn't arrived by the time I got there. Lord Gabriel and Lady Eleanor were there already discussing some detail with Brother Joseph. Chloe was standing a little apart from them and she waved at me so I headed over to join her. We were chatting when Perry bounded in, Andrew trailing along behind him. Perry pulled me close, nuzzling into my neck and leaving a fairly decorous kiss on my cheek. "We're here," he said.

I caught a glimpse of Andrew over Perry's shoulder and decided he didn't look too much the worse for wear – a little weary perhaps. He winked at me. "Your problem for now," he mouthed.

I stifled a giggle.

Perry was still clearly euphoric, bouncing on his toes with excitement. I wasn't sure a rehearsal was necessary, but at least it gave everyone involved a chance to understand where they should be and what they should be doing when. Nor was I sure that Perry paid any attention. He stood where he was supposed to, said the things he was meant to say and appeared to be listening when Lord Gabriel spoke. But he couldn't stand still; some part of him was always on the move, whether he was rocking from foot to foot, waving his hands around or just fidgeting with whatever he'd found in his pocket. Whenever he was next to me he leaned down and whispered in my ear odd snippets of the conversation he'd had with his parents. I doubted he'd remember any of what he'd been told this evening. I'd have to rely on Andrew to be sure Perry was in the right place at the right time tomorrow.

Afterwards, Perry walked back to my room with me, and kissed me goodnight, his hands sliding into my hair, his lips warm and soft on mine.

"Next time we meet, it'll be at the Old Chapel, to be married," he whispered. "I will be there, no matter what. I love you."

"Me, too," I replied.

I stood in the doorway watching him walk away, down the stairs. I couldn't believe that this time tomorrow I'd be married to Perry. Despite everything that had happened, all that had gone before, I found I wasn't nervous; I didn't want to run away. I was excited and looking forward to it. Since that last major nightmare, I was starting to believe in what both Andrew and Perry had told me; I was wanted and I didn't need to be alone no matter what.

I shut the door and turned to look round my room. All I had left were the things I needed that night and my outfit for the next day. Edward had moved all my stuff and no doubt he'd arrange for these last few items to get to our new rooms, too. I assumed it was the same for Perry, not that he had much in the way of personal belongings.

My dress was hanging by the window, shimmering like a rainbow as it moved slightly in the light breeze. It was beautiful, exceeding even Edward's usual high standards. It had a deep neckline that mirrored the shape of my necklace, with wide shoulder straps and no sleeves. The bodice fitted closely down to my hips and then it flared out into a mid-calf length skirt. It fastened down the back with a long line of delicate buttons. I didn't have a veil, just a white circlet to wear in my hair, but I did have a shawl to wear over my shoulders. It was finely woven in silver and white in a typical Trader style and light as gossamer. Edward had cleverly made it so it fastened to and draped from the shoulder straps of my dress so I wouldn't have to worry about it falling off.

I couldn't wait for the next day.

Andrew

Andrew chose to stay in the staff accommodation with Perry the night before the wedding. If Perry was going to have a nightmare – and no one, not even Perry, disputed the possibility – then this was the most likely time and Andrew would be there to calm it. And if Leonie had a nightmare – a subject no one was going to bring up in her presence – both Andrew and Perry would be nearby.

But as far as Andrew could tell, Perry had calmed down and went to sleep quickly.

***

Andrew woke to find Perry squatting by his bed, shaking his shoulder.

"I can't sleep, Andy. I can feel the nightmares hovering. I need you to stop them." Perry's fear was clear in his voice.

Andrew blinked at him sleepily. "Of course. Come here."

Perry curled up against him, their bodies fitting together, Perry's back to Andrew, and Andrew's arms around him as they had done so many times before.

"I love her so much. What if she changes her mind? What if she decides she doesn't love me? I can't do this on my own. What if I can't cope, what if everything goes wrong again?" Perry asked, his voice a whisper.

Andrew tucked the blanket over both of them as he replied, "It's going to be alright. She's not going to change her mind, and we all know she loves you. You won't be alone, no matter what. I promised her that and I promise you that."

"Are you sure?"

"Yes, I'm sure. Shush, sleep now. I'll be here."

Reassured as much by Andrew's presence as his words, Perry fell asleep again without trouble. Andrew lay awake longer sorting out his thoughts and feelings. It had been years since they had last slept like this, but it was still instantly familiar, instantly comforting, for him as well as Perry. He had long ago come to terms with the fact that Perry would never feel for him as he felt for Perry, but their relationship didn't need to be anything more than it was. It was still close, loving and satisfying. It was oddly validating that tonight Perry had needed him; from tomorrow it would be Leonie that Perry turned to, but tonight it was him.

The last few months had been difficult to say the least. Of course he trusted Lord Gabriel and had done what had been asked of him without complaint, but not without concern. From the start he'd felt that they were placing Perry in a vulnerable position, playing on his weaknesses and exploiting him, and he had been protective of his friend. He had grown jealous of Leonie as she'd clearly aroused in Perry those feelings that he couldn't. But he had quickly come to know her and had seen the scared, lost, hurting girl behind the brave front. And despite his skill at hiding it, Leonie had soon understood that he felt the same way over Perry that she did.

He'd been able to acknowledge, at least to himself, that he loved both Perry and Leonie, that he was deeply concerned that they were both being exploited by Lord Gabriel's plans, whatever those plans were, and yet he'd still been jealous – of both of them! It had taken him some time to address this and even now he wasn't quite sure what his feelings were, although he had expressed to Leonie what he wanted them to be.

Lying awake, he tried to set it out logically in his head. He loved both Perry and Leonie; Leonie knew how he felt about Perry but he was quite sure that Perry didn't, and almost as certain that neither of them knew how he felt about Leonie. He had wished he was the one arousing feelings in the other, but he didn't want the full consequences of arousing such feelings. He didn't want to be responsible for someone else's happiness or wellbeing, or to depend on them for his own. Nor did he want anything that would distract from his relationship with God; he was both content and happy with his place in the Order and his monastic life. For him at least, what he had there was infinitely better than what the secular world could offer. Jealousy out of the way, he could love both of them properly, and want only what was best for them – and they were clearly in love with each other.

That left his concern about Lord Gabriel's plans. Whilst

there was nothing false about how Perry and Leonie felt for each other, Gabriel had clearly encouraged matters, and Andrew did not understand his reasons. He could accept that encouraging two adepts of such abilities to work together could lead to considerable benefits – that had been Gabriel's initial position – but that needed no more than a working relationship. Once Perry had started to develop feelings for Leonie, of course his emotions had to be addressed. But surely Gabriel's actions had caused their relationship to develop faster than it would have done, like a hot house flower? If it had happened more slowly somehow it would have felt more genuine.

And now that it was all out in the open, Andrew certainly didn't understand why they needed to marry so fast. It wasn't like Leonie was pregnant – he could be certain of that – nor, despite the rumours, was she on death's doorstep, or an heiress about to be married off elsewhere and her fortune lost to the House. Gabriel had said that if they were going to do this anyway, they might as well do it quickly and minimise the disruption. Okay, that was perhaps the easier option, and Leonie might well have far fewer nightmares once they were married but since when had Gabriel ever chosen easy over right? No, his gut feeling was that there was far more to all this than Lord Gabriel was admitting and that was what concerned him. Of course he trusted Gabriel, and he was sure Gabriel was following God's lead, it was just that sometimes this had a high price and he was afraid that his friends would be the ones to pay it.

There was nothing he could do about this other than to be there for either, or both, of them, if, or when, it became necessary. In the meantime he could simply pray for them both and he did that before settling back to sleep again himself.

Chapter 20

Saturday morning

Leonie

I stood in the middle of my room, dressed only in a towelling bath robe after my shower, turning slowly on the spot as if somewhere I would see a solution to my problem. What was I supposed to do about breakfast? The wedding was to be merged with the normal late morning service and followed by lunch for all our guests. But I wanted to eat before that and I could hardly wear a bathrobe to the dining hall. I'd dumped yesterday's clothes in the laundry without thinking. The only other outfit I had was my wedding dress. I couldn't wear that to breakfast either. Why hadn't I thought about this earlier?

I was still puzzling over this when there was a knock on the door. Before I could move to answer it, the door opened and Chloe bounced in, her arms full of unidentifiable packages. She was closely followed by Lady Eleanor, carrying a tray piled high with food.

"We've come to help you get ready," Chloe said, with her usual beaming smile.

Chloe was going to be my only bridesmaid. I'd been told that someone, usually a parent or sibling, normally escorted the bride into the church and down the aisle. But Traders considered that it was for the bride to give herself to her husband and vice versa. So, I had decided that I would walk alone, followed by Chloe. However, Pedro had asked if he could escort me to the door of the Old Chapel and I had happily agreed.

Now, I looked at Chloe, barely comprehending. Normally I just had a quick shower, put on whatever I was supposed to be wearing and dragged a comb through my hair – and I meant dragged. My hair's default position was curly and tangled. I hadn't been planning to do much more than that.

"But there's hours to go yet," I protested. "It won't take that long."

Lady Eleanor put the tray down and grinned at me. "We'll have breakfast first. But it should take long. It's a special day. And it'll be fun."

Fun? Really? Well, at least they've solved the breakfast problem.

We did take our time over breakfast, but eventually, Lady Eleanor leaned back in her chair and looked me up and down. "Nails first, I think," she said. "Do you agree, Chloe?"

Chloe nodded and pointed towards one of her packages. "I've got just the colour." She seemed to know exactly what she was doing, massaging my hands and feet, trimming my nails, and then painting them with liquids out of several different bottles.

"Base coat, colour, top coat," she said, tapping each bottle in turn. "Do it properly and it'll last much longer." She looked up from where she was sitting on the floor with my foot in her lap. "Don't worry, Edward's made sure you've got some remover in your rooms, should you want it."

I was amazed at how relaxing I found the process. Once she was done, I turned my hands and feet this way and that, admiring them. She hadn't used a colour, exactly, but when the light caught my nails they sparkled, a rainbow, just like my dress.

How does someone who always wanted to be a nun turn out to be a skilled manicurist?

"Now stand up," said Lady Eleanor. "And take your robe off."

I did so, a little puzzled, and she started to massage body lotion into my skin.

"That's a Trader custom," I said.

She smiled. "I know. I was fostered to the Traders in my early teens."

I looked at her with new eyes. Perry had said once that there were Traders – or at least ex Traders – at House St Peter. I'd never thought that Lady Eleanor might be one.

"What have you chosen?" I asked. The lotion always contains rosemary to symbolise remembering your vows and myrtle for true love. But the bride's friends choose two or three other ingredients to represent their views of the bride and the marriage.

Lady Eleanor smiled again. "Thyme," – that meant courage or bravery – "coriander," – hidden worth, much valued – "and honeysuckle." That one symbolised an unbreakable bond of love. I was speechless. Lady Eleanor just carried on with the lotion. When she'd finished, my skin felt soft and silky, darker than usual, almost glowing, a deep gold.

Hang on. If she lived with the Traders then did she learn what I learnt…?

I glanced at Lady Eleanor with curiosity. She met my eyes and hers were full of mischief. *"I think Prospero is in for a particularly interesting day,"* she said in my head.

That's a yes, then. I hadn't known she was a telepath.

As I put my robe back on and sat down, she took one look at my hair and sighed. "Chloe," she said. "Pass me that bottle, please." She sprayed something all over my hair.

"What is that?" I asked, sitting up straighter, sniffing and trying to deduce the ingredients in it from the scent.

Chloe giggled. "Sister Elizabeth calls it witchcraft," she said.

Lady Eleanor laughed. "It's perfectly innocent. Sister Soraya makes it, although she keeps the recipe secret. I used to use it all the time on Melanie."

She waited a moment and then tackled the tangles. The spray was definitely magic because the tangles just gave way before her. She combed and brushed each ringlet carefully until my hair shone and then she fastened the circlet in it. When they were both satisfied and there was nothing left to do but put my dress on they stopped to change into their own formal wear. Chloe's outfit was pretty much what she wore every day – brown trousers, white undershirt, brown tunic, but it was new and I think Edward had made it from slightly finer material than usual, with more elaborate stitched detail round the hems. Lady Eleanor looked very impressive, with a formal tunic in blue silk, embroidered to highlight her position in the House.

Lady Eleanor slipped my dress over my head and Chloe did up all the little buttons at the back and made sure my necklace sat just right. Today I had chosen to wear my Trader bracelet high around my upper arm where it could be seen. Once I was ready they let me look in the mirror. Clearly both Lady Eleanor and Chloe were in league with Brother Edward in terms of weaving magic with my appearance. The girl who looked back was truly beautiful, not me and yet it was me. This vision took my breath away. The others were just amused at my astonishment.

"Did you not realise how beautiful you are?" Chloe asked me, but I could only shake my head at her, robbed of all power of speech.

I was still speechless when there was a knock at the door.

Chloe opened it a little and stuck her head out for a moment. "It's Pedro," she said, turning back into the room.

"Let him in," instructed Lady Eleanor, "and then you and I had better be off."

Chloe did so, and very soon Pedro and I were left alone.

"You are the most beautiful woman I have ever seen," Pedro told me with a smile.

"I didn't know you were a nestling," I told him, finding my voice again. I didn't know why I'd chosen now to bring the subject up. "When did you know about me?"

"From the beginning, when you hid in the stores. I just didn't know it was you until Prospero brought you into the kitchen that first time."

I looked at him, puzzled. "But you didn't treat me any different."

"That's because it doesn't make any difference." He offered me his arm. "Now, my Lady Leonie, would you allow me to escort you to your wedding?"

I took his arm and together we walked down the stairs, across the courtyards and over to the Old Chapel. At the door, Pedro melted away, leaving me to Chloe's care.

"Take a deep breath," she said.

I did so, and then looked down the aisle towards Perry. He had turned towards me and the look on his face said everything about how he felt about me. It was as if there were only us present, being drawn inexorably together. My heart singing, I fixed my eyes on his face and walked towards him.

Perry

Perry was captivated by the vision of Leonie as she walked down the aisle towards him, calm, confident and beautiful. Both his nerves and his surroundings disappeared as he held out his hands towards her. She placed her hands in his, allowing herself to be drawn close to him. He breathed in her sweet scent, fresh and herbal.

"Hello, beautiful," he said softly, his voice trembling as he tried to control emotions he couldn't begin to name. "You came then."

"I did," she replied, equally softly, smiling up into his eyes, her voice so certain that he was instantly reassured. Together they turned to face Lord Gabriel.

Perry remained captivated by Leonie throughout the service.

He made his vows first, his promises to her, so different from his vows as a monk, and yet so similar. When he'd made his vows as a monk, he had been so certain of what he was doing, so convinced it was for the rest of his life, so sure he was doing the right thing but it had been all about him. Last night and today his uncertainty came from wanting to be sure this was right for Leonie.

In his oath as a monk, he had promised a lifetime of faithfulness and service to God and that vow continued, no matter what. Now, he turned towards Leonie, taking her hands in his, and promised to love her, care for her, cherish her and be faithful to her for the rest of their lives together. He was enchanted by the sound of her voice as she repeated the same vows to him. Did she realise that she had publicly declared that she loved him?

As he became a monk, he had promised poverty and

chastity. Now he was almost bewitched by the touch of her skin as she held his hand and he gifted her with everything he would ever be or own, and vowed to worship her with his body. As she reciprocated, his mind was overwhelmed with thoughts of what was yet to come. He could barely wait; it was as if he could already feel the warmth of her body against his.

They sat for a reading, the passage he'd quoted to her only a few days ago. A cliché for a wedding, perhaps, but it meant something special to both of them. He squeezed her hand, her fingers entwined in his and tucked between them as they sat, and she turned her head to glance at him with a sweet, shy smile.

Then, somehow, the time had passed and the service was over. They walked back down the aisle to cheers, everyone wreathed in smiles. He didn't watch where he was going; he couldn't take his eyes off Leonie, scarcely able to believe that she was now his wife. Lady Eleanor had a camera and took pictures of them, standing in the doorway to the Old Chapel, and still he had eyes only for Leonie.

He was hardly aware of anything or anyone else all through their wedding lunch. He was simply aware of Leonie's presence, wherever she was in the room, eating, laughing, chatting with friends and guests. He came back to reality only when Lord Gabriel proposed a toast to them both, and, with some carefully chosen words, sent them both packing.

He grabbed Leonie's hand and left the dining room as fast as possible, running and giggling with her down the corridor, across the courtyard and up the stairs to their rooms. Leonie reached for the sensor pad that formed the lock, eager to be safe inside but Perry lifted her off her feet and into his arms.

"You're my bride," he said. "It may be old fashioned and a superstition but I'm still carrying you across the threshold."

He did just that, before kicking the door shut behind them and sweeping through into their bedroom. There, he placed her down, keeping his arms around her. Her palms were flat against his chest and she was trembling slightly.

"It doesn't have to be now," he said. "We can take all the time we want."

She looked up into his eyes. "But it is allowed, now?" she asked.

"Oh yes, most definitely," he told her.

"Then I don't want to wait." Her voice was little more than a whisper as he touched his lips to hers, and he had waited too long already.

He felt for the buttons down the back of her dress, but there were so many and his patience failed him. He couldn't undo them fast enough, causing several of them to part company with the fabric in his haste. He brushed the straps off her shoulders and half stepped back as the dress fell to the floor, pooling in a rainbow around her feet and leaving her standing naked before him.

He breathed out in awe at the sight of her—golden skin like velvet, red curls tumbling almost to her shoulders, deep dark eyes filled with trust in him. "Leonie, you are so beautiful."

She reached for the fastenings on his tunic, unbuckling them and pushing his tunic back off his shoulders to fall unheeded. He let go of her for a moment to pull his undershirt over his head. Now her palms were once more against his chest, this time electric on his bare skin. She moved her hands down towards his trousers but he caught her wrists, afraid that if she continued he would lose all control. Instead, she stroked upwards until her fingers were on his temples and sliding over his hair. He wrapped his arms around her, pulling her close, her skin hot against his own, her scent filling his nostrils as he buried his nose in her hair.

Already overwhelmed by his own desire, it was a moment before he realised that he was also sensing Leonie's desires as she reacted to his hands stroking her back. Somehow their minds were linked. Not as they normally did; this was different. He was experiencing everything that she was feeling and he understood just how much she wanted this too. She looked up at him, smiling.

"See," she said. "You won't hurt me. You can't."

He shook his head, not truly understanding what was happening and unwilling to trust his voice.

"You won't," she insisted. "This is us, together."

He still didn't understand but now he didn't try; he explored her body with his hands and lips, experimenting with the sensations he – and she – were feeling. Somehow he took his hands off her for long enough to remove the rest of his clothing, keeping his lips on her, nuzzling her ear, her cheek, her neck, as he did so. She twined her hands round his neck, then ran them back down his chest. Were the electric sensations flooding through him her feelings or his? It didn't matter. He guided her towards the bed, not sure that he could remain upright much longer. He pushed her down, falling with her, arms and legs wrapped around each other. Greedily he tasted her lips, her mouth, her skin – or was she doing that to him? Their minds were linked, twisted together as one; he couldn't distinguish between them nor between his body and hers. He let go of all conscious control and allowed his instincts to take over, his body flooded with sensations more intense than any he had felt before.

**

Afterwards they lay together, complete, their bodies still tangled. Leonie was sprawled across his chest like a cat and he had one hand twisted in her hair. The explicit mental link they had earlier was broken, but her contentment was almost a presence in his mind. Her breathing whispered against his chest where she enhanced the cat-like image by giving a very good impression of purring. If Leonie oozed contentment, his own smile had to be several feet wide. The mental link had been deeper than he'd thought Leonie had intended. He now knew from her exactly how she felt about him, even if she had trouble vocalising it. He was surprised by how much better that made him feel; he'd thought he'd understood and accepted her reasons for not speaking. Idly he wondered if he might have given anything away himself and then decided he didn't care.

Leonie stirred and lifted herself up on his chest to look in his eyes. "Perry," she said, and it did indeed sound like a purr. "See," she continued. "You did remember how!"

Perry still couldn't stop smiling. "I did, didn't I? But that was different. It was never like that with anyone else. How, where did you learn that mind linking?"

"Surely you've heard that Trader women make the best lovers?" She was teasing him, her eyes lit up.

"I thought that was just a rumour, an exaggeration."

She shook her head, which caused ripples all along her body. Every movement she made was arousing him again.

"All Trader women learn how from their early teens in preparation for their marriage. But the men don't; I never heard of a Trader man who could even sense the connection."

"Perhaps that's because they aren't telepathic? I could feel it." He wasn't particularly concerned about the reasons. Instead, he wrapped both arms around Leonie and rolled them over so that he was once more on top. "Shall we see what else I can remember?"

Leonie answered by arching her back, her hips pressing up against his and suddenly their minds were linked again.

"You are going to have to teach me how to do that," he managed to say before giving way again to their mutual rising passion.

***

Perry watched as Leonie started to explore their new accommodation. Still naked, she flung open the doors to one cupboard and glanced back at him. He slid off the bed to stand behind her. Edward had provided all they could need – trousers and tunics in soft, muted blues and greens for Perry, greys and blues for Leonie. This drawer was full of lingerie, that shelf held a pile of undershirts in a rainbow of colours. And all of a quality suggesting the family of a High Lord.

They showered together, dreaming of the future. Another day, another time, he would... For today it was enough to wash each other, continuing to touch and learn about each other's body. They lingered over dressing, trying things on as he suggested outfits for Leonie and she did the same for him. Once dressed, he followed her into the living space unable to take his eyes off her as she ran from window to window, exclaiming at the view as the sun set over the courtyard. He still couldn't believe that this beautiful, gorgeous creature was his *wife*.

Remembering his promise to care for her, he moved to the kitchen area, opening all the drawers and doors, looking for food. He found bread, cheese, fruit, a cold pie and, yes, that was a big tin of chocolate chip cookies. He put them on the kitchen table and looked up to call Leonie over. She'd found the bookshelf and was stroking the spines of the books with care, pulling first one and then another out for a closer look. He breathed her name and she turned round, her face beaming, glowing with pleasure and happiness.

"All my favourites are here," she said.

He'd probably find many of his favourites too. He gestured at the food and she flowed across the room.

"It looks like a picnic."

He didn't want to meet anyone else, to have to share anything of Leonie with others, not today. But he knew how much she liked to be outside and how she loved picnics so he nodded his agreement and together they packed it up. Despite the incipient dusk, they took this down to the river, to a favourite spot rarely frequented by others. Perry half lay back on the ground, supporting himself on one arm, listening to the sounds of the night, and getting far more pleasure from watching Leonie eat than from his own meal. Soon, very soon, he would take her back through the darkened courtyards to their new home. Tonight he wouldn't have to leave her at her door. Tonight, their wedding night, he would share her bed, sleep with her in his arms and wake with her in the morning.

He couldn't wait.

Eleanor

Eleanor stood at Gabriel's office window watching Perry and Leonie walking across the courtyard, arms around each other, heads touching, a picture of happiness and togetherness. Gabriel came over to see what she was looking at. She turned towards him.

"Is it worth it, Gabe?" she asked. "A little happiness now, in exchange for all the trouble you see coming? Does the end ever justify the means?"

He sighed deeply. "I love them both," he told her. "They are the son and daughter I could never have. I don't want to sacrifice either for the greater good. I would rather it was me, not them, paying the price for the opportunity that's coming. But I am doing what God requires of me. Of that, I am certain." He turned away. "You remember the story of Abraham and Isaac?"

She did. God had asked Abraham to sacrifice his son and heir, Isaac. Abraham had trusted God enough to do so and God had spared Isaac at the last moment.

"Are you hoping that one or both of them will be spared?"

"I was," he confessed. "But what I hope doesn't matter. It might give me strength, but it makes no difference to what I have to do. I still have to face the consequences of what I do. And one of the things we have to do is meet with Lord Leon. I want you to do that."

Chapter 21

Sunday morning

Perry

Perry woke early on Sunday, his body still attuned to the rhythms and routines of monastic life. He was disorientated for a moment, thrown back in time, by the presence of a warm, naked female body curled against him, and then the memories came flooding back. He smiled with pleasure and twisted so that he could watch Leonie sleep. He wanted to reach out and stroke her, touch and caress her skin, but she was sleeping deeply and peacefully, and he was loathe to disturb her. Instead, he lay still and let his eyes traverse her body, drinking in every detail – the length of her eyelashes, the way her hair twisted around her ears, the deep pink of her lips curved in a happy smile as she slept. As he watched, she opened her eyes and smiled at him.

"Perry," she said contentedly, almost purring again.

She reached for him and once more he forgot all conscious thought as he drowned in the pleasure of her body. They lay together listening to the bells that signalled the end of the early service.

Leonie lifted herself up on Perry's chest to look him in the face as she asked, "Are we going to the next service?"

He replied with a question, "Would you like to?"

She nodded. "Yes, only..." her voice was hesitant. He waited and she continued. "Won't everyone know what we've been doing?"

He smiled and sat up further, gathering her onto his lap and into his arms. "Well, yes, I should think they'll have a pretty fair idea. Does that matter? We've got to face everyone sometime, and at least at the service they should be concentrating on worship rather than what we might have done."

Fleetingly, he remembered many previous Sundays when he'd fallen out of bed with some woman, hungover but driven to attend the service by a need he hadn't understood. He understood the desire now, but it was still there, just as strong as it ever had been. It wasn't an external pressure – even as a monk attending services had not been compulsory – but an inner compulsion, a need to worship with others in God's presence. He wanted to do that, and he wanted to do that with Leonie but he certainly wasn't going to pressurise her into doing anything she felt uncomfortable with. She tucked her head into his neck.

"Won't they tease us?" she asked, her words whispering across his skin.

He shook his head. "Maybe, a little. Not much and it'll be me rather than you. I won't let anyone be mean to you."

She smiled a little at that and they decided to risk attending the service.

"Meanwhile," Perry said, "I'm going to get us some breakfast to fortify us."

"You can cook, too?" Leonie asked, in mock amazement.

"I happened to notice a jug of batter in the fridge and I can certainly cook pancakes," he claimed.

Leonie

Perry certainly could cook pancakes. I felt braver after some breakfast, but I was still concerned about being teased. A lot of teasing went on after a Trader wedding. A newly-wed couple wouldn't set off on their own with their waggon because a single

waggon simply wouldn't be safe. So a Trader's wedding night –
and subsequent nights – would be spent in camp or on the trail
with everyone else. But they wouldn't be the only ones teased the
next morning; the party after a wedding usually ended with a
number of couples finding somewhere to bed down together. And
those on guard duty would get teased just as bad for not having
had the opportunity to do so. I was so unbelievably happy with
Perry, spending time together, making love; I didn't want
anything to taint it or even interrupt it.

But I knew how much attending worship meant to him,
and it meant a lot to me now, so we risked it and went.

***

A few days later

I stood in the shower and stretched, enjoying the warm
water pouring over my body, running in rivulets down my skin,
an echo of what Perry had done with his hands earlier.

We had woken early and made love, slow and satisfying,
the rising sun caressing our skin through the window.

Making love with Perry was everything I'd hoped it would
be and totally different from what I'd expected. The mind linking
that every Trader girl was taught in her teens wasn't about
controlling or manipulating one's partner. It was more about
gently nudging and amplifying actions and reactions, timing and
feelings to enhance sexual pleasure. I'd heard theories about it; the
enhanced pleasure enticed men to join the Trader community,
bringing the new blood essential to a small breeding group and at
the same time it dissuaded them from straying, or at least from
straying outside the community.

As far as I knew, no Trader man could sense it, although
they knew that their women had the ability. Perry had worked out
how to use it from our wedding night. Our lovemaking had

become a time when we communicated without words. It could be hot and deep and passionate, or slow and luxurious, or comforting and reassuring.

These days and weeks of marriage were the happiest time of my life. We had been welcomed back into the community as a married couple, no teasing, just love and congratulations and a real sense of belonging. And thinking of the community, my next class started soon. I had maybe half an hour before I was supposed to be in a lecture over at the college.

I turned off the shower, shook the water out of my eyes and the daydreams out of my head, wrapped a towel round myself and headed back into the bedroom. Perry was there, sitting on the end of the bed half dressed, still topless. He looked up at me with a smile and came towards me.

"Hello again, beautiful," he said, stroking his fingers over my wet shoulder and teasing the edge of the towel. He gestured back at something on the bed with his other hand. "It's going to be warm today. I've found some cream to protect your skin. The scars are more delicate, more vulnerable. They need to be looked after."

I looked round him at the tub of cream on the bed. He took advantage of my distraction to loosen my towel further and it fell to the floor.

"Perry," I said, trying to sound reproving.

He just grinned.

I ran my fingers up the scar on his chest. "What about these?" I asked.

"I don't plan to expose that one," he said. "Or the ones on my legs or back. But Edward seems to have provided me with short-sleeved shirts for some reason. You could help me cover the scars on my arm."

I hadn't ever thought about the fact that he always wore long sleeves; after all it had been the colder weather for most of the time I'd known him. He was still running his fingers down my back, tracing the damage there, white lines and fine ridges.

"Do you mind them?" I asked. "My scars, I mean?"

He shook his head. "I mind the pain they represent," he said. "But they are part of you and I love you. I don't see them as ugly or anything like that."

He took me by the shoulders and turned me round, then reached for the cream and started to rub it in.

"How did you get your scars?" I asked. "You've never told me."

It was a moment before he replied. "An argument with a window, or so I'm told," he said. "I don't remember. All I know is, I started drinking one lunchtime. The next thing I remember clearly is waking up in hospital forty-eight hours later and George telling me he'd lost count of the number of stitches he'd put in me. I had some broken bones, too. I wasn't unconscious the whole time, I just don't remember it. All I remember is the fear."

He'd covered my back and shoulders with the cream and now he slid his hands round to the front.

"I don't have any scars *there*," I said.

"I know," he breathed in my ear. "I just like holding you there."

I twisted round to face him. "If you carry on like that, we're both going to be late."

"Not that late. And anyway, I know loads of short cuts across the campus."

Chapter 22

May

Eleanor

Lord Leon, now well into his eighties, sat down with care, sinking onto the garden bench and resting his cane beside him. "I'm getting old, Ellie," he said. "Not like you young things."

Eleanor smiled at the compliment. "I've got grandchildren, you know," she told him.

"Hmph. That's nothing," he replied. "I've got a quiver full of great-grandchildren. And while several of them are smarter than their parents, they're too young to rely on as my heirs. I've not got that long left, and I've no confidence that my House will be well looked after when I'm gone." He turned in his seat to look Eleanor full in the face. "So, tell me, what's got Gabriel so worked up?"

Instead of replying she handed him a photograph taken on Perry and Leonie's wedding day.

He squinted at it. "My eyes aren't what they were, either, but that's Neville's lad," he said. "The one who defied him to join Gabriel's monastery. There's a fair few rumours going around about his sudden wedding."

"I dare say there are," agreed Eleanor. "But it's not him it's about. Look at the girl."

Lord Leon's eyes widened as he studied the photo in silence for a long time and then handed it back. "She's as beautiful as her mother."

"Did you know?"

He sighed and rested his hands on his knees, his shoulders

hunched. "When we found Augusta's body, I knew the dead child beside her wasn't Helena's kid, that's all. I thought she'd be safer if I acted as though it was. I didn't know what had happened to her. If she's anything like her mother, I'd be happy to leave my House in her hands." He paused, sitting up straighter and gesturing around the garden. "When my youngest son, James, wanted to set up Taylor House here I encouraged him. I thought it would give us an excuse to look for her, to try and find her. He doesn't know that and I didn't tell Gabriel either. Obviously it didn't work."

Taylor House was where Lord Leon and Lady Eleanor were meeting, a joint enterprise between their Houses, located on their mutual boundary. Lindum provided the land and much of the resources whilst St Peter provided all medical staff. Its role was to find, rescue and provide for children in need – orphans, slaves, refugees and runaways. Today it had provided Eleanor and Leon with a meeting place that wouldn't arouse suspicion.

"It saved a lot of others," Eleanor told him.

"I suppose it did," he agreed. "Where was she?"

"You had the right idea. She was a slave then a runaway but we don't know in which House because she doesn't know. Then she joined up with the Traders and eventually reached us about seven or eight months ago."

"And you recognised her?"

"No. No one did. No one thought about it. Everyone looks at her hair and thinks Chisholm, not Lindum."

Lord Leon winced at Eleanor's easy mention of his ancient enemies, but she ignored it and continued, "Before the wedding Brother Benjamin did a DNA test, just to be on the safe side. That told us."

"So who knows?"

"Me, Gabe, Benjamin. That's all."

"Not the girl? Nor Neville's lad? Or Neville himself?"

"Not as far as we know. We've not told them." That was strictly true, thought Eleanor. Best not to get into what Gabriel had done to Prospero.

"And yet you went ahead with the marriage. There's more to this than meets the eye. Gabriel is up to something. What is it?"

"She's your heir. What you do about it is up to you. Marriage to Prospero may make it slightly more likely that she will meet with those who might recognise her, but they intend to remain quietly in House St Peter for the foreseeable future."

Leon nodded, and Eleanor continued, "Gabriel has been having visions again. Something is going to happen – very soon. It's vitally important and it centres round her. He doesn't expect her to survive it."

"So, you give me back my heir with one hand and take her away again with the other?"

"We felt it wasn't right to keep her from you. You don't have to do anything, but it needs to be your choice as to whether to acknowledge her or not. It's not for us to decide that."

Lord Leon sighed heavily, shoulders slumping again. "Acknowledging her won't do anything for her safety. It wasn't me that wanted her dead. But now I know, I can't ignore her." He straightened his back, resting his hand on his cane, and tapping it on the ground. "Six months, Ellie. I'll keep it quiet for six months. That'll give me time to plan should she survive and Gabriel time for whatever he thinks is going to happen."

Ellie nodded her acknowledgement of his decision.

"What do you call her?" Lord Leon asked quietly.

Eleanor smiled. "She's known as Leonie."

Leon closed his eyes for a moment. "Helena always wanted to call her that. Augusta would have known. It was definitely Augusta's body we found, by the way. No doubt about that. She'd just turned twenty one and Leonie would have been between four and five years old. I recorded her birth. I called her Leonie Helena Augusta. I don't suppose there is any way I could see her?"

Eleanor shook her head and her voice was sympathetic as she said, "That wouldn't be very wise right now, would it? However carefully we arranged it, someone would put two and two together."

Lord Leon had to agree. He stood to take his leave of Eleanor, their meeting over. "Thank you, Ellie, and thank Gabriel for me. Keep me informed, as best you can."

***

Eleanor headed for Gabriel's office as soon as she returned home, finding both Gabriel and Benjamin in there. "Six months we've got," she told them. "Six months while he decides what to do."

For a few minutes they discussed the detail of what Lord Leon had said. "He wanted to see her," Eleanor said at the end. "I wish we were able to let him."

Gabriel looked at her with sympathy in his eyes. "I'm sorry, Ellie. I wish he could meet her too, but it just can't be done. I'm doing everything I can to protect her but that would just be too risky."

"I know," she agreed. "I just wish it was different, that's all."

Benjamin glanced at Ellie for a moment before turning back

to Gabriel. "We've been looking at the records from the Shield over Prospero and Leonie's rooms," he said. "And they're not what I was expecting."

He laid the records in front of Eleanor and Gabriel. They showed peaks of intense energy, which weren't hard to match to a likely pattern of sexual activity. But the energy hadn't needed to be contained by the Shield; far from broadcasting it was turned inward, intense and powerful but over a very narrow range.

Eleanor understood the record traces instantly and burst out laughing. "I don't suppose anyone has ever used a Shield to monitor the Traders," she said. "It makes sense if you think about it. You wouldn't want a Trader couple broadcasting, not in such close quarters. I guess Leonie knows what she's doing. We didn't need to worry, did we?"

Benjamin looked at her blankly and then raised his eyebrows in surprise as Gabriel snickered slightly. She took pity on him and decided to explain.

"Trader women use their Gifts to enhance sexual pleasure for their partner and themselves," Eleanor said. "Clearly it uses the energy generated during sex so they don't broadcast."

Benjamin raised his eyebrows even higher. "Well, that would make a very interesting research topic," was all he found to say.

"There's also the tracker that's implanted in Leonie. Do we still leave that?" he asked clearly looking for a safer subject. "I don't understand why anyone would implant an expensive tracker and then leave the child as a slave."

"We leave it," Gabriel confirmed. "I think we have to accept this is the work of more than one person or group. We know there are some who want Leonie dead because of her father, and some who want her alive because of her mother. There's someone – whoever substituted the other child – who knew she was alive but wanted everyone to think she was dead. And there's someone – whoever placed the tracker – who wants her alive and wants to know where she is but either doesn't care that it's here or is already out of the picture. I think there's a clue in what Leon told Ellie – that Augusta had just turned twenty one."

Eleanor looked at him blankly, not understanding what he meant.

"Assassins," Gabriel said. "In my opinion there are Assassins involved in this."

"I thought they were just a myth," Benjamin said, voicing Eleanor's own thought.

"No, they're very real," Gabriel replied and went on to explain what he knew. "They're nomads," he said. "For sale to anyone who can afford to hire them to kill someone. Only when it comes to children, things get a bit complicated."

"They'll take money to kill children?" Eleanor was aghast.

Gabriel shook his head. "Not exactly. They'll accept a contract, but they won't carry it out until the child is over twenty one. If the child dies of natural causes before that, they still expect to be paid. But if someone else kills that child before they reach twenty one, the Assassins don't get paid. So they guard their intended victims closely – secretly and unobtrusively but very jealously."

"Hang on," said Benjamin. "Doesn't that mean those kids would be really well protected? At least until they're twenty one?"

Gabriel nodded. "Absolutely. Some High Lords even do that deliberately to protect their offspring. But it's a gamble. Only the person who made the contract can cancel it, and it will cost twice the original price to do so. If a High Lord can't cancel the contract in time..."

"So, what do we do?"

Gabriel sighed. "The first option is to find whoever took the contract out – if there is one – and persuade them to cancel it. If we can't do that, then we need to find the Assassin who holds the contract and both persuade and pay them to break it. Which will cost a fortune, although I'd happily pay it. On the plus side, at least we have nearly three years to do so. And in the meantime, they are likely to protect her as much as we can."

Eleanor was still puzzled. "If they don't kill children, what about the body of the child that was found with Augusta?"

"That wouldn't have been Assassins," Gabriel said. "Whoever did that must – like Lord Leon – have thought that Leonie would be safer if everyone thought she was dead. And they must have had access to the body of a child that would not be missed and yet could be mistaken for Leonie."

"So, who would want her alive?" asked Eleanor.

"No," said Benjamin, "that can wait. Right now we need to be thinking about who wants her dead. If Gabriel is wrong, that's who we have to protect her from and if he's right, that's who we'll need to negotiate with to cancel the contract."

"That's pretty easy," Eleanor retorted. "Some of House Lindum and some of House Chisholm for one reason or another. Plus anyone who thinks they could curry favour with either House by removing a potential problem. But, if Gabriel's vision has her dying anyway in the next few months, Assassins aren't relevant, are they?"

"I don't know why or how she dies, or whether the vision will happen or change," Gabriel said. "Or whether it's to do with her heritage, or totally unrelated. We need to plan and act for all eventualities."

"And what about Chisholm?" Eleanor asked. "Do we need to contact him? She could be his heir too?"

"No, I think not," Gabriel replied. "She's not a direct heir, merely an option for him and he keeps a close eye on his descendants. I wouldn't put it past him to have placed her as a slave orphan to get rid of her without the guilt of killing her. And the tracker could be him too, so that if she survives he can find her and use her."

"Wouldn't he have wanted to keep her? He could use her to claim House Lindum."

"She's a double-edged sword. Lindum could use her to claim House Chisholm. William of Chisholm is pretty cautious."

Benjamin summed it up, "So basically, anyone in Lindum or Chisholm might want her dead or alive, depending on their particular outlook and loyalties? Nothing like narrowing it down, is there? How do we move on from here?"

"I'm going to speak to Tobias and Leah," decided Gabriel. "See if the Trader network can find anything out for us. In the meantime, if you have any contacts that might be helpful, see if you can make discreet enquiries."

"There's something else, too," said Benjamin. "I'm concerned about the impact on Prospero of what is happening and what may happen. I don't think he's dealing very well with some of the changes."

Gabriel looked surprisingly unconcerned as he replied, "We've already said we'll deal with the impact of Leonie's death on him when, and if, it happens."

Benjamin shook his head. "It's not that. I think he's struggling with leaving the Order, with losing the framework it puts on his life. I think he's coping fine with being married, it's the loss of the pattern of the last years that's the problem."

"I suppose he has attended at least one service almost every day since," Gabriel conceded.

"Exactly."

"Well, you can't expect me to discourage someone from participating in worship, surely?"

"No..." said Benjamin. "I just think in this case it may be a symptom that he's not adjusting as well as we could hope. I wonder whether staying in the same environment wasn't the right thing for him after all, whether a complete change would make it easier?"

"Perhaps when they visit his family in July, that'll help?" Eleanor asked.

Gabriel touched her hand. "I don't think they are going to make it that far, Ellie. Everything is getting closer and closer. The crisis is soon," he said in a quiet voice. "Maybe even before the end of June."

Eleanor looked at him in horror. "Really? So soon?"

He nodded.

"Even so, I'd like to do something," Benjamin said. "There's a medical conference coming up at the beginning of June for a few days. If we sent Prospero as our delegate, even sent Leonie with him, gave them a few days extra away together, either before or after the conference, it might just help break the cycle?"

Eleanor agreed enthusiastically, thinking that at least it was another good experience they could give the couple. Gabriel just shrugged but gave in to her wishes.

Chapter 23

May

Leonie

I took Perry's hand, leading the way as we walked through the woods to one side of the town. I'd decided it was time I took him to meet the nestlings that I'd been providing for. It was another beautiful day, the sun breaking through the branches and dappling the ground with shadow, but I was too concerned to really appreciate it.

"You're not to come all the way with me," I told Perry. "They trust me now but any other adult will scare them off. I'm surprised they even agreed to come and meet you. They'll never trust me again if I lead you to their nest."

I pulled him to a halt in a clearing not far from the nest. "You sit here," I said. "Stay still and wait for them to come to you. Don't move towards them, let them do it all."

"I do know what to do," he said, his usual over-confident self, so I wasn't at all certain that he would sit still.

I headed in the wrong direction for the nest and doubled back on myself.

Han and Att – the closest to leaders that the group had – were waiting and came straight up to me. "Whatcha got today, Lee?" they asked, hands searching for my pockets.

"I've left it with Perry," I said. "Remember, today we're going to meet Perry?"

Han nodded. "Peh-Ree," she said, sounding out the syllables, rolling them round her tongue. "Perry." She looked up at me. "Safe? Not scary?"

I grinned back. "Safe. Not at all scary."

Att nudged me. "Perry has food?" he asked.

"Yes," I confirmed.

"Okay," Att said. He was always curious about everything, and Han wasn't much different, so they followed me back to the clearing. All the younger ones trailed along behind trying to decide whether they were also brave enough to do this.

We stopped at the edge of the clearing, still in the shelter of the trees. Perry hadn't moved and the food and clothes were enticingly set out beside him. I looked down at Han and Att. "Still want to do this?"

They nodded and took my hands, one on each side. Step by step we walked across the clearing to Perry. The little ones stayed in the trees, ready to run when things went wrong.

But things didn't go wrong. Att let go of my hand, sat down and picked up some of the food. Han took a moment longer but then she followed suit. Perry was doing exactly what I'd told him to, so I sat down myself. I felt a warm breath and little hands on my back. Eth tucked his head under my arm, Dan pushing in beside him and then Aim squeezed in between me and Han. Eth was looking longingly at some bread, but Perry was between him and it. Before I could do anything, he scrambled out from under my arm, climbed across Perry and grabbed the bread. Then he settled down on Perry's lap to eat it. Dan followed him – she always did exactly what Eth did. Their spots under my arm were filled by Zac and Tre, and soon all the nestlings had joined us. I could feel Perry radiating calm and reassurance, of course, which the children would be affected by without knowing but I hadn't expected it to be that effective.

Some of them started talking to him, and Zac asked him if

he was the angel. There was nothing I could do; I hadn't told Perry about the angel because I hadn't expected it to be mentioned. The angel was a story that spread among nestlings as they moved from group to group; I'd known it myself as a child. It was a mythical creature that brought food and warmth and safety and family, all the things any nestling dreamed of, but it wasn't real. Perry smiled at Zac and denied it.

"No, I'm not the angel," he said, and I relaxed for a moment until he continued, "But I know where the angel's house is."

The nestlings – even the shyest ones – were all over Perry in a moment pressing him for details.

"Perry," I said telepathically. *"It's not real. Don't lead them on."*

"Yes, it is," he replied, sure he was right as always. *"Trust me."*

I didn't really have any choice, but I fumed quietly as he started to answer all the nestling's questions and tell them about the angel's house. Only, the more he spoke the more I got involved listening to what he described. The nestlings were entranced, because it was just what they dreamed of, and I supposed it wasn't that long since I was one of them, dreaming of just the same things. For me, Perry clinched it right at the end.

"It's called Taylor House," he said. "Like the Angel Taylor."

That was the angel's name, but none of us had told him, so he had to know from somewhere else. What the nestlings wanted to know next was whether he would take them there.

"It's a long way," he said. "Several hours, maybe more, with a horse and cart. I could find one of the people who live there and get them to come and fetch you, but it will be a couple of days before they get here."

The nestlings were eager, of course, so we agreed that we'd meet them again the next day to tell them what would happen and when. I waited until we were well out of earshot on our way back before I turned on Perry.

"Angel. Taylor House. Tell me!" I demanded.

He grinned at me, smugness written all over his face. "You're generating energy," he pointed out.

I should think I was, with frustration, and if he wasn't careful I was going to aim it all at him. Perry could be many things, but he wasn't stupid. He knew what I would do.

"Okay, okay," he said. "I'll tell you everything. Just breathe slowly and calm down a little."

He slipped his arms round me and oozed calmness, touching my mind with his and absorbing and dissipating the excess energy. Although he acted calm, I knew he worried when I got overexcited like this, afraid it would lead to nightmares beyond his ability to control. But I did find it easier to be calm when he was holding me close and he clearly wasn't going to tell me anything until I was calm, so I breathed slowly and deeply as instructed and he started explaining.

"It's a rescue home for children in need – usually ex slaves, refugees or runaways. It's based between House Lindum and House St Peter but it rescues children from wherever it can. Every medic, monk and nun from St Peter's works there for at least six months as part of their training."

"So you've been there?" I asked Perry, somewhat in awe.

"Yes," he confirmed. "A couple of times. I've spent well over a year there in total."

No wonder he knew how to approach the nestlings. I almost asked him why he hadn't told me before, but there was something I wanted to know more. "And the angel? Is the angel real then?"

He grinned with amusement and shook his head. "No, I guess not. Unless you think Lord James is the angel, perhaps. He set up Taylor House. The stories about the angel started spreading maybe seven or eight years ago. I don't know where they started but they make things a lot easier."

"I dreamt I saw the angel once," I said slowly. It was such a distant, vague memory. "He gave me food."

"Did you?" Perry smiled indulgently. "I wish Taylor House or the angel had been there to find you. I hate to think of you as one of those nestlings, lost and cold and hungry."

His hands were in my hair now and he bent his face to mine and kissed me. We both needed a little distraction from these revelations and where we were was very quiet and private, so we took advantage of it.

***

Perry

Perry led his horse out of the stable, mounted and looked down at Andrew. "Keep an eye on Leonie while I'm away, won't you?" he asked.

"Of course," Andrew agreed. "I don't know why she isn't going with you anyway."

Perry shrugged. "I wanted her to. Meeting Lord James and collecting these nestlings and taking them to Taylor House – I'm sure her being there would make it easier. But Gabriel said no and he wouldn't change his mind whatever I said."

Or whatever Leonie had said, although most of Leonie's views had been expressed to Perry rather than Lord Gabriel. She was still a little in awe of him.

"And what if she has a nightmare?" Andrew asked.

Perry grinned. "Gabriel said you'd cope."

Andrew made a noise of disbelief and patted Perry's horse on the neck. "Be off with you then," he said. "Have a good trip."

Although he missed being with Leonie almost as soon as he left the campus, he enjoyed the outing. The weather was pleasant and he rode across beautiful countryside, the sun on his back and a slight breeze in his hair. It wasn't long before he met up with Lord James who was driving two horses pulling a small waggon. Perry tied his horse to the back of James' cart and joined James on the driving seat.

There was quite an age gap between them – Lord James being older by ten or twelve years – but the two had struck up a firm friendship during Perry's visits to Taylor House. In many ways they had similar backgrounds and a number of common acquaintances. As youngest son of a High Lord, although he had no chance of inheriting, Lord James had been brought up as part of the ruling family of a Great House. Perry too, had grown up in and around a Great House after his uncle had picked him as a potential heir.

James grinned at Perry. "So what are you now? Monk or married man?" He nudged Perry with his elbow. "Had enough of celibacy had you?" He laughed. "Or are you bored with the quiet life and ready to upset your uncle again? Spread scandal and gossip across the Great Houses once more?"

"Good to see you too," Perry replied, returning the nudge with a friendly push.

"Seriously," James said. "I saw you, what eight months ago, and there was no hint of this then."

"Eight months ago I hadn't even met her. I only found her just before Christmas," Perry confessed.

"So you met her, courted her, left the Order and married her in less than five months? There's got to be a good story behind that. There's any number of rumours going round."

"Are there?" Perry was both interested and amused. "Like what?"

"Well, most have you seducing her, or making her pregnant or compromising her in some way and then Lord Gabriel or her family or even Lord Neville insisting you marry her. One or two vary that with her trapping you into marriage. There's some that say she's an heiress and either Lord Gabriel or Lord Neville or both have had you marry her to get their hands on her fortune. There's even one that says she's seriously ill, and that when she dies Gabriel will snaffle her fortune and you'll go back to the monastery."

Perry laughed. "I didn't seduce her, she's not pregnant, she didn't trap me, she's not an heiress, she's not sick, and she's got no family and no fortune. Does that cover it all?"

James grinned back in return. "Yes, I think so. In that case, what happened?"

"I fell in love with her, and she with me. We didn't want to be apart. That simple."

"Really? Why so quick then?"

Perry shrugged. "We didn't want to wait. But mostly it was Lord Gabriel. He felt a long delay would be unsettling and disruptive to the House. And Leonie's very Gifted and was having terrible nightmares. He thought being married would ease them, which it has."

"How old is she then? If she's still having nightmares?"

"She's eighteen."

"Only eighteen? And Lord Gabriel still rushed you into marriage?" James was surprised. "That doesn't sound like him at all. Are you sure there's no ulterior motive?"

"None that I know of, though you can never be quite sure with Gabriel. But I wasn't going to argue against him."

"And what did Lord Neville say? He does know, right?"

"He knows. I don't think he cares. I understand his words were 'He can marry who he chooses'," Perry said dryly.

"But you're still one of his heirs?"

"If I return to his territory, yes. The only concession Lord Gabriel got was that he will put both Lilyrose and Brin before me."

James raised his eyebrows. "That's actually quite a concession. Everyone knew you were his first choice. Will you return?"

Perry sighed. "Yes, we'll go back. I want to see my parents and brothers and I want to take Leonie to meet them. Gabriel has suggested we take the next quarter session out, July to September, to go and visit, make a thing of it. And Leonie wants to go, so I guess we will."

It was James' turn to laugh. "Hen pecked already, are you?"

Perry grinned at him, acknowledging the teasing.

"Go on, then," said James. "You've got a picture of her,

haven't you? Let me see."

Perry prevaricated for a few moments, but it wasn't long before he fished in his pocket and handed over a copy of his favourite picture of Leonie, taken just after their wedding. They had reached the nestlings' clearing and Lord James brought the horses to a halt before looking at the photo.

"Ah," he said slowly. He studied it for a while before speaking again. "She's very, very beautiful, isn't she?" he said, handing the picture back.

"You'll not get me to argue against that," Perry agreed. "Although getting her to believe it is a different matter altogether." He glanced around the clearing. "Look, there are nestlings hiding in the trees. You wait here and I'll see if I can get them to come to me."

He climbed out of the cart and sat quietly in the middle of the clearing, waiting for the children to summon up the courage to come to him. He didn't have to wait long; soon they were surrounding him, asking him about the horses and the waggon and whether James was the angel. Cautiously, James came to join them, bringing food.

Once the children had eaten their fill, the two men encouraged them to explore the waggon and introduced them to the horses. They didn't set off on the return journey until all the children were happy and comfortable and content to come with them. As well as food and clothes and blankets, the waggon contained small toys and books to keep the children amused and for a while Perry drove while James read to the children. They discovered that Han and Att could both read – that shouldn't have come as a surprise, Perry thought, given how much Leonie liked books. She was bound to have shared that with them. After that, he rode alongside, giving the children turns at riding with him, whilst James drove and Han read out loud.

It was a long journey, as Perry had told the children. They stopped to eat, and some of the children dozed from time to time, lulled by the rhythm of the waggon as they journeyed. Perry and James didn't have a chance to continue their conversation until long after they had arrived at Taylor House and the children had been fed and washed and settled in to sleep, together for now. Before they too went to sleep, Perry and James took a well-earned break, relaxing with a drink in one of the comfortable lounges.

"Is she happy, then, your Leonie?" James asked.

Perry thought that a slightly strange question, but he answered it in the context of her past, thinking of the children they had rescued that day, and forgetting that James knew nothing of Leonie's history. "Yes," he said simply. "Very happy. So am I."

James smiled at that. "So, how did you come across her in a monastery? Where did she come from?"

"She was masquerading as a male student. Only she had a nightmare and we found her out, and discovered just how Gifted she was. Gabriel made her his ward and after that she and I got rather thrown together as I was involved in managing her nightmares and things just developed from there."

"And before that?"

"Before that, as a small child she was brought up by an aunt. When the aunt died, she ended up in an orphanage, in one of the Houses where they treat the children as slaves. I don't know which House. She ran away and became a nestling, like these, but she got hunted." Perry's voice turned hard as he mentioned that, and the pain and anger he felt on Leonie's behalf surged up, a hot ache in his chest until he got it under control. "They chased her straight into a Trader caravan, and the Traders rescued her. She stayed with them for years and then with Settlers in the town until she came to the college."

James listened, rubbing his chin. "So you know nothing of her parentage then?"

Perry shook his head. "Nothing. Except she's obviously of Chisholm descent." Belatedly, he added, "Sorry." remembering the adversarial relationship and recent history between Chisholm and Lord James' House, Lindum.

To his surprise James laughed. "Don't worry. I'm not as anti-Chisholm as the rest of my family. At least they look after their orphans properly, which is more than can be said for a number of others. I'm just sorry we weren't there for your Leonie."

"Chances are she was in one of the Houses you can't get access to. How are you progressing with those by the way?"

Although Leonie was one of his favourite topics of conversation, one he could talk about all night, Perry was starting to feel a little uneasy about this conversation. There was something nagging at the back of his mind, something crucial that he should know but couldn't remember. It wouldn't come to him, and given that James could talk all night on the shortcomings of those Houses that didn't treat their orphans properly, the conversation took a different turn.

**

Perry spent the whole of the next day dealing with the medical needs of the children, both the ones they had just brought in and ones already living at Taylor House. It wasn't until the morning after that, as Perry was about to set off on the ride home that the subject of Leonie came up again.

"Take care of that wife of yours," James said by way of goodbye.

"Don't worry, I will," Perry replied.

"Next time bring her along. I've got a wedding gift for you. Well, mostly for her. It's back home at the moment, but I'll bring it next time I know we're going to meet."

Perry smiled his thanks, waved goodbye again to the children and set off, eager to be heading back towards Leonie. A single rider tended to move faster than a waggon, and by mid-afternoon he was within just a few miles of the Abbey. He started to look for Leonie with his mind, eager to reassure himself that she'd been fine and then had to laugh as he spotted her much closer than the campus, less than a mile away, clearly coming to meet him. He found a small, sheltered clearing just off the track, tethered his horse and then spread the blanket from his pack on the ground. Knowing that Leonie was now just a few minutes away, he sat down facing the direction she was coming from and waited.

She dropped from a tree, landing on the blanket in front of him, making him jump. He grabbed at her, reaching out with both arms and she tumbled laughing into him. He twisted her round so their lips met and kissed her hungrily. She responded, sitting astride him, stroking her hands into his hair, her mind claiming his. He ran his hands down her back, then up under her shirt, eager for the silken touch of her skin, for what that would lead to.

Chapter 24

Late May

Perry

Perry sat on a chair outside Benjamin's office, waiting for Leonie. Benjamin had insisted on another examination to see how Leonie was progressing and, again, Perry had not been allowed to join them. This time, he didn't mind. Leonie had blossomed since their marriage both physically and emotionally. She looked as well as Perry had ever seen her, putting on weight and her skin and eyes glowing with health. She was far more confident and clearly felt accepted and secure. He wasn't worried about her, or the results of any tests, not with all his own senses telling him she was fine.

He leaned back in the chair, tipping his head back and closing his eyes as he thought about what his life had become. He had his work which he enjoyed, his faith which fulfilled him, he was surrounded by friends and, best of all, he had Leonie in whom he delighted. He was looking forward to the years to come with a bright hope. His almost daily attendance at services perhaps contained an element of reluctance to step back from something that had been such a large part of his life for many years. Mostly it was the only way he could find to express his joy and his thanks to God for what his life had become now. He opened his eyes at the sound of the office door opening. Benjamin stood there, smiling at him. "You can come in now," he said.

Perry took the seat next to Leonie and she reached for his hand, giving him a shy smile.

Benjamin sat down behind his desk. "Everything's fine with Leonie," he said. "Excellent progress, good health, no worries. Keep up with what you're doing."

He looked down, searching for a paper. Perry felt the warmth of Leonie's blush.

"You have a one track mind," he told her. *"That's not what he meant. But I'm up for it anyway."*

That made the blush deepen, but it had faded by the time Benjamin looked up at them. He passed over some papers. "We're sending you to this conference at the beginning of next month. Leonie, you can go too. You can take a bit of extra time, before and after to enjoy yourselves."

Benjamin went on to tell them about the arrangements that had been made before Perry and Leonie left his office, heading for the main reception where Perry was supposed to be on clinic duty.

They stopped by the main desk to say goodbye. Leonie reached up and kissed Perry's cheek and then went dancing off out of the entrance hall heading back to the college area for her next class. She bent down beside a small boy who had just dropped his toy, picking it up and handing it back to him with a smile but barely breaking her stride. Perry watched her until she'd left the building, dancing, happy, and by herself, no longer afraid, he realised. Smiling to himself he looked down at the chart in his hand to call his first patient. It turned out to be the small boy who had also been watching Leonie leave.

"Is she your girl?" the boy asked him.

Perry grinned back at him. "She's my wife."

The boy peppered him with questions as they found a consultation room – "Why was she here? Why didn't she stay? Where's she going?" – despite his mother trying to quiet him.

"It's fine," Perry said to the mother, not minding at all. "She was here because we've just been to see her doctor. Now she's left because I've got my work to do here with you, and she's gone back to her classes."

"But she's a grown up," said the boy, somewhat indignantly. "She shouldn't have to go to school."

Perry couldn't help but be amused by him. "How old are you?" he asked. "Seven?"

The boy nodded.

Perry carried on, "When Leonie was seven she didn't have parents to look after her and she didn't get to go to school then. So now she's catching up on everything she missed."

The mother nudged her son. "See, Jemmy," she said. "You have to work hard at school or you'll still be going when you're grown up."

Jemmy subsided, but his mother looked up at Perry. "That was Leonie, then. You're the one who married her."

Perry was unable to keep the proud smile off his face. "Yes. Do you know her?"

The mother shook her head. "I've heard of her. I've not met her myself though I have friends she's helped. She should be here with you. I've heard she's a very good healer."

"She certainly knows a lot more about medicinal herbs than I do," Perry conceded. "But I think she wants to concentrate on her studies first and then decide about the future." He decided to ask her about it that evening.

***

He sat in the armchair in their bedroom reading, or at least pretending to read while he watched Leonie. She was wandering round the bedroom, tidying up, putting things away and getting ready for bed.

"Have you worked with healers, before?" he asked. "With the Traders, perhaps?"

She came and perched on the arm of the chair. "Lots," she said. "I was Katya's apprentice."

He listened, enthralled and impressed as she told him all about her experiences. Trader women were the healers of their tribe and Traders were a tough and healthy people. Leonie had learned what any other Trader girl would learn to deal with accidents and injuries, childhood fevers and childbirth. But Leonie had been apprenticed to a Headwoman, one of the longest serving and most revered across the caravans. Headwomen dealt with the more complex health issues, the more serious injuries, the most difficult births, and Katya even more than most. Leonie was in the strange position of having more experience with complex and serious issues than with simple ones. Even after she'd come to join the local Settlers, she had used her knowledge and experience to help those in the community, again often with more complicated situations.

"Do you want to work in medicine longer term?" he asked her.

She shrugged. "I don't know. I never thought about the future like that. Mostly all I was aiming for was to stay alive. Make the most of today and not worry too much about tomorrow."

"You must have planned ahead to come here?"

"I guess. Even here all I wanted was to learn how to control my gifts. I wasn't looking further ahead than that." She hesitated. "What I would like to do is help others like me. Like those nestlings. Rescue them like the Traders rescued me."

He smiled at that – so like Leonie to want to help those worse off than herself – and he pulled her down onto his lap.

"Suppose we work out which courses and modules the college offers that would help you do that? Then we can plan what you can study and when, after we get back from visiting my family?"

She wriggled deeper into his arms, as if she couldn't get close enough to him. "I never thought I'd be able to plan that far ahead," she whispered.

He stroked her face gently, trailing his fingers down her neck and along the bare skin of her arm. The limitations by which she'd been forced to live tore at him once again, but right now, with her body so close to his, so inviting and responsive, he was distracted by other things.

Early June

Leonie

I heard the door open and then shut as Perry came back into our apartment one afternoon, head bent over some papers as he walked into the living room. He raised his head to look at me, waving the papers. "These are all about that conference we're going on," he said.

I took the papers off him and spread them out on the table. "Look, it's in House Eastern. How do we get there?"

"There's train tickets in there somewhere and details of where we're staying. Chloe's organised it all," Perry told me. "And she's booked theatre tickets for the night after and found somewhere we can go dancing."

"I love dancing," I said, trying to take it all in.

Perry stood behind me, putting his arms round me. "I'm just worried you'll be bored while I'm doing the conference bit," he said.

"I won't, I really won't," I replied. "I'm going shopping. Edward's given me a list of stuff he wants me to get – there's some lace specialist there. And I'm going to find the Settler and Trader area and see if there's anyone I know."

I was really looking forward to that bit. Even though I was an Outsider I'd still be welcome, my Trader bracelet showing my identity. The Gathering was happening later this summer so every Settler group and Trader caravan would be humming with the latest news. The Gathering happened every five years, with caravans from all over the world meeting together in one place for a few weeks. I'd been once, not long after I'd joined the Traders. It had been a hubbub of colour and noise and excitement. That time I'd still been scared of everything and had only ventured out into the crowds a little, mostly hiding in, or on, or under Katya's waggon. Five years later I was sorry I wouldn't be going but I would enjoy hearing all their plans.

"Why are you doing Edward's shopping?" Perry asked, his voice suggesting he wasn't particularly bothered. He reached forward to shuffle through some of the papers.

"He's going to make me some stuff in return, and he gave me buttons to replace the ones on my wedding dress..." The way he'd raised his eyebrows at me had made me blush from head to toe, but he'd found me the buttons anyway and handed them over with a grin.

Perry wasn't listening. He'd picked up one sheet of paper and was staring at it.

I nudged him. "What is it?"

"It's the delegate list for the conference," he said as his finger highlighted one name.

"Dr Lesley Walters," I read, then looked up at him. "Is that your Lesley?"

He nodded. "I'm not sure I want to go now," he said. "But Andrew would say it was an opportunity to meet her and apologise and try and make things right."

"Andrew would be right," I told him. "Better to sort it than avoid it." I wanted to meet Lesley; she'd clearly had such an influence on Perry in the past which had affected his whole life. I wanted to see what she was like, what sort of a person she was. She'd obviously (well obviously to me anyway) loved him deeply so we already had that in common.

Perry frowned, looking doubtful. "Well, maybe," was all he would concede. But we went on preparing to go.

***

The night before we were due to leave I felt the nightmare starting. Unusually, I woke up immediately, but then realised I could still feel the power curling around me. It took me several moments to realise that it was Perry's nightmare I could feel, and I didn't know what to do. Instinctively, I reached for him to wake him, shaking him gently with my hands, and twisting my mind into his. He sat up suddenly, his eyes open but clouded. Until he spoke I wasn't even sure he was awake.

"What is it?" he asked. "What's the matter?" Then, as he felt the power in the room, "Is it a nightmare?"

I nodded. "But it's not my nightmare, Perry," I said.

He looked bewildered. "It was me? It was, wasn't it? It was me."

I wrapped my arms round him, holding him as he'd done for me so many times. "It's okay, nothing happened, it barely got started."

He moved round to sit on the edge of the bed, shaking his head, still confused. "It's been so long..."

I decided we both needed a hot drink to settle us, and he followed me through to the kitchen. As I was making them there was a knock on the door.

"That'll be the watch team," Perry said. "It'll have shown on the monitors and they'll think it was you and come to check we're okay."

He went to answer the door; I could hear there were several people there but not what they were saying. After a moment or two Andrew came through to the kitchen so I made a drink for him too. At least it was Andrew who'd stayed, I thought with relief; I figured Perry would be most open with him, and – possibly – agree to Andrew examining him.

Andrew seemed fairly unconcerned about what had happened and unsurprised that I'd stopped the nightmare. I said that I hadn't known what to do, but they both said I'd done the right thing – damp down the power as much as possible, try and wake the person affected, and wait for the watch team. Andrew did manage to check Perry's pulse and temperature, and then asked him if he wanted anything to help him sleep again. He shook his head, but I muttered that he'd make me take it, if it were me.

"That's different," Andrew said. "Your Gifts haven't stabilised yet. Perry's have and this was only minor."

Perry looked at me, his eyes full of concern. "You'd worry less and sleep better if I took it, wouldn't you?" he asked.

I nodded, knowing I was going to worry about him anyway.

"Okay, then," he decided. "But just a half dose, okay?"

Andrew insisted he went back to bed before taking it, and he didn't argue, which was a little worrying in itself. I sat beside him while he took it but when I started to get up to see Andrew out, Perry held onto my wrist.

"Don't go," he whispered so I stayed and let Andrew find his own way out.

Perry pulled me into bed beside him, sliding one arm under my shoulders and the other round me to hold me close. He was almost asleep already as he rested his cheek on my head and settled himself comfortably.

"Don't ever leave me," he said quietly. "I couldn't cope without you."

He was definitely asleep before I could answer. It took me longer to fall asleep again. I was worried about why he'd started having a nightmare again after so long. Andrew had told me some time ago that Perry's last major nightmare had been shortly after he'd discovered that Lesley had married. Now he'd had one – nearly, anyway – just a day or so before he would meet her again. I couldn't help but think there had to be a connection. I knew he had to meet up with her, that there were things he needed to resolve. I knew that she was in the past and that he loved me. And I wanted to meet her. But now it was getting closer, I was afraid of how he might feel when he met her again, that there might still be something between them, that he might come to think of me as a mistake. I knew if I told him he'd reassure me, tell me not to be so silly, tell me all the things I could tell myself but that didn't stop me fretting over it.

What did help was the even rhythm of his breathing, the warmth of his body next to mine, the security of his arms around me. Despite my worries it wasn't long before sleep overcame me, too.

Perry seemed fine the next day, a little fidgety perhaps, but okay. We attended the morning service which calmed him – actually it calmed me too. I felt a lot less apprehensive about everything afterwards. By the time we'd had lunch, finished packing and made our way to the station, I was definitely excited, though once I saw the train I was totally in awe of the sheer size of it. I'd seen them before, but not this close and I'd never realised they were quite so big.

While we were waiting to board the train, and I was sitting close to Perry and therefore feeling brave, I confessed to him. "I thought about using the train to get away from you, back at Easter."

He grinned smugly at me. "You'd never have got away with it."

"You can't see me that far," I protested.

"I can see you a long way," he insisted, slipping his arm round me and pulling me close. "But that's not what I meant. You need paperwork to cross into another House, and you wouldn't have had it."

"I've travelled across no end of Houses with the Traders," I said, feeling rather puzzled.

"Traders are different," he said. "A High Lord is responsible for those who live on their land. If he or she allows more people onto the land than the land can feed, they're in trouble, so they control the border crossings. But everyone knows Traders take care of their own, and bring economic benefits, so they travel freely. They're never going to be a burden, quite the opposite." He looked to see if I was taking this in, and then carried on, "House St Peter takes in anyone who needs it, papers or not, but they expect everyone who stays to contribute in whatever way they can. House Eastern's much smaller, so we have papers to promise we're not going to be a burden on them. House Tennant's a Sanctuary House, so that's much like St Peter."

"What's a Sanctuary House?" I asked.

He was well into his stride now. Perry loved teaching as long as his students listened. "Sanctuary Houses are neutral in any war or dispute and often act as mediators. They provide a safe haven to anyone who is running away from anything, whether they are guilty or innocent, and give them a fresh start. Any pursuers who enter the territory will be severely dealt with, but again everyone is expected to contribute to the extent that they can."

I thought about this for a moment. "So what's the catch?"

"Is there always a catch?" he asked quizzically.

I nodded.

He shrugged slightly. "A Sanctuary House doesn't deal with the pursuers. You're still in danger if you leave the territory. If you're escaping injustice you'll be protected, but if you're escaping justice then the moment you break the Sanctuary House's laws, or try to freeload you'll be handed back to where you came from."

I wish I'd known about Sanctuary Houses when I'd been a runaway.

A whistle blew, and Perry stood up. "Time for us to get on board," he said.

He guided me to our seats and sat me down by the window so I could look out. I watched the scenery rolling past; I'd never travelled so fast before. That amused Perry, who clearly had. "When we go to visit my parents," he said, "that train will go quite a lot faster than this. And we'll be travelling overnight, so we'll sleep on that train."

"We'll sleep on it?" I asked him in amazement. "Will it have beds?"

He nodded, smiling. "Yes, it will." Then he leaned over me and breathed in my ear. "And believe it or not, I've never made love on a train."

I twisted towards him, my lips brushing over his, more than ready to remedy that but he pointed out there was no lock on the door to our compartment.

"Wait till we go to House Tennant," he whispered. "There'll be locks then."

I curled happily against him, his arm round my shoulders and went back to watching out of the window. Perry read for a while, at least I think he did; I wasn't sure he turned over many pages. I just enjoyed the view – fields and farms, houses and gardens, forests and roads all sweeping past.

The town we arrived in was very different from the one surrounding our Abbey. House St Peter was a rural and farming society and the population was quite spread out. Transport was generally on foot or horseback or by horse and cart. As we'd got closer to our destination, the houses I'd seen had become more tightly clustered together, interspersed with much larger buildings that Perry said were factories, workshops and shopping centres. I'd even seen powered vehicles buzzing around. Once we got off the train, there seemed to be so many people around, so many buildings and even more powered vehicles weaving between them all. The last time I'd seen such crowds had been at the Trader Gathering. I gripped Perry's hand and followed in his wake.

The hotel had me open mouthed in wonder. It was higher than anything at House St Peter, even taller than the hospital. To one side was a smaller building which Perry said was where his conference would be held. Inside, it was luxurious, opulent even, and I just stopped in my tracks, gawking at it all. I found House St Peter very comfortable, not extravagant but definitely comfortable. This hotel had silk and velvet where we might have cotton and linen and it was all a bit overwhelming. Perry didn't seem discomfited by it; I thought men perhaps didn't notice such things as much. Or perhaps he was more used to it in his past. I asked him about that when we were settled in our room, which was equally opulent. He looked around as if seeing if for the first time, rather confirming my theory about him not noticing.

"I suppose it is rather grand," he said slowly. "And yes, I've stayed in places like this with Lord Neville. Sometimes you have to present a certain appearance for the people you are dealing with to take you seriously."

I could understand that. Traders dressed appropriately to the community they were trading with. Sometimes Merchant Ethan had worn simple, muted clothes, other times he had dressed in brilliant flamboyance. And it fitted with something Lord Gabriel had said to me. He'd said he had a future role for me that required I was used to living in a way that was appropriate for the daughter of a High Lord.

"Is this how a High Lord lives?" I asked Perry.

"Some of them, yes," he said, "and some even more luxurious. But Lord Neville's home and my parents' home are much plainer and simpler, much more like what we have back home." He shrugged. "A bed's just a bed, whatever it's covered with." Then he grinned at me, a wicked light in his eyes. "Care to try this one out?" he asked.

He pulled me into his arms, his lips brushing the edge of my ear and then down my neck, warm and soft, leaving me in no doubt as to what he meant. The touch of his skin on mine, his body against my body sent tingles of anticipation flooding through me. He twisted his mind into mine and I responded. Of course we tried the bed out.

Chapter 25

Monday – Early June

Perry

They started the next morning with the swimming pool. Perry was already vibrating with amusement at the recollection of Leonie's reaction to the news that swimming costumes would be required. He had mentioned it a couple of days ago only to find that Edward had already brought the subject up, and rather more bluntly. Brother Edward might appear quiet and reserved, shy even, but he loved to tease those he cared about, and teasing Leonie was a temptation he couldn't resist.

Apparently, he'd just looked at her and had said straight out, "You won't be able to swim naked, you know."

Leonie's face when she'd recounted this to Perry had been such that he dearly wished he'd been present for the original conversation. Of course, Leonie had never needed clothes for swimming – she'd never swum anywhere but lakes and rivers, and nestlings wouldn't have bothered and Traders were quite comfortable with casual nudity. And as for the times they'd been up to the lake together since they'd been married, those had been very private and there would have been little point to any swimming costume.

Edward had found Leonie a swimming costume and the sight of her in it not only amused Perry but also aroused him. He jumped into the pool sharpish as a result. Leonie stood on the edge for longer, looking down at him, appearing unsure about the whole situation, but she jumped in happily enough when he reached his arms up to encourage her. Once in, she was at home straightaway, relaxed and enjoying it, loving both the main pool and the spa bath beside it. Perry – foolishly with hindsight – challenged her to a race over a couple of lengths and found himself hard pushed to beat her. He was slightly suspicious that she might even have let him win.

He was ready to get out long before she was, so he lay on one of the couches next to the pool, half watching her, half reflecting on the conflicts he was feeling. He knew his nightmare had been generated by his fear of ever losing Leonie; he was afraid it indicated he wasn't coping with life outside the Order as well as he had thought. The private compartment on the train and the luxury of the hotel had flustered him too. They reminded him of times with Lord Neville and he was concerned that he'd taken Leonie to bed yesterday as a distraction even if it had led to a genuine expression of his love for her.

And then there was Lesley. He knew that he owed her an apology and he was still struggling with his guilt over the way he had considered her for so many years. Yet she had also treated him badly and on top of all that he had some very happy memories of their time together. Reconciling all these feelings was beyond him. Lying beside the pool, he spent a few moments in prayer about it all and then decided to concentrate on the delights of today.

He enticed Leonie out of the water with promises of lunch and took her to a friendly little café in the town centre. They spent the afternoon ambling round the shopping area, window shopping. They found the places where Edward had commissioned Leonie to buy lace, and also located the Settler area. Perry knew that Leonie could have found both of these on her own. He just wanted to see for himself where she would be and assure himself that she would be safe. In return, once they were back at the hotel, he showed her round the conference centre so that she could visualise where he would be.

Tuesday

Perry woke first the next morning, a little unsettled still by sleeping in a strange bed. He pulled the sleeping Leonie into his arms, reassuring himself just by holding her.

She opened her eyes. "Perry," she purred, her face alight with happiness.

He responded by running one hand down her back, cupping her bottom and pulling her even closer.

They made love slowly and gently but with a deep passion, luxuriating in each other's body, stroking and kissing, pleasuring each other. Perry didn't want to let go of Leonie, didn't want her to stop touching him.

She nudged him, giggling. "Breakfast will be here in a minute. One of us has got to be able to answer the door."

"They can wait," he mumbled, nuzzling into her neck, tasting her skin and teasing her ear with his tongue. "Besides, I'm just going to eat you. That'll take care of breakfast."

"But I'm hungry," she pleaded just as a knock came at the door. Groaning, Perry rolled out of bed and grabbed a robe before answering the door to room service. Leonie ate breakfast in bed, flushed, dishevelled and naked with a sheet partly wrapped around her. Watching her, Perry could easily have passed on breakfast, conference and indeed anything else just to get back into bed with her. Instead he summoned up all his restraint and self-control to prepare for both the conference and his likely meeting and conversation with Lesley. With even greater reluctance, he left Leonie in their room, still preparing for her day out, and headed towards his duties.

He was looking for Lesley from the moment he entered the conference building, his eyes sweeping from side to side, scanning everyone present. He couldn't concentrate on anything else until he'd spoken to her, apologised and asked her to forgive him. He saw her almost immediately, near the refreshments, standing alone, her back towards him.

He went straight over, touching her arm as he said, "Hello, Lesley."

She turned towards him and shock rippled through him. Lesley was pregnant? How had he not known, not heard? Why keep this child and not his?

"Perry," she said, looking up at him and then following his eyes towards her belly.

He kept his face straight, battling not to let his feelings win. His relationship with Lesley was a long time ago and everything was different now. He had no reason to be jealous. He had Leonie. He should be pleased for Lesley.

"Congratulations," he managed to say. "When are you due? Should you even be here?"

"Two or three weeks," she answered. "This is my last outing. I nearly didn't come when I saw your name on the delegate list."

With that, he understood the impact he'd had on her life, how it had mirrored her impact on him. He let go of his jealousy over the baby with relief. "I'm glad you did come," he said. "I want to tell you how sorry I am about the way I treated you. Can you forgive me?"

"A long time ago," she told him. "I shouldn't have kept it from you. I should have talked to you. Can you forgive me?"

"Also a long time ago," he said with a smile. "But it's only recently I realised how badly I treated you."

"It's okay," she said, shaking her head a little to dismiss the subject. "I thought you'd become a monk." She glanced at his clothing, clearly not that of the Order.

"I did. I left the Order a couple of months ago and got married soon after."

"You, married?" Lesley couldn't keep the surprise from her voice. "Was that to please your family?"

"No, to please myself." He grinned. "And my wife, of course."

"I'd like to meet her."

"She'd like to meet you. In fact, she came with me. Not to the conference, but to stay here. Would you like to meet up with us one evening?"

Leonie

I wandered out of the hotel lobby and ambled down the street, feeling happy and relaxed and sure that I was loved. Had I been trying to stake my claim on Perry when we made love, before he met up with Lesley? No, I was sure I hadn't. Perry loved me and that was that.

I fished in my pocket for Edward's shopping list. The things he'd offered to make for me in return for getting his shopping definitely fell in the category of things monks shouldn't be expected to know about. Perry was going to enjoy them, though. A lot. And so was I. My mind drifted off in anticipation and my skin started to heat.

There was a noise behind me, so loud all other sounds were drowned out. Wind gusted around me, tearing at my hair and clothes, dust obscuring my vision and forcing me to cover my eyes. I turned towards the noise but had to crouch down, head tucked in, wrapping my arms round myself for protection. A building groaned in agony as part of it gave way. Then, for a moment, there was silence.

Sound returned. Alarms, sirens, voices, shouting. Cautiously, I lifted my head, shaking the dust from my hair and eyes, and looked towards the hotel. At first glance nothing seemed wrong. Then the dust settled further. The conference centre had collapsed, roof caved in, crumpled like a discarded sheet of paper.

Where's Perry? Is he safe? Is he hurt?

I reached out with my mind and found him inside the damaged building. He was shocked but unhurt and there was space around him. Without thinking twice, I locked my mind around him and teleported to where he was. I found myself under a table which had protected him, bearing the brunt of the debris that had fallen. Perry was sprawled across a woman, his body protecting her. She saw me before Perry did and her mouth dropped open. I recognised her immediately.

"Hello, Lesley," I said, my voice sounding far calmer than I felt.

Perry twisted towards me at the sound of my voice. "Leonie," he exclaimed. "What the... What happened? What are you doing here?"

Isn't that obvious?

"Something exploded. I came to find you," I told him. "Now, please can we get out of here?"

He looked at me like I was crazy. "Just what exactly did you have in mind for getting out of here?" he asked.

I would have thought that was obvious too. "Teleporting, of course. How do you think I got here?"

"Leonie," he said in a tone which also said I was crazy.

"There are three of us."

I interrupted him, indicating Lesley's bump. "Four, actually."

He brushed that off. "Three, four, either way it will take an incredible amount of energy."

"So we link and do it together," I told him. "Right now you're generating energy, Lesley is, and I'm pretty sure I am. Can't you feel it? And anyway we don't have to go far."

"Can anyone join in this debate?" asked Lesley, from where she was lying, still partly under Perry. Her tone definitely held notes of amusement, no matter how serious the situation was. "Because I'm up for this. I want out of here."

Perry looked from one of us to the other. "I'm outvoted aren't I? You're going to gang up on me?"

He gave in after that although he pointed out all the dangers, especially to the baby. If anything went the slightest bit wrong the child could be fatally ripped from his mother's womb then and there. I refrained from pointing out the dangers of staying where we were. It wouldn't have helped; he knew them anyway.

Lesley and I both mind linked to Perry who managed the actual teleport. I wrapped my mind around Lesley and particularly around the baby, holding him – and her – tight and close with both my mind and my arms. Perry wrapped his arms round both me and Lesley.

"Ready?" he asked.

We nodded. There was a brief moment of disorientation and then we were outside lying on a grassy slope, looking back and slightly down at the damaged building. We all collapsed with relief. I felt Perry in my mind, just checking I was okay before he turned to Lesley to check properly on her and the baby.

I stared at the buildings. The hotel seemed unaffected and pretty stable. The conference centre didn't. I could feel so many people in there, trapped, injured, hurting, scared and dying. And I could feel the building shaking, collapsing, fires and leaks starting. I needed to rescue those people and I didn't know where to start, who to get first, how to find the energy. The only way I could get people out was to teleport them and I didn't even really know how to teleport people safely. I'd only ever moved myself and small inanimate items. Perry felt me searching the building and turned back towards me.

"Leonie, no, you can't do it. You can't get them out. You can't rescue them all." His voice was full of panic.

"I have to try," I told him. "I have to do all I can. I'm sure I've the energy to move at least one more person, but I need you to help. I need you to show me, to make sure I do it right. And to tell me who needs it most."

He shook his head, but he gave in. Our minds linked together, we started to scan the building. That glow meant a man, panicking and in pain.

"Him?" I asked.

"No, he's conscious, his image is bright, strong. He's hurt but he'll keep."

Two women together, more pain, less panic.

"No," Perry said again. *"Look for a faint image, dull, little pain. That means they're unconscious. They'll be the most in need."*

I stretched my mind through the building, scanning,

searching. So many people, so much pain. There was a flicker. I looked closer. *"Here, this one,"* I called to Perry.

"Yes," he said. *"This one. Wrap your mind round him and visualise the ground in front of us. Hold him absolutely still like this. We don't know where he's injured. Ready? Move him."*

A man appeared in front of us, early fifties, hair greying a little at his temples, a little overweight. I'd seen him at our hotel. He was unconscious, his skin white and clammy. Perry bent over him, and Lesley knelt down awkwardly beside him. They worked together, conversing in whispers, a practiced team. Was this how it had been when they'd been an item?

I fretted at my uselessness and tried to search the building again. Perry felt what I was doing and tried to stop me. "Leonie, you can't. Lesley's contacted emergency services. You have to leave it to them."

"There must be more I can do," I pleaded with him. "I can see what needs to be done and I can't do it. I'm helpless and I shouldn't be. I need more energy, more power."

Lesley touched his arm. "That's a power stone, in her necklace," she said quietly to him.

He glanced at her. "No, it's not," he said, quite definite about it.

She clearly didn't believe him, but neither of them said anything more and I didn't know what they were on about.

"Perry," I pleaded again. "What can I do?"

His eyes were unfocused, staring at the ground without seeing it, as if he was deep in thought, undecided about something. Then he raised his head and touched the central stone in my necklace with the tip of his finger. "Do you know what a power stone is?" he asked.

I shook my head impatiently. I needed help, not instruction. We didn't have time for one of his lectures.

"It aids the transfer of energy between people," he told me, regardless. "When you and I share energy, just two of us, that's easy. Even three, like we did just now, isn't too hard but the more people you connect the harder it gets. Power stones aren't jewels, they're constructs that allow many people who are fairly close to one another physically to connect and share energy, all controlled and then used by one person.

"Each person needs a power stone and the stones protect the individual wearer, preventing them from being too drained by it. This, though"—he tapped the jewel again—"this is a master stone. It'll pull energy from anyone wearing a power stone in a matching setting, however far away, from anyone they can connect with, and from any other power stone or master stone it can reach. And it can reach a long way. It's not a continual connection but once it's drawn that first burst of energy it's almost self-replicating, almost inexhaustible. If you can access it and control that energy, you can use it."

I only needed to know one thing. "How do I access it?"

He didn't answer straight away, but looked at me, his eyes dark and sober. "First, you have to know there'll be a price for using the stone. It doesn't come cheap. Master stones are greedy. Power stones protect their users but this won't protect you."

There was always a price for doing something, but when I looked at his face – pale and drawn – and Lesley's face over his shoulder, eyes wide, shocked and silent, I realised what this price would be. Now I knew why he hadn't wanted to tell me, and just how much it had cost him to do so. I had no choice, though; I had to use it, just as he had had to tell me about it. I nodded and he accepted that.

"Just touch it with your mind, like we touch minds," he said. "If you can use it, it'll respond."

Hesitantly, I reached out to it, feeling its warmth, and it opened up like a flower in my head. I had a moment to look up at Perry and then the power flooded in. I could taste the touch of Lord Gabriel, see the scent of Settler Leah, hear the colour of Headwoman Katila, and sensed so many other colours and tastes and scents and sounds that I didn't recognise. They swirled around my head, a whirlwind of awareness that threatened to overwhelm me. Then my stones were there, *mine*, two of them, not just the one in my necklace, spinning as a balanced pair, spinning all these sensations into a thread, a cord, a rope of power that I could use. I took hold of it and reached for the building to find and save the trapped. Something touched my hand and I looked down to see it was Perry. I wrapped one strand of the rope around him, a thread connecting us. I could see all his thoughts, his plans, his hopes and worries, his very being laid out like an open book and a strength – a golden thread – running through him that I realised was prayer.

We didn't need words to communicate. The emergency services were on the way – indeed I could feel them approaching. Perry would liaise with them and organise the medical care of the rescued. I couldn't heal with the power, but I could set broken bones or put pressure on bleeding wounds. As my power wrapped around the building, I created a translucent image in front of me, showing the building, the damage, how I was supporting it and where the victims were. Steadily, slowly, carefully, I wrapped cords of power around, into and through the damaged building, holding it up, preventing it collapsing further, smothering fires, and sealing leaking pipes. As I reached victims, I teleported them out and into Perry's care. I assigned a strand from the power rope, a tiny piece of me, to each victim as I rescued them to help with any medical care that I could. This ability to multitask was incredible. One thread, one task – and unlimited threads.

Perry

As Leonie accessed the master stone and all that came with it, Perry pushed the consequences from his mind. The best thing he could do for Leonie now was to make sure her actions counted for as much as possible. Leonie's mind was linked to his which he found comforting. At least they would be together for all the time they had left. Her master stone hadn't drawn energy from him because he wore no stone of any sort. His power stone had been in the cross that he had forfeited when he'd left the Order and he hadn't replaced it yet with something else. In a way, he was grateful; being outside the union gave him more freedom, more options later.

Lesley spoke quietly to him, "You do what you have to do. I'll take care of Leonie. I know what to do."

He nodded, trusting her, and went to liaise with the emergency services, acting as a translator, a connection between them and Leonie. He didn't hesitate to use his rank and position in both House Tennant and House St Peter to achieve what he had to. There would be a reckoning for that and a price to pay but that could come later.

For a moment, just a moment, he knew Lesley's mind was touching his and he felt an overwhelming sense of forgiveness. Automatically, he looked across at her though he was too far away to see her face, and knew that they were at peace with each other.

He couldn't do that much directly as a doctor but he worked in triage, allocating each injured person to the most appropriate available care. Through it all he prayed, constantly, non-stop, for the victims, for the workers, for the perpetrators and for Leonie.

Leonie

Something else was clamouring for my attention, so I diverted another thread to it – Lesley. I wrapped a thread around her as I had Perry and she too was an open book to me. For a fraction of a second I linked the two of them together so each could know, deep in their hearts, that the other had forgiven them for all that had happened in the past. Then I paid attention to what Lesley was trying to tell me. This body, *my body, this frail human body* – for a moment there were two competing views in my head and I didn't know who I was – my body was overheating from all the power. Lesley gave me cool fresh water to drink and poured cold water over me. I left a fraction of my attention with her, doing what she told me, looking after this body.

We talked too, about Perry, about her baby – I could sense him.

"He's going to be such a fine, strong boy," I told her.

"That's good to know. I won't have long with him."

"You know that? I didn't want to tell you."

"Treatment would have harmed him. He deserves his chance to live."

My heart went out to this child who would grow up without a mother. At least he'd have a loving father.

Lesley had loved Perry – she still did, I could see that in her mind, though she tried to keep it from me. She visualised the power differently from me. I saw woven threads, a rope. She saw a flowing river. Perry perceived it as fire, a consuming flame.

As I grew used to this woven rope of power, learning how to use it, how to read it, I realised it was filled with all the knowledge of the original contributors. I wanted to dive into it, wrap it around me, learn all I could, and yet there was too much— I would never have the time to study it all. I roamed around, dipping in and out of all this knowledge. Sometimes I found a thread whose knowledge would enhance or aid that of another totally unconnected thread, a connection that no one else had made or could make. Each time I tried to link those threads together, to reweave the rope so that they touched. I don't know if it made any difference but perhaps they would be able to help each other.

I found that if I thought about a specific subject the threads with knowledge in that area glowed and I could feast on what they knew. There was so much to learn and so little point; one of the things I learnt agreed with what Perry's face had told me earlier. I wasn't going to survive this. And if by some miracle I did, I would forget all this, forfeit my gifts, struggle to cope again with living in the everyday world. I searched for information that might help, and the references led me back to…Lesley.

"The experts say doing this will kill me," I said.

"Yes," she agreed.

"The experts say you are the most expert. That you may know how to beat this."

"I don't know," she said. *"I've been researching for years and I'm still not sure. Physically, it's draining you and overheating your body. I'm trying to keep you cool but that's not really the critical bit. At the end you've got to separate from all the power you're using, break the connection with the master stone. If you try and take control it will fight back and destroy you. Or you let all the energy flow through you and it will take you with it. If you can somehow anchor the bit that is you so the rest flows past you*

and leaves you behind, then maybe you have a chance. That's all I can offer you. I'm sorry."

"Perry," I said to her. "He's my anchor."

She nodded slowly. "That might work," she agreed. "You know that he will try to join the union in your mind? To take your place to protect you? That he has no chance if he does that?"

I did. We planned a solution together. It wasn't ideal. If we pulled it off, Perry was going to be furious with Lesley. If I died, it would take him a very long time to come to terms with it and forgive her – and she really didn't have that long.

"It's okay from my side," she said. "I did something dreadful to him. This is something I can do for him to make up a little. But if he doesn't forgive me, that could destroy him."

I was worried about that, too. "I'll just have to survive," I told her.

I didn't notice the passage of time. My perception of it was askew anyway as I could do so much more, so much faster with all this power. But I came to the point where I could feel no more life in the building. I reached instead for the bodies, those who had died in the explosion, and laid them carefully near Perry. He turned to the first to examine it before realising.

"I couldn't save them," I told him, mind to mind. "I didn't get there soon enough. I let them down."

"You did all you could," he reassured me. "No one could have done more. They would have died instantly."

I moved on to stabilising the ruins, adjusting them, laying them down so they wouldn't collapse further when I withdrew my support. I found experts in the rope of power and learnt what I should do. Bit by bit, I withdrew from the building.

Chapter 26

Perry

It was over. There was nothing useful left to do. Perry stopped and surveyed the scene around him. To a casual observer at a distance Leonie appeared to be standing still, looking across at the now derelict conference centre. To those who looked more closely she was slightly blurred by the power enveloping her, and any adept would have felt the static crackle of the power in the air. Her feet were not touching the ground; instead she hovered about a foot above it. Lesley was close by but they appeared to be ignoring each other.

Perry moved to stand in front of Leonie. Her eyes, on a level with his for once, were glowing green with power but she smiled at him and he knew with relief that she was still there, still herself, not subsumed in the union of energy.

"There's nothing more you can do," he said. "Everyone is out and the building is safe for now. It's time to stop."

She nodded. "I know," and then turned to look at Lesley. "I'm so sorry," she said.

"It's not going to be long, is it?" Lesley responded.

Leonie shook her head, and her eyes dropped to Lesley's belly.

"He's going to be such a fine, strong boy," she said with sadness in her voice that Perry didn't quite understand. She raised her eyes to him again.

"Are you ready?" he asked.

"No," she said peacefully, smiling at him. "I don't think I'll ever be ready. But it's time."

"I love you," he said as he took her hands in his, holding them close and touching his lips to hers.

The power coalesced into ribbons of light which encircled them, twining around their bodies, the energy teasing him, tantalising him with all it could offer, and tormenting him with all it would take. Gradually, they rose into the air, arms stretching out to the sides, still hand in hand, spinning slowly and their bodies becoming ever closer. They kissed, passionate but tender, moulded together as if they could never be separated.

Then Perry heard Lesley shouting his name, both vocally and telepathically, her voice full of urgency and desperation. It gained his attention only for a fleeting second, but that was enough. Leonie used that break to push at his mind, disengaging him from her and the power, making him stagger slightly as he landed next to Lesley.

He turned to her, shouting in bewilderment and anger. "You distracted me! It should be me there! Not her! Me!"

Lesley didn't take her eyes off Leonie as she replied, "You wouldn't survive. She might. Look!"

He turned back towards Leonie who had risen higher in the air and was spinning faster and faster. The ribbons of light were twisting and turning and being absorbed into her body. As the last ribbon disappeared, she curled into a ball, tumbling and spinning in place, end over end. The air around her shimmered and lit up as the power arced from her, earthing in the ground beneath. For a moment Leonie hung motionless in the air and then she began to fall.

Perry leapt towards Leonie. The air seemed like treacle, his legs wouldn't respond, he couldn't get there fast enough. Then he was there, beneath her, reaching for her, she was in his arms and he was using every sense and skill and ability he had to search for that little spark that meant she was still there, still alive. Finding a flicker, finding a spark of hope, he wrapped himself around it, protecting the spark, encouraging it, feeding it with his own life, living for both of them.

Sharing his own life energy, his own will to live, with Leonie to give her a chance at life was dangerous for both of them but it was all he could do. He knew it was strictly regulated both within the church and the medical profession but he didn't care. It took every ounce of his concentration, every fibre of his being; he couldn't focus on anything else.

Leonie

Am I ready? Ready to let go of all this power, this ability to do anything, this feeling of invincibility? Ready to deceive Perry to try to save him? Ready to destroy the newly healed relationship between him and Lesley? Ready to forfeit the joy and happiness of the last few months? Ready to leave Perry behind? Ready to die?

No, I'm not. But it's my turn to put my hand on the wheel of life and move with it. I know I am doing the right thing and I've had my reward already, these last weeks with Perry. The price will be whatever it is and I will pay it gladly, and God will go with me. No, I'm not ready, but it's time.

Perry touched his lips to mine and I felt his love spread through me.

Somewhere, in the middle of the woven rope of power was the thread, the single strand that was me. I wrapped the end of that thread around Perry, using everything I had left to protect him. I made sure he was safe, and then gave my self up to the power and whatever came next. The world spun around me, my master stones continued to spin, faster and faster until they were just light themselves, consumed by the power of the rope. The power leapt free and I was torn away. My thread spiralled down, ripped raw where I had been woven into the rope and so damaged that I started to disintegrate. A second thread wrapped around me, holding the broken pieces together, and then everything faded away.

Chapter 27

Tuesday

Gabriel

Gabriel was sitting at his desk when he became terrifyingly certain that the deciding event of his visions was about to take place. He prayed with all his heart that he was wrong – in which case he'd look a fool – but feared deep in his soul that he was right, which would be much worse. Urgently, he gave verbal instructions to Chloe and telepathic ones to Eleanor and Benjamin. Then he pulled off his Abbot's ring and placed it on the desk in front of him. He opened his desk drawer and took out the Deathstone that Merchant Ethan had sent him for Leonie, turned it over in his hand, then dropped it into his pocket. He reached a little further into the drawer and pulled out a twin to his Abbot's ring which he set on the desk beside the first one.

He stared at both rings, finding it difficult to comprehend that he was even thinking of doing what he planned to do next. Then, knowing he had very little time, he sighed and put the second ring on his finger. Picking up the original Abbot's ring, he twisted the jewel and setting until it separated from the ring part. He spread his left hand, palm uppermost, on the desk and placed the jewel from the original ring in the centre of his palm. He returned to staring at it, praying urgently all the time.

The call on his energy came as a sudden ache through his chest which eased just as Eleanor and Benjamin erupted into the room. Their imminent questions were silenced as the stone on his palm started to glow, projecting a wide beam upwards in which they could see indistinct figures and shadowy movement.

"What on earth...?" whispered Benjamin in awe.

Gabriel took a deep, calming breath, ignoring the residual

ache and tried to explain. "This stone is the twin of the one in Leonie's necklace, designed to work in partnership," he said.

"You gave her the original necklace?" Eleanor interrupted. "I thought that was the copy."

"It was the original," he confirmed. "I know you thought it was the copy. Only Prospero recognised it. I saw him realise, though how he even knew about the necklace in the first place I have yet to find out. I suspect Melanie."

Eleanor pulled a face which suggested she agreed, and Gabriel went on, "As a twin master stone that is not being actively used, this one is projecting what the other one is doing. Which means Leonie is using the other one."

They watched the projection avidly, starting to pick out details and people, recognising both Perry and Lesley as it became more focused and expanded to the width of Gabriel's desk. Chloe rushed in with the first reports of what had happened and stayed to watch, equally in awe.

Gabriel turned to her. "Is everything in place?"

She nodded. "All in hand," she confirmed.

"I sent for Melanie," Gabriel told Eleanor belatedly. "Whatever happens we may have need of her skills."

Eleanor shrugged, still concentrating on the projection. "This is why you had us take our power stones off, isn't it?" she asked.

He agreed. "I want you both – and Henry, George and Andrew – at full strength should Leonie need you."

"But you kept yours on?"

"Even used passively like this, the master stone is

dangerous. I had to have the power stone as a layer of protection despite the cost."

The projection sparked and flashed, little flecks within it coalescing to form larger bubbles and streams of light.

Gabriel breathed in, amazed. "She's reading the energy, not just using it but manipulating it, making connections, learning from it. Practically no one can do that and she's doing it instinctively, with no training."

Over the next few hours Chloe flitted in and out, bringing updates. The news spread across the campus and others came in and stayed, watching the projection, until the room was filled and people spilled into the outer office, all other tasks forgotten.

It was easy to tell when matters started to come to an end. The projection filled with an image of Prospero and then blended into patterns, colours and ribbons of light.

"Chloe," Gabriel called urgently. "We need direct contact with the site. Now!"

She hurried to obey. There was a blinding flash of light. The stone went dark, Gabriel gasped and closed his hand tightly over it, his upper body bent over his desk.

Silence hung over the room for a long minute, then Chloe shouted, "They've got her. It's a patchwork of phones and telepathy but I have the team leader. They've got her. They say it looks like soul sharing."

Benjamin leapt to his feet, pushing Chloe back into the outer office and started to issue instructions. Gabriel gave his own instructions to those who remained. Rapidly, they dispersed to carry them out until only Eleanor was left with Gabriel. His hand remained clenched.

"Show me," Eleanor said quietly, reaching for his hand.

Much as he wanted to, he couldn't deny Eleanor. He opened his hand to show her.

"Oh, Gabe," she said softly, her voice full of pain and sympathy.

"Just you, Ellie," he said. "Don't tell anyone else, not yet."

Perry

The High Lord of House Eastern had two transcopters, both of which she had assigned to help with the emergency. The first was her personal transcopter, today doing duty as an air ambulance. The second didn't normally carry passengers, instead carrying spare fuel cells for the first one along with many square metres of flexible solar power generation material. Now that material was spread out across any spare ground, fuel cells stacked around it, some full, some recharging, leaving the transcopter free also to act as an ambulance, albeit a rather bare one. In his role as liaison, Perry had delegated transport arrangements to the transcopters' team leader and forgotten about them.

Two of the team were beside Perry as he caught Leonie, helping him to his feet, pushing her more firmly into his arms, guiding him towards the transcopter whose engines and rotors were already running. Perry went without resistance, unable to concentrate on anything but supporting Leonie.

I must not let go. I will not let go.

Two of the team tried to take her from him; he held her tighter, knowing that he needed to touch her closely to have any chance of saving her. From somewhere he heard a voice.

"Don't separate them. Whatever you do don't separate them. Strap them down together however you can but don't separate them."

In relief that someone at least understood, he allowed himself to be pushed onto a seat, and didn't fight the straps being placed around them. He barely even noticed the transcopter taking off.

The voice continued. "We're to think of him as her life-support system," it said. "There's no point in monitoring her because we'll just get his readings. But they don't share circulation so if we can get a drip on her that'll help. But don't disrupt his concentration."

That was right, Perry thought as, somewhere on the periphery of his mind, he became at least partly aware of what was going on. He was her life and she was his. Without her, he couldn't function. He flexed his fingers slightly, and she mirrored the movement. Someone gasped; he didn't know why. He knew only that there were medics around him, and the voice's instructions reassured him that they accepted his actions. One of the team knelt in front of him and very gently reached for Leonie's arm. Perry didn't try to stop them, nor did he let it disturb him. He equated medics and intravenous drips with help, and, as it was his mind living for both of them, he didn't even think about Leonie's past reaction to such.

He wasn't aware of the passage of time until the transcopter landed. The team rapidly released the strapping and assisted him out. He still clung tightly to Leonie, body and mind, guarding and nurturing the tiny spark of life. Then he felt a mind slide in beside his, taking over the support of Leonie, protecting that delicate spark.

Benjamin, I can give her to Benjamin. No one knows more about how to take care of her. Benjamin will look after her.

Andrew

Andrew watched as Benjamin and his team disappeared with Leonie, staying beside Perry who blinked and looked around as if waking from a dream, puzzled to find himself somewhere other than he expected. Rather than landing on top of the hospital, the transcopter had landed expertly in the main courtyard of the Abbey complex.

"We're caring for her in your rooms," Andrew explained. "It'll be better for her, and it's easier to protect. Come on, let's go."

He pulled Perry's arm over his shoulders and slipped his own arm round Perry's waist to support him before leading him into the building. The guards at both the main entrance and the door to the apartment acknowledged them and let them pass, though Perry barely seemed to notice them. He noticed the one at his bedroom door, who would not let him enter. He pulled away from Andrew's support.

"I should be with her," he said, his voice filled with the emotions he hadn't let himself feel.

"She has the best care, you are not her doctor." Andrew tried to be calming.

Unable to restrain himself after all that had happened, Perry slammed both fists into the wall beside the door in frustration.

"She is my wife!"—or was it—"She is my life!"? Either way his shoulders sagged in exhaustion and Andrew led him to the kitchen area and sat him at the table there.

"She has the best care," he repeated.

"She doesn't have me and she doesn't have you!"

Andrew could hear the desperation, fear and loss in Perry's

voice. "You have done all you can for her, more than anyone else could," he said. "Besides, she is not the only patient here. Let others do what they can now."

"If she... Without her... I can't..." Perry's voice broke on the words and Andrew reached over to place his hands on top of Perry's.

"Remember," he said. "When the darkness closes in, still I will say..." He paused hoping that Perry would complete the phrase.

Instead Perry shook his head. "It's never been this dark before."

"All the more reason. Say it. When the darkness closes in, still I will say..."

"Blessed is the name of the Lord." They completed the phrase together even if Perry's voice was little more than a whisper. It seemed to give him some strength for he repeated it.

"Blessed is the name of the Lord." He looked up at Andrew and continued, "Let me be singing when the evening comes."

Andrew smiled encouragingly. "That's right. Evening maybe here but dawn isn't far away, and we will still be singing."

From their early days in the Order, this had been a reminder to themselves and each other that God was with them no matter how bad things seemed. Perry found music a particular comfort and the desire to still be singing God's praise no matter how dark things got had seen him through some real problems. Andrew could only hope and pray it would help him now.

He spoke again. "Soon, Leonie will need you and only you will do. You need to be ready, rested, fed, your injuries treated by then."

Perry looked at him blankly. "I'm not hurt," he said.

Andrew found that hard to believe. "You're covered with dirt, dust, blood. Is none of it yours?" When no answer was forthcoming he continued, "Never mind. You need to clean up anyway. We'll use the bathroom and I can check you over."

Perry was uncomplaining and compliant but seemed unable to initiate any action. Andrew took charge, unfastening Perry's top, removing his clothes and setting the torn and damaged items aside for cleaning, mending or disposal. As far as Andrew could tell, Perry had not been hurt much; a few minor cuts and grazes and some developing bruises were all he could find. Satisfied that he had done all he could in this respect he propelled Perry towards the shower to wash the rest of the dust and dirt off. The hot water seemed to revive Perry somewhat but then he slumped against the wall, clearly hit by the enormity of what Leonie had done and what was still at risk.

Andrew sighed. Obviously today was going to continue to be difficult, to require that he did things that he had tried very hard not even to dream about. Fleetingly he wished that the circumstances had been different, then stripped off his own clothes and stepped into the shower. He held Perry closely until the juddering sobs eased, and then washed him as gently as any mother with a small child. As he ran his hands over Perry's body he prayed for the strength to do this from love and not desire; he also prayed for both Perry and Leonie as he had very little hope of anything but a tragic end to events. When he was done he pushed Perry out of the shower and found them both towels and then clean clothing.

By the time they'd emerged from the bathroom the guard had moved away from the bedroom door and nodded at Andrew to indicate that they could now go in. The room was less busy than Andrew had expected; only Gabriel and Benjamin remained there with Leonie. The sight of Leonie, unconscious, lying in bed, jolted Perry out of his all-but-somnambulant state and he hurried across the room towards her. Benjamin turned to Andrew, raising his eyebrows in a mute question as to how Perry was coping. Andrew simply shook his head in reply and stayed by the door, reluctant to enter the room and witness Perry's raw emotion and deep love for Leonie any further.

Perry sat on the bed beside Leonie, murmuring to her with one hand stroking her face and hair. Andrew took it as a positive sign that Perry's other hand was checking her pulse and temperature, whilst his eyes were seeking the monitor screen propped on a table. At least his medical training was coming to the fore, some sign that he was able to function despite everything he had to be facing.

Benjamin went over to sit on a chair near Perry, leaning towards him to get his attention before he spoke. "There are few physical injuries, but..."

Perry looked at him and finished the sentence. "But the power beat her."

Benjamin didn't quite agree. "Well, it drained her, left her with insufficient energy or desire to carry on living by herself. You supported her, got her home to us, which was quite something, and we're carrying on with that, but we can only do it for so long."

Perry nodded. "I know. Thirty-six hours."

"Well, we'll see how long she needs. We have to hope and pray that by then she'll have recovered enough to be able to make it on her own. She'll need you then; if you're with her, talking to her, encouraging her at the point we have to stop supporting her, it could tip the balance."

Perry nodded again, then turned his head towards Leonie,

away from Benjamin, attempting to hide his feelings. No hope of that, Andrew thought. They were obvious to anyone who so much as glanced at him. Benjamin looked towards Andrew, tilting his head towards the kitchen. Understanding, Andrew left to find a glass of juice for Perry. In the background Benjamin was still talking.

"What you need most right now is to sleep. You need to recover your energy too."

Perry answered him, "I understand. I just…don't think I can sleep. And I can't leave her. I can't."

"No one is suggesting you do. You can sit or lie down next to her and rest even if you can't sleep."

As Andrew returned with the juice, Perry was making himself comfortable beside Leonie. He obediently took the glass Andrew held out, drinking it without suspicion.

Benjamin spoke again. "Prospero, I can't promise that Leonie will live, but I can promise that I will not let her die while you sleep."

Perry nodded his thanks. "I'm just going to stay here with her," he said.

In moments, he was deeply asleep.

Gabriel spoke, "I didn't think he'd fall for that drink given how often he's done it to others."

"He's just focused on Leonie, not really aware of what's happening," Andrew volunteered, and Benjamin agreed.

Gabriel nodded. "I'll watch them for now; you both get some rest while you can."

Although Benjamin stayed a moment longer, Andrew

slipped quickly into the next room. It had been re-equipped as a medical resource, with somewhere comfortable for those supporting Leonie with their Gifts, as well as duplicate monitors for her vital signs, and a bed for anyone to catch a quick nap. He gestured to the monitoring technician to go for a break, and took over her place, pulling on the headphones and feeling almost relieved by the brief solitude.

Consequentially, only Andrew heard Gabriel apologise to the sleeping couple for what had happened, what he felt he had driven them towards as sacrificial offerings. And only Andrew heard Gabriel pray for them, something he joined in with wholeheartedly.

Chapter 28

Wednesday

Perry

Even as Perry woke he thought of Leonie and turned towards where she should be, one arm reaching for her.

"She's still with us, and getting stronger," came Benjamin's voice from somewhere in the room.

Perry pushed himself up on one elbow, stroking Leonie's cheek with the other hand, checking that she was still warm, still breathing. Then he turned towards the voice.

"You drugged me, without consent," he said, although without rancour.

"Oh, I had consent," Benjamin confirmed. "Just not yours."

"Gabriel's I suppose," said Perry as he sat up and swung round to sit on the side of the bed. He swayed a little as his head swam, and Benjamin moved to support him.

"Take it easy," he said. "You've been out for a while."

"I'm okay. What time is it?" He looked around the room at the dimmed lighting. "What day is it?" he added.

"It's about six in the morning," Benjamin said. "You slept through the night. Now you need to eat. Do you think you can stand?"

Perry tried to stand up, swayed a little, and put one hand back down to stabilise himself before straightening up. "Yes, I'm okay."

"Right, you go and freshen up, and I'll arrange some breakfast for you. Once, you've eaten I'll talk to you about Leonie."

Benjamin moved towards the door.

Perry felt a rush of panic. "Don't leave her alone!"

"Don't worry, I'm not even going to leave the room." Benjamin fitted actions to words, opening the door and speaking to someone on the other side.

Satisfied, Perry went to use the bathroom. As he came out he noticed for the first time that he was wearing a patient's ID bracelet and monitor disc.

"I'm a patient?" he asked, surprised, waving his wrist at Benjamin.

"Indeed you are. Did you really expect anything else after what you did?"

"I suppose not. Am I in real trouble?"

Supporting someone in the way Perry had saved Leonie was highly regulated. What Perry had done was so far outside the regulations that he shouldn't even have contemplated it. He expected that he would never work as a doctor again, and there would be some form of punishment as well. He found he didn't care, it just didn't seem important. If Leonie lived it would be a small price to pay, if she didn't... He couldn't complete the thought.

"No. Did you expect to be?"

Perry looked at him, disbelieving. "No?" he echoed.

"She's your wife, Prospero," Benjamin said gently. "Didn't you listen to the words of the wedding service? Or consider the theology of marriage? What God has joined together...? Two shall become one...? If you are one already, how can what you did be a problem?"

Perry shrugged in bemusement, not knowing how to respond, but at that moment the door opened and Alan came in with a tray of food. Benjamin made him sit and concentrate on eating, and he found he was hungry; he realised he'd only had a sandwich since breakfast the day before. It seemed a lifetime since he'd sat eating breakfast yesterday, watching Leonie, flushed and relaxed from their lovemaking. Leonie hadn't eaten anything since then, and his eyes drifted to the feeding tube and to the drip attached to her arm.

"She won't like that," he said to Benjamin.

"She needs it, though, and right now she doesn't know."

Perry had to acknowledge that he was right. He finished eating. "Now tell me," he demanded.

Benjamin nodded. "Very well. Do you remember any of what I told you yesterday?"

Perry shook his head. "Not really. I barely remember getting back here."

"I suppose that's hardly surprising. The first thing is that there are very few physical injuries, just a few scratches and bruises, some minor burns. However, she is totally exhausted. Using the master stone raised her metabolism which burnt off every ounce of fat on her, not that there was much in the first place. It would have raised her body temperature too, but that doesn't seem to have had too much of an effect."

He paused, and Perry spoke, "Lesley kept pouring water over her to cool her down, and making her drink. She couldn't get around easily to help anyone else, but looking after Leonie, she knew what to do."

"Yes, she clearly did, and it's made a difference, given Leonie a better chance, physically anyway. The amount of power coursing through her has destroyed all the connections in her brain that enabled her to access her Gifts. On the good side, we think they are just disconnected, blown out rather than burnt out, which means they could reconnect. And given that she's at the age when the connections are normally being made anyway, well that might also give her an advantage."

Perry nodded to show he was taking this in. "Then there's some hope that if she lives she could recover some of her skills?"

Benjamin continued. "Yes, there is. But at the end the power drained her, leaving her with insufficient energy or desire to support life. What you did, supporting her, whatever the rights and wrongs of it, was very skilful, it kept her alive. You did well getting her back to us."

"It was instinctive. I didn't even think about it, or what I was doing, I just did it."

"Well, it was well done, whatever. Now we are supporting her, and we plan to do that until tomorrow morning."

"That's longer than thirty-six hours," Perry said in surprise. Thirty-six hours was normally the limit of such support; it was generally agreed that if a patient had insufficient energy by then to maintain life for themselves, more support was unlikely to help. Providing support beyond forty-eight hours had proved to be detrimental to both patient and supporters.

"Yes it is," Benjamin agreed. "It's at the far end of what is beneficial, but we wanted to give her the best possible chance. So we will withdraw support tomorrow morning; after that she will sleep, and we will manage things so she wakes up about twenty-four hours later."

"You make it sound certain that she will live."

"She's responding very well, I'd say we are cautiously

optimistic. Those who are supporting her are getting very vivid memories from her, which is a good sign." He paused a moment. "Some of her childhood memories are horrific."

Perry winced. "Yes, she's shown me what she could remember."

"On the other hand, her recent memories are both... interesting and instructive."

This time Perry blushed. "Who is supporting her?" he asked hurriedly.

"Well, Henry and George to start with," Benjamin told him.

Perry thought them a good choice. Henry and George were both doctors in their fifties, each with several Gifts, both calm and reliable. George was a monk, like Benjamin and Andrew; Henry was a member of the lay House, married with teenage children. Neither would have been overwhelmed by either set of memories.

"After that, Andrew, Gabriel and I have each taken a share, but Gabriel had to stop Andrew, he was putting too much into it. But the bulk of the support is being done by Eleanor and Melanie."

For a moment it seemed entirely natural to Perry that Melanie – Eleanor's daughter – should follow Lesley in his life. She'd been a young doctor when he had first been a student at the college. After his break up with Lesley she had introduced him – and naturally Andrew – to her rebellious life of partying and more. They'd never been a couple, but they had been lovers, on and off, for more than a year.

Then something jarred and Perry looked up sharply. "Melanie's here?"

She shouldn't be here. She lived with her husband and their children a long way away. Mostly Lady Eleanor visited her, not the other way around. Why was Melanie *here*?

Benjamin looked a little apologetic. "We needed to find women who could support her. There aren't many and you know that gender matching works better."

Perry agreed, "Yes, I suppose it does." Then he lapsed into silence, trying to remember and process all he had been told.

***

The next twenty-four hours passed in a dream for Perry. He sat beside the bed watching Leonie, scarcely daring to take his eyes off her. He tried to pray but his prayers were incoherent; he tried to read his Bible – actually he'd picked up Leonie's Bible, he realised at one point – but he couldn't take in the words. He ate and drank when food was put in front of him, slept when he was forced to. There was always someone sitting with him and Leonie, caring for her, which he found a comfort. He'd told Leonie once that if anything ever happened to him she'd be surrounded by people who would love and care for her; now he found this was true for him.

He learnt of the number of people in the next room, watching monitors, supporting Leonie, prepared for any eventuality. He discovered that both Pedro and Richard had supplied a rota of staff to ensure that those looking after Leonie were in turn cared for and fed. He was told of the steady stream of brothers and sisters praying in the Monks' Chapel, ensuring that there was always someone praying for Leonie. He found that a comfort, too. Mostly, the activities of others simply flowed around him, like a stream around a boulder.

Some of the time Gabriel sat with them. Perry tried to articulate the thought that was pressing heavily on him.

"I did this to her."

"No," Gabriel said firmly. "You didn't. It was using the power that did the damage."

"But I told her about the master stone and I knew the consequences. She had no idea." The words burst from him.

"In the heat of the crisis you made a lot of decisions, calmly and rationally, and they were the right ones. Think about this—if Leonie had known that death was likely, and injury certain, would she have chosen to use the power anyway, to save others?"

Perry didn't even have to think about the answer. "Yes, she would."

"So you made the right decision for her. If she hadn't had the power from the master stone, what would she have done?"

"She'd have used every ounce of power and energy and skill that she had to help as many as possible."

"And the consequences of that would have been?"

Perry's reply was slower this time. "It would have left her equally drained, possibly injured, and distraught that she hadn't been able to do more. But I could have stopped her."

"Could you? Really? And how would that have left her feeling?"

Perry sighed. "Really? No, I suppose not. She's stronger than I am, and she'd have resented it."

"Yes. There was never going to be a good outcome for Leonie from this. Knowing that, you chose the right course of action, the one that would do the most good for the most people."

"That makes me sound cold and calculating and uncaring."

"No. You did this instinctively because you have good instincts and good judgement. And how can it be uncaring to sacrifice what you love for the good of others?"

"I could have been the one to use the master stone; I could have taken the necklace from her. That would have protected Leonie."

"But Leonie couldn't have done what you did, treating others, could she?"

"No, she doesn't have the training."

"And could you have done what she did?"

Prospero was close to claiming that he could have done, but honesty took over. "No," he said quietly. "I couldn't have done all that she managed. And the stone wouldn't have responded like that for me. I've touched it before."

"You see, that's another good instinctive decision." Gabriel ignored the confession about the stone to carry on. "At the time you probably didn't consciously realise it, but you chose the best people for each task. Tell me, if Leonie hadn't done what she did, would there have been more deaths, more serious injuries?"

"Yes, you know there would have been many more."

"And each one of those people has family, parents, siblings, spouses, children, whose lives will have benefited from her actions."

"I suppose so."

"So, if you want to feel responsible for anything, you can feel responsible for all that good as a result of your choices, not the harm to Leonie over which you had no choice."

"I planned, at the end, I was going to take on the power, so it was me, not her, but I let myself get distracted."

Gabriel smiled. "Prospero, do you really think that, with all that power at her disposal, Leonie was unaware of your plan? It's my belief we'll find that distraction was a set up."

Perry was incredulous. "She read my mind? And tricked me? And got Lesley to help?"

"You were planning to protect her. Is it so surprising that she would plan to protect you?"

Perry shook his head in disbelieving wonder, and again lapsed into silence, exhausted by the discussion.

Later Melanie came into the room and Gabriel slipped out, tactfully and quietly. Perry stood up to greet her, kissing her cheek and motioning her to the chair he had just vacated. He sat on the edge of the bed and reached to stroke Leonie's hair.

Melanie kept her voice low, "She's a lovely girl, Perry. I'm so glad you found her."

"I'm glad you could meet her."

"I'm sorry I couldn't make it to your wedding. It was rather short notice."

"That was Lord Gabriel. He said that if we were going to do this we might as well get on with it instead of disrupting his House for months."

"I know."

"Do you?" Perry was mildly surprised. "Most people outside assume there must have been some nefarious reason. There are any number of rumours. I'm glad he insisted; at least we've had the last few weeks."

"You forget I've been seeing her memories. These last months have been the happiest of her life."

"They don't have a lot of competition," he said ruefully.

"She loves you very deeply."

"She can't say it, did you know that?" He looked up at Melanie for a moment, then back at Leonie. "Everyone she loves has died, sometimes brutally, so she's never dared to tell me. I told her and look…"

His voice broke for a moment. He was still stroking Leonie's hair with one hand, the other resting on his leg, and Melanie covered it with hers in sympathy.

"She's doing really well, Perry. She's a real fighter, she has a very good chance."

He nodded. "I know. But this is just the first hurdle, isn't it?"

"She has such faith and confidence in you, Perry. All she wants is to be with you. That must make a difference."

He shook his head slightly. "I hope so. It's a lot to live up to."

"If you are half the person she thinks you are, then you'll manage," Melanie assured him.

Andrew spoke from the doorway, surprising Perry by his presence. "You want to be careful basing your views of Perry on Leonie's memories, Melanie. She over exaggerates his good points and ignores all his faults."

Melanie looked up and smiled at him. "But you made sure she knew all about his faults?"

"I tried, but you know how it is. He'd brainwashed the poor girl before I had a chance to tell her the truth."

Even Perry had to smile at that wild accusation. "Andrew, you of all people know how hard I tried to keep away from her."

Andrew ignored his comment. "Seriously though, Melanie, she does bring out the best in him."

Perry couldn't respond.

Melanie stood up to leave. "Try not to worry, Perry, Leonie really is doing well."

Andrew sat down in the other chair, the one Gabriel had recently vacated. "My turn to be here with you," he said simply.

"There's a rota, is there?" Perry asked.

"It's one anyone's lucky to get onto," Andrew informed him. "Everyone wants to be here, doing whatever they can to help."

Perry looked at him gratefully. "I'm glad you're here anyway."

"I'm sorry I couldn't do more for Leonie. Gabriel stopped me, said I was doing too much."

"I know you've done all you can and more, and you don't want to end up a patient yourself." He thought for a moment. "Melanie and Lady Eleanor need to be careful, or they'll end up in hospital themselves."

"Oh they will," Andrew replied. "Twenty-four hours rest and observation, as soon as they aren't needed here. That's already agreed." He looked at Perry. "You ought to be in hospital yourself."

"How come I'm not? You tricked me readily enough with that spiked juice before."

"You would be if anyone thought for a moment you'd stay there. But mostly, Gabriel simply won't allow you and Leonie to be separated, no matter what Benjamin thinks should happen."

Perry was surprised. "I didn't know."

"And Benjamin suggested Leonie would have a better chance cared for in her own home with her own things around her. Especially given how she feels about hospitals."

"That's why she's here, not in hospital then. I hadn't even thought about it."

"You didn't think about it because you knew. I told you yesterday. Apparently there's also a lot of interest in Leonie from all sorts of people. It's easier to protect her here than in the hospital."

"Did you tell me that too? I'm sorry; I don't really remember much about yesterday after Leonie collapsed."

As ever, Andrew understood. "That's okay. You weren't really with it once you got here."

"I don't think I'm really with it now. I can't focus on anything."

"No one expects you to. Just sit here with Leonie. We'll do the rest."

Taking that as permission, Perry moved back to his chair, holding Leonie's hand in his, while they sat quietly together.

They made him sleep that night. He consented, aware that he had little real choice, and on condition that he could stay beside Leonie.

Chapter 29

Thursday morning

When he woke, for that moment before he opened his eyes, Perry was happy. He could hear Leonie's breathing, feel the warmth of her body close by, and he smiled at the thought of how he might wake her. Then he sensed the presence of others, the memories of the last few days hit him and he sat bolt upright, eyes wide. Benjamin was watching him. Perry closed his eyes again, hiding his face in his hands.

"She's still doing well. We're still optimistic," Benjamin said, his voice low.

Why does everyone whisper? They're not going to disturb her. They could shout and she wouldn't wake.

Perry looked up. "How long?" he asked.

"Not long. Wash and eat and then we'll talk."

Perry complied; it was a quicker and easier route to what he wanted and he seemed to need all his energy to focus on hope for Leonie. He managed to get hold of Leonie's notes and read them while he was eating, an activity which Benjamin tolerated, perhaps because they didn't tell him much he didn't already know. Physically she was stable, all her vital signs normal. There was really only one thing he needed to know.

"How long?" he asked again.

"It's early yet," Benjamin replied. "Another couple of hours or so. For the last few hours she's only needed minimal support."

Perry nodded, acknowledging the information. For him, another two hours was both too short and too long. He didn't want the time to pass and yet he couldn't wait. He picked his Bible up, then put it down, aware that reading was beyond him. His chair was uncomfortable; he couldn't sit still and yet there was nowhere he could go and no real room to pace. Benjamin was sympathetic – Perry found this disconcerting, being somewhat out of character – and suggested that he went over to the Abbey to join the early service.

Perry shook his head. "I can't leave. It's not that I won't, or that it isn't a good idea, I just...can't."

Benjamin looked at him thoughtfully. "In that case, what you need is something to do."

He left the room for a few minutes. Perry found he was less panicked by this than he had been twenty-four hours earlier. He didn't really understand what Benjamin had meant but it didn't bother him. Like so many things over the past hours, it just didn't seem relevant or important.

Benjamin returned carrying a tray that held some of the small wooden handheld crosses that many people had, along with a bottle of oil and a polishing rag. "There's a number of people too worried to concentrate on anything," he said. "Gabriel got Richard and Edward to find little jobs they could do to calm them. It should work for you too." He laughed slightly. "I don't think the silverware or jewellery has ever been so well polished. And you wouldn't believe how much knitting is going on."

Perry set to his task steadily, ignoring others as they came in and out of the room. He found the rhythmic movement soothed him and enabled him to pray. By the time he had finished with the tray of crosses he was in a much more peaceful state of mind. When he looked up, both Benjamin and Andrew were sitting with him. Andrew took the tray and put it to one side.

"We're going to start in about ten minutes," Benjamin said quietly. "Gabriel's supporting her now and he'll be the one to manage it. We need you to talk to her, tell her she's loved and wanted, encourage her."

"I want to hold her," Perry said. "Whatever happens, I want to be holding her."

"Okay," Benjamin agreed slowly. "That won't hurt and it might even help."

Perry didn't wait for more but made himself comfortable on the bed then lifted Leonie gently on to his lap, cradling her in his arms. At a nod from Benjamin, Andrew wrapped a blanket around her to keep her warm.

"You're to talk to her," Benjamin said again. "It doesn't matter what you say, it's the sound of your voice that's important."

Perry nodded. "I understand."

Benjamin spoke again, his voice serious. "Whatever happens, you aren't to try and support her or soul share with her. You won't be able to help her that way any longer. Do you understand that? Give me your word you won't try?"

Perry looked up at him slowly. "I understand," he repeated. "You have my word. Is that enough? You trust me not to?" He frowned, both puzzled and surprised.

"I trust you," Benjamin replied softly.

Perry shook his head. "I don't think I would. Trust me, I mean. Not if I were you."

"But I do. So that's all I need. We'll be working from next door. You just need to talk to her."

Benjamin left, but Andrew stayed, sitting on the side of the bed. "I can stay here, if you'd like me to?" Andrew asked.

"No," Perry said, quite definite. "Right now, I'd rather it

was just me and her. But thank you for offering."

"You're welcome," Andrew said. "If you need me, just call. I'll be there."

As Andrew also left the room, Perry pulled Leonie more closely into his arms and started to talk to her. "I love you. I can't bear to lose you. Stay with me. I know you love me. You might never have said it, but I know it's true just the same. You have so much love to give and so many people love you. Do you have any idea how many people love you? This place is full of people who love you, people who are desperate for you to live. Choose to live, Leonie. I need you so much."

He stroked a stray curl back off her forehead. "I'm going to take you to meet my family, my parents. My mother will love you and you'll get on so well with her. And my father will think you're amazing. And I'll show you all the places I grew up. There's a lake; it's so beautiful. The water's clear and it's so warm in the sun. We can swim as much as you want to and whenever you want to. Or we could ride, just the two of us, up into the hills. Take a picnic, maybe even camp out. I used to do that a lot, riding from home to Castle Tennant."

He paused, swamped for a moment by childhood memories.

"Is there anywhere you'd like to visit? Because we could, anywhere at all. We could travel, see the whole world, if you'd like to. Maybe catch up with your Trader caravan? Meet up with your friends there?"

Leonie might not have much in the way of happy childhood memories, but they could make so many for their own children. "And then we'll settle down somewhere. Wherever you like, here, Castle Tennant, near my parents, anywhere that takes your fancy. And we'll have children. Lots of children if you like.

As many as you want. Sons and daughters, maybe twins even, like my brothers." He smiled at the thought. "I hope our kids are like you. Strong and courageous. I don't care if they're Gifted or not, just healthy and happy."

When he ran out of words, Perry moved into song, starting with some of Leonie's favourites. Then he chose those hymns which had deep meaning for him, ones that gave him comfort and strength to face whatever he had to.

Andrew

Andrew found himself a space in the next room where Gabriel had made himself comfortable before taking over support of Leonie from Melanie. Melanie didn't leave; even if they weren't taking an active role, the room was full of those who loved Leonie, desperate to know whether she was going to live.

Benjamin was talking quietly to Gabriel. "I could do this. It doesn't have to be you."

"Yes, it does. If she dies, it will be on my watch. Did Prospero promise not to try to support her?"

"He did. Not that he could anyway. Right now he's too drained. He doesn't have the capacity."

"That's not the point," Gabriel told him accepting his assurance anyway. "You have monitors on both of them?"

Benjamin nodded and indicated Mark who was sitting with a bank of equipment and screens in front of him. Gabriel spoke again, this time to Mark, "Can you turn the sound off please, and turn them away from me. I don't want to be able to see or hear what they report until it's over."

Andrew wasn't sure whether he wanted to see the monitors

or not. In the end he positioned himself where he could see them, deciding that he couldn't handle the suspense.

Gabriel took a deep breath. "Right," he said. "Here we go."

For the next few minutes there was absolute silence as Gabriel slowly withdrew support from Leonie. Most people were huddled round the monitor screens. Andrew found himself continually glancing between the screens and Gabriel who had closed his eyes. When Gabriel opened them again, the room was still hushed. Benjamin reached for the screens and turned them towards him.

"Look at the monitors," he said.

"Yes." Gabriel nodded as he looked at both sets of information. "I had better go and speak to Prospero."

Without thinking, simply responding to an urge to be with Perry, Andrew stood up. "Let me, please?"

Gabriel nodded again. "You go then. That might be better."

Perry was sitting on the bed with Leonie held closely in his arms, still singing to her as Andrew entered the room. Andrew sat down beside him, and Perry turned his head.

"Andrew, go away."

"You know that I can't." Gently Andrew placed his arm around Perry's shoulders. "The key moment is over. It's time to put her down. I'm here. You will be alright."

Perry leaned towards Andrew and, for a moment, placed his head on Andrew's shoulder, while he attempted to master his emotions. Then, very carefully, he lay Leonie down on the bed, and Andrew covered her with a blanket. Clearly unable to comprehend what to do next, Perry remained sitting on the bed. Andrew passed him a small glass of liquid.

"Drink this, and sleep, just a couple of hours. I will stay with Leonie. I promise you, she will not be alone and nor will you."

Andrew had expected difficulty, argument, but Perry simply drank and lay down. "Andrew," he said, before sleep claimed him. "What if—"

"No what ifs," Andrew replied firmly. "Just sleep."

But as Andrew sat beside him, watching him sleep, he could not help the 'what ifs' running through his own mind.

Leonie

Where am I? I am...somewhere, I can't tell where. I know my eyes are open, but there's nothing to see, no light, no dark, just nothing. I can't hear; there's absolute silence. Nor can I smell, or feel or move. My Gifts don't work.

Is time passing? How can I tell?

Perry is looking for me. I'm sure of that. He promised he'd always find me but how can he? I can't call out, and if I can't use my Gifts can he use his?

More time passed, possibly.

Gradually I became aware of sound entering my world. Dim and distant, it could be Perry's voice and I found I was able to choose to turn towards it. As it became louder I was sure it was Perry – I still couldn't make out the words, but I could hear the tone and the sound. He was looking for me, and he was close. As hope twined around me, other senses started to return. It seemed to me that I could now catch the scent of Perry's skin—warm, musky, male, with undertones of both the hospital and the church. His voice became clearer and moved into song. I was safe, loved; I could almost feel the touch of his arms around me.

If Perry is singing then all will be well, all is well with my soul. I can relax and wait for whatever comes next.

Secure in that knowledge, ready to face whatever happened, I closed my eyes and drifted off.

The story continues in

Weave of Love

Choices and Consequences Book 3

Release date : October 2019

What if your choices have devastating consequences for others?
How can anyone know the right thing to do?

Leonie chose to sacrifice everything to save other people. Now those around her have to face the consequences – and those consequences are not what they expected.

Prospero must deal with his own guilt. He was the one who gave Leonie the tools she needed – her life was in his hands. To make the most of what she did, he will have to face up to all the family issues he has avoided for so long. Whatever he chooses to do, someone he loves will be hurt. For Leonie's sake, is he now strong enough to make the choice he couldn't make before?

The crisis predicted by Lord Gabriel has come and gone. But his task isn't over. Leonie's very existence maybe out in the open but Gabriel discovers that the past is never what it seems – and nor is the present. How can he use what he now knows to bring together those who have been enemies for as long as anyone can remember? If he fails in this, everything he's had to do so far will be in vain.

Can't wait? Sign up for my occasional newsletter to get a preview of Weave of Love. Just visit my website at www.racheljbonner.co.uk or go directly to the sign up page at https://www.subscribepage.com/weave. You'll also get the latest news, sneak peeks and early extracts for:-

Cloth of Grace

Choices and Consequences Book 4

Release date : February 2020

Please consider leaving a review! Reader reviews are crucial to a book's success by helping other readers discover them. Please consider taking a moment to review Thread of Hope at whichever e-retailer you purchased it from. Your review doesn't have to be long or detailed – one sentence about how the book made you feel would be great.

Want to make contact? I'd love to hear from you. Please visit my Facebook page at www.facebook.com/rachelbonnerauthor or connect with me on Twitter at www.twitter.com/racheljbonner1 – or both!

Not read Strand of Faith yet? It's available at all the major ebook retailers and can be ordered at all good bookshops.

Strand of Faith

Choices and Consequences Book 1

A girl. A monk. An unthinkable sacrifice.
When the choice is between love and life, how can anyone decide?

In a post-apocalyptic future, a girl and a monk, both with extraordinary mental powers, have compelling reasons not to fall in love. But their choices will have consequences for the rest of the world.

After the troubles of his youth, Brother Prospero has found comfort and fulfilment in the monastery. Then he discovers something that forces him to reconsider his whole vocation. How can it possibly be right to leave a life of worship and service for human desire? And if he does leave, will the pressures from his past destroy him?

Orphaned and mistreated, Leonie has found sanctuary and safety at the Abbey. When she comes into contact with Prospero everything spirals out of her control. Everyone she's ever loved has died. She can't do that to him. But how can she walk away from the first place she's truly belonged?

Abbot Gabriel is faced with an impossible choice. He can do nothing and watch the world descend into war. Or he can manipulate events and ensure peace – at the cost of two lives that he is responsible for. Is he strong enough to sacrifice those he loves?

Acknowledgements

Writing a book is a journey, and once more I have been accompanied on that journey by so many people. I couldn't have done it without all of you and I am so grateful to you.

Like Strand of Faith, the cover for Thread of Hope was designed by the very talented Oliver Pengilley. Once again, Ollie, it's exactly right for the book. I know that this time I gave you even less idea of what I wanted it to be like and you still came up with just the right cover. If you'd like to see more examples of Ollie's work, visit his website at www.oliverpengilley.co.uk or his Etsy shop at www.etsy.com/uk/shop/oliverpengilley .

Sarah Smeaton has been my editor again (and thank you to www.reedsy.com for introducing us). Sarah, you have an outstanding ability to point out where and how my manuscript needs altering and polishing. This would be nothing like as good without you, so you have my thanks.

The other Rachel, of www.rachelsrandomresources.com has my thanks for once again leading me through the nightmare of social media marketing, blogs and reviews and making it easy. Social media has its critics but I have found nothing but encouragement and support from book bloggers and the writing communities on Facebook and Twitter.

I will never be able to express my gratitude for the support I have had from family and friends. So many of you bought Strand of Faith – even when it wasn't your 'normal read'. And then you enjoyed it, and told me how you couldn't wait until Thread of Hope was available. Thank you from the bottom of my heart. Friendship is an amazing thing that transcends age, gender and culture. In particular, thank you to my house group and my church for your enthusiasm and encouragement.

The love and support of my husband, David, my sons,

Adam and the other one, and my first readers, Mum and Kathy has been invaluable. You may not realise it but neither Strand of Faith, nor Thread of Hope would have happened without the input from each one of you. I cannot describe how much I love and appreciate each of you. Thank you for everything.

Finally, thank you again to you, the reader. Without you my books would have no purpose. I hope you've enjoyed reading it as much as I enjoyed writing it and will be back again to read the next in the series as soon as it is available.

Deo gratis.

Rachel J Bonner

April 2019

CPSIA information can be obtained
at www.ICGtesting.com
Printed in the USA
BVHW080838060519
547457BV00002B/195/P